Born in Lincolnshire in 1912, **Michael Francis Gilbert** was educated in Sussex before entering the University of London where he gained an LL B with honours in 1937.

He joined the Royal Horse Artillery during World War II, and served in Europe and North Africa, where he was captured and imprisoned – an experience recalled in Death in Captivity. After the war he worked in a law firm as a solicitor, and in 1952 he became partner.

Gilbert was a founding member of the British Crime Writers Association, and in 1988 was named a *Grand Master* by the Mystery Writers of America – an achievement many thought long overdue. He won the *Life Achievement Anthony Award* at the 1990 Boucheron in London, and in 1980 was made a Commander of the Order of the British Empire. Gilbert made his debut in 1947 with *Close Quarters*, and has become recognized as one of the most versatile British mystery writers.

BY THE SAME AUTHOR
ALL PUBLISHED BY HOUSE OF STRATUS

Inspector Hazlerigg Series

Close Quarters		1947
They Never Looked Inside	alt: He Didn't Mind Danger	1948
The Doors Open		1949
Smallbone Deceased		1950
Death has Deep Roots		1951
Fear To Tread	(in part)	1953
The Young Petrella	(included) (short stories)	1988
The Man Who Hated Banks and Other Mysteries		
(included) (short stories)		1997

Patrick Petrella Series

Blood and Judgement		1959
Amateur in Violence	(included) (short stories)	1973
Petrella at Q	(short stories)	1977
The Young Petrella	(short stories)	1988
Roller Coaster		1993
The Man Who Hated Banks	(included) (short stories)	1997

Luke Pagan Series

Ring of Terror		1995
Into Battle		1997
Over and Out		1998

Calder & Behrens Series

Game Without Rules	(short stories)	1967
Mr. Calder and Mr. Behrens	(short stories)	1982

Indivudual Works

Death in Captivity	alt: The Danger Within	1952
Sky High	alt: The Country House Burglar	1955
Be Shot for Sixpence		1956
After the Fine Weather		1963
The Crack in the Teacup		1966
The Dust and the Heat	alt: Overdrive	1967
The Etruscan Net	alt: The Family Tomb	1969
Stay of Execution and Other Stories	(short stories)	1971
The Body of a Girl		1972
The Ninety-Second Tiger		1973
Flash Point		1974
The Night of the Twelfth		1976
The Empty House		1979
The Killing of Katie Steelstock	alt: Death of a Favourite Girl	1980
The Final Throw	alt: End Game	1982
The Black Seraphim		1984
The Long Journey Home		1985
Trouble		1987
Paint, Gold, and Blood		1989
Anything for a Quiet Life	(short stories)	1990
The Queen against Karl Mullen		1992

MICHAEL
GILBERT

THE CRACK IN
THE TEACUP

HOUSE OF
STRATUS

This edition published in 2011 by House of Stratus, an imprint of
Stratus Books Ltd., Lisandra House, Fore Street,
Looe, Cornwall, PL13 1AD, U.K.

www.houseofstratus.com

Typeset by House of Stratus.

A catalogue record for this book is available from the British Library
and the Library of Congress.

ISBN 0-7551-0515-X

From all that terror teaches,
From lies of tongue and pen,
From all the easy speeches
That comfort cruel men,
From sale and profanation
Of honour and the sword,
From Sleep and from Damnation
Deliver us, good Lord.

G. K. Chesterton

This verse from *O God of earth and altar* is reprinted from *The English Hymnal* by permission of Oxford University Press.

Chapter One

Anthony Takes Tea

"Another cup of tea, Mr. Sudderby?"

"Thank you, Lady Mayoress, but two cups are all I ever take. Even of your truly delicious China tea."

"Mr. Brydon?"

"No more," said Anthony. "What beautiful cups."

"They are Royal Worcester," said Mrs. Lord, "and are just over two hundred years old. As you see, they have no saucers. In the days when they were made, saucers were thought rather common."

Anthony Brydon examined his cup curiously. It was so shallow that it hardly held any tea. The vivid greens had faded to brown. The gold had almost disappeared. Like everything about Mrs. Lord it was old, precious and very slightly impracticable.

"About your cricket field. Or pitch, do you call it?"

"The pitch is the bit in the middle, actually."

"Sporting terms are confusing. I received a deputation last week. They wanted to discuss bowling. I was under the impression that bowling was something which took place in the open, on a bowling green. Nowadays, apparently not. It is an indoor occupation, and involves elaborate machinery. Will croquet go the same way, I wonder?"

"I was once very fond of croquet," said Mr. Sudderby, tugging at his short beard. "I had a trial for Sussex."

"You're a man of unexpected accomplishments, Mr. Sudderby. But we were talking about cricket. How large is a cricket field?"

"The smallest possible area would be a circle of fifty yards radius from the middle of the pitch. Sixty would be better."

"And you could fit one into my home meadow?"

"Oh, easily."

"You are sure that my windows would not be in danger?"

"It's rare for a cricket ball to be hit full-pitch for more than three hundred yards."

"These technicalities are beyond me. But if you assure me that my windows and glass-houses are safe, you shall have your field."

"It's very kind of you."

"I feel I owe it to you," said Mrs. Lord. "Since the Corporation, of which I have the honour to be head, are taking away your own field, it's appropriate that I should offer you a replacement. When will it be required?"

"We shall be able to go on using the one we lease from the Corporation until the end of this season, and we shan't want to start playing on the new one until next May. We'd like to come and do some work on it in the off-season – particularly if we're going to return the square."

"The square?"

"The square is all the different pitches."

"I don't pretend to follow you. Tell me, Mr. Brydon, do you not find it dangerous, playing cricket in glasses?"

Anthony Brydon smiled. When he did so he looked even younger than his twenty-three years. "It's an advantage," he said. "It makes the fast bowlers sorry for you. Actually I have a special pair of glasses for cricket. The lenses are plastic."

After tea, he gave Mr. Sudderby a lift back into Barhaven. The gentle, bearded Town Clerk was an old friend. As a small boy, and later, in holidays from school, Anthony had gone for long walks with him over the downs. He was an enthusiastic, if inaccurate, ornithologist and local historian.

2

All around them Dollington Park slept in the late afternoon sun. The home meadow would make a fine cricket field. A bit farther from Barhaven than their present one, and off the bus route, but almost everyone had cars nowadays. They would have to think about traffic control. Mrs. Lord wouldn't want a stream of cars coming down her front drive every Saturday afternoon. Could they open an exit from the far side of the field into Cow Lane?

"It's wonderful how she keeps the place up," said Mr. Sudderby.

"Most of her money comes from the toll bridge," said Anthony. "If the Government ever took the tolls away she'd be in the soup. They're tax-free, too. I've never understood why."

"The original Act of Parliament makes it quite clear. The tolls were to be regarded as returns of the capital sum expended on constructing the bridge."

"I don't know how much it cost to put a bridge over the River Barr in 1790," said Anthony, "but since she must now be getting five thousand a year out of it, I don't call it a bad investment."

"It's a very good investment," said Mr. Sudderby. "Good for her, and good for the town. Particularly as the Act authorises us to raise the tolls on any three days in the year which we choose. It's my belief that the half-crown toll we impose on Bank Holidays is all that saves Barhaven from an invasion of those horrible young men—" Mr. Sudderby screwed his face up— "known, for reasons I have never been able to fathom, as Mods and Rockers. Mod, I suppose, is short for modern. But *what* do the Rockers rock?"

"Their elders and betters," said Anthony. "Of course, they haven't *got* to come over the toll bridge, but if they don't use it, it means a detour of nearly thirty miles, and that's enough to put them off, I expect."

"Do you know, I nearly had a fit this morning. I thought I had seen a Kirtlands Warbler."

It took Anthony a few seconds, his mind being on teenagers, to realise that this was the ornithologist, not the Town Clerk, speaking

"Would that have been exciting?"

"Epoch-making. It's the only warbler that is entirely yellow underneath. The global population of Kirtlands Warblers is hardly a thousand individuals. They winter in the Bahamas and are only commonly found in Michigan."

"I take it that it wasn't."

"I'm afraid it turned out to be a canary. It must have escaped from one of the pet stores on the Parade. Our Friday influx has well and truly started, hasn't it?"

At that point the by-road from Dollington Park and village joined the coast road. The tide had set towards Barhaven. There were sedate family saloons, crowded station wagons, rakish sports cars, impudent Minis, cars with luggage piled on roof racks, cars towing caravan trailers, cars towing boats.

"Not too many motor-cycles, thank heavens," said Mr. Sudderby. "Do you think you could pass that car ahead?"

"I expect so. There's not a lot of point in it, though. We shall only be held up by the next one."

"I wanted to see the people in it. I thought—yes—they are—" As Anthony drew level with the car ahead, a well-preserved 1960 Hillman, Mr. Sudderby leaned dangerously out of the window and waved. The driver and the plump little woman beside him looked up in surprise at the bearded figure, then smiled and waved back.

"The Burgesses," said Mr. Sudderby. "He's a chartered accountant. He works for a big firm in the City. His wife's name is Doris."

Mr. Sudderby reseated himself.

"They told me they might be coming down here for their summer holiday. I'm so glad they've managed it. The Burgesses are *just* the sort of visitors we ought to encourage in Barhaven."

"They looked a nice couple," said Anthony. He had been so busy with his driving that he had not actually seen them at all.

"They're not only nice," said Mr. Sudderby. "They are the *right type*. People with a bit of money to spend, and who like to spend it quietly. Not like *that* sort."

He looked with distaste at a boy in a black leather, brass-studded jerkin, wearing a red scarf round his neck and a crash helmet on his head, with a similarly dressed figure, male or female, it was hard to say which, on the pillion. He was threading his motor-cycle through the stream of traffic with the insolent verve of a destroyer needling a convoy of laggard merchant-men.

"Not quite the Barhaven type," agreed Anthony. "This is your turning, isn't it?"

"It's very kind of you. That will do nicely. Unless you'd care to come in and take a glass of sherry."

"I'll have to get home. I want to see how my father's getting on."

"Of course. I hope he's no worse."

"He's no worse," said Anthony. "But I should be fooling you if I said he was any better. He's had to take things very quietly after that last attack, and he hates it. Left to himself, I think he'd much rather go out on to the golf course, play a strenuous eighteen holes of golf, and drop down dead on the last green."

Mr. Sudderby looked faintly shocked. "You mustn't talk about death," he said. "He'll be with us many years yet, I hope."

The older you got, thought Anthony, the less you *did* want to talk about death. As if, by averting your eyes from him, you could placate the quiet, grey man who sat in the corner of the room, waiting to come forward, at the chosen moment, and tap you on the shoulder.

Chapter Two

Anthony Plays Cricket and Witnesses an Assault

From the bowler's action Anthony judged it was going to be a fastish ball, swinging away to the off, which would keep low and ask to be cut. Too late, he saw that it was going to be straight, but short and hookable.

Five seconds later the ball was safe in the hands of deep square leg, and Anthony was walking back to the pavilion.

He arrived to an ovation.

"The youthful hero," said Chris Sellinge," blushed, removed his cap to acknowledge the cheers of the crowd, and—"

"Bloody silly way to get out."

"When you've made eighty-five, you're entitled to get out in any way you like."

"It was a cow-shot," said Anthony. He started to unbuckle his pads. "My feet were in the wrong place."

"Speaking for myself," said Sellinge, a thick rufous estate agent with rather less hair on his head than when he had left the Royal Navy at the Armistice, but the same unsinkable optimism which had made him a menace in most of the navigable waterways of the world, "I never have time to worry about my feet. I think of two things only. The bat and the ball. My concern is that they shall make contact."

"In any game," said Anthony, "the thing that matters most is to have your feet in the right place."

"When you're old enough to go out with girls," said Sellinge, "you'll realise how wrong you are. Did you have any luck with the Lady Mayoress?"

"She's going to let us have the home meadow."

"Ah! A bribe to stop us squealing when they turn us out of this one."

"It'll make a very nice ground."

"It'll take ten years to make a playable square."

"Less than that if we work at it. Anyway, I thought it was very decent of her to offer it at all."

"You're young," said Chris. "You go round in rose-tinted glasses. When you grow older, you'll cultivate a decent cynicism."

"I can't see that there's anything to be cynical about."

"Don't you realise that what is being perpetrated in Barhaven is the biggest and most barefaced land grab since Bishop Poore moved his cathedral from Old Sarum to Salisbury – having first taken options on all the best building plots along the River Avon."

"You're always looking for ulterior motives."

"You don't have to look for things when they hit you in the eye."

"Cover point *is* going to get hit in the eye if he crowds Charlie Roper like that."

But Chris was not to be diverted.

"In the first World War," he said, "there were, I understand, two bitterly opposed factions, the Westerners and the Easterners. That's the position in Barhaven in a nutshell. There *are* only two ways the town can develop. It can't go inland, because that's all farmland, and untouchable. And anyway, in a coast resort nobody wants to build inland. Therefore, the town must spread east or west. Correct?"

"Your reasoning," said Anthony, "is irrefutable."

"The sensible way to develop is to the west. There's a three-mile stretch up to Dollington and the river. It's handy for the station. It's the residential side already, so you've got the services laid on. And a lot of it belongs to my clients."

"I guessed you weren't entirely disinterested."

"Of course I'm not disinterested. Who is? Certainly not the Council. You know *why* they want to develop east, don't you?"

"To spite your clients."

"It's because a lot of the property on the east of the town belongs to them already – clear out, you stupid little bastards!"

A couple of youths who were strolling unconcernedly across the sight screen stopped as Sellinge shouted, and started to retreat. The batsman lashed out wildly, and skied the ball into the hands of mid-off.

"If I was Charlie Roper," said Chris, "I'd get after those boys with a stick."

"About time we declared, anyway."

"Bad luck, Charlie. It was those kids walking across the screen."

Charlie Roper, the Barhaven wicket-keeper, was a larger man, with a red face and a shock of light hair. He said, "It wasn't the boys, Chris. It was you bellowing like that. You've got a voice like a bloody foghorn. Come here, you two."

The youths approached.

"This one's my Terry," said Charlie. "He's my eldest. He's got no more sense than a wooden rabbit."

Terry grinned, showing a tooth missing in his upper jaw.

"What did you come up here for, anyway? I didn't think you were interested in cricket."

"Nor I am," said Terry. "I came up here with a message from mum. She said, don't be late tonight, because her mother's coming over."

"You can tell her from me that if she thinks I'm going to go without my wallop just to listen to my mother-in-law nattering, she can think again."

"Do you really want me to tell her that, dad?"

"No."

"Tea," said Anthony. "A hundred-and-ninety-four for six. Good enough. If Seaford can get half that in the time that's left, they'll be surprising themselves."

As they got up, Chris said, "That little matter I was talking about. If I came to see you, officially – would you be interested? I could manage eleven o'clock on Monday, if that suited you."

Anthony paused, with one foot on the pavilion step. Behind them, the players, umpires and supporters were drifting across the green field towards the tea tent. It was always interesting, he thought, when an acquaintance turned into a client.

"Why, yes," he said. "As far as I know I'm free at eleven. Come along and we'll talk about it."

The last Seaford wicket fell soon after six with the score a hundred-and-eleven. By half-past eight Anthony was sitting on a bench in one of the shelters on the sea-front wondering what he was going to do with the rest of his evening.

At that hour the Marine Parade was full of strolling couples and family groups. Mostly they were the sort of people James Sudderby would have approved of. Solid folk, with money to spend, and no idea of kicking up a shindy.

And surely – yes – there were the Burgesses. They were going into the Pleasuredrome, Barhaven's newest attraction, which offered a heated swimming-pool and ten-pin bowling, with Bingo and dancing in the evening.

Behind the Burgesses, two girls were loitering, arm in arm. Both wore their light hair dressed in a way which suggested an unconvincing sort of wig. One was wearing what looked like a sack, belted at the waist. The other wore very narrow, light blue jeans and a short black leather jacket.

They were clearly waiting for someone to take them into the Pleasuredrome.

Well, why not? Not both of them, of course. One of them. For preference the one in the leather jacket. But suppose you couldn't separate them? And how would you start? "Would you care to accompany me into the Pleasuredrome?" He knew exactly what would happen. A haughty stare. "As a matter of fact, we're waiting for a friend." And, as he moved off, they would giggle. How they would giggle. The whole thing was fantasy, anyway. Could he, a professional man, a partner in the old-established firm of Brydon & Pincott, Solicitors and Commissioners for Oaths, start picking up girls on the front? Well, could he? That was a question which had puzzled and worried him before, and which now presented itself afresh. *How did you start?* What was the opening move which culminated in those desirable joys, those scufflings in the secluded corners of the Odeon, those intimacies in the back seats of parked cars, those rollings in the short grass behind the ninth hole on the Municipal Golf Course? Other people did it. Look at Chris Sellinge. When he cut away early from the pub everyone had known where he was going. It was an open secret that he was running a girl from the Sea-Side Stagers who were in the middle of their Mammoth Summer Season at the East Pier Pavilion. Chris was older than he was; and − let's face it − not terribly attractive. How had *he* started? How did anyone start? Was there some trick, some knack, or gimmick, something unaccountably left out of the syllabus for the Law Finals; some key which, once grasped, unlocked this final door? His theoretical knowledge of sexual practices was detailed and comprehensive. He had built it up from jokes heard at school (jokes at which he laughed conscientiously, afterwards analysing them to extract the hard grains of fact round which their fancies were built); from graffiti on lavatory walls; and from those useful paper-backed American novels which could be bought on railway station bookstalls and thrown away at the end of the journey. Straightforward love-making; love-making not so straightforward; perversion; masocho-sadism, transvestism, narcissism, fetishism; he knew it all.

He had never kissed a girl in his life.

He decided to go to the cinema.

When he came out, the sky was bright with stars. The Marine Parade was emptier. There were couples in most of the shelters along the front; two or three couples in some, intent on their own business, unmindful of each other.

The Pleasuredrome was still open, and busy. The foyer was a blaze of lights and he could hear the band playing. A babble of voices. Louder voices. Screams of laughter. Screams.

Anthony quickened his pace.

As he was passing it, a door at the side of the building opened with a crash, throwing a fan of light across the pavement. A man backed out, dragging someone. It was a body, which the man held under the arms. He straightened his back, heaved, and the body skidded across the pavement and ended up in the gutter.

Anthony took half a pace forward, then stopped. A drunk was being thrown out. It was none of his business.

Now the man had gone inside again, but the door was still open. There was a clatter of footsteps, a stamping, an exchange of obscenities, and the man reappeared. This time there were three people involved.

One man was holding a struggling boy. He held him easily. His right hand had twisted the boy's right arm behind his back, locking it in an upward position, his left hand was holding the collar of the boy's jacket. With his knee, he was frog-marching him forward in a series of spine-shattering jerks. The victim's free left arm whirled in a circle, but failed to connect.

The second man stepped close to the boy, and put a finger under his chin, tilting it back. "He's young to be out without his mum, isn't he? What'll we do with him? Cool him off in the sea?"

Using the only weapon available to him, the boy jerked his head forward. His forehead hit the second man on the bridge of the nose. The man rocked back on to his heels, came forward again, and hit the boy full in the face with clenched fist. Then, swinging his arm well back, he hit him again. At the second blow, the boy screamed.

"St—st—stop it," said Anthony. The stammer which afflicted him in moments of crisis rendering him almost speechless. "S—stop it at once."

Both men looked up.

"I should — off, if I was you," said the man who was holding the boy.

Anthony was shaking with rage.

"If you hit that boy again," he said, "I'll g—get the police."

"No bother," said the second man. "There's one right behind you."

Anthony swung round. A constable was standing in the mouth of the alleyway. With him was a stout man in a dinner-jacket.

"These the boys, Mr. Marsh?" said the constable.

The man in the dinner-jacket came forward and peered down at the first boy, who was climbing slowly out of the gutter and back on to his feet. Then he looked at the second one.

"That's them," he said. "Rotten little bastards."

"You're sure of it?"

"Dead sure. I noticed 'em when they came in. I didn't like their looks. I ought to have turned 'em out."

"I take it you'll be preferring a charge."

"You're damn right I'll be preferring a charge. If they've damaged the machinery it might cost a couple of hundred pounds to put it right. I'll say I'm charging 'em."

"You'd better ring for a car. Barhaven 2121. Ask for the duty officer."

"Right," said Mr. Marsh.

"Are you going to charge these men, too?" said Anthony. He had got back control of his voice.

The policeman looked surprised.

"I beg your pardon, sir?" he said.

"I wanted to know if you were going to charge these men."

"Charge them?"

"With assault."

"Assault on who, sir?"

"On these boys. I know this one, by the way. His name's Terry Roper. One of these men held him, and the other hit him, twice."

"It's a lie," said the second man. "We were having a fight. He hit me, and I hit him."

"If he cuts up rough, we've got to get a bit rough too," said the first man.

The constable said to Anthony, "I don't see how you come into this at all."

"I saw it happening. I saw this man hit the boy in the face, while the other one held him."

"If that's right, how did he hit me?" said the second man, and pointed to his own face, where a bruise was already developing on the cheekbone.

"He butted you with his head."

"It sounds like a real mix-up," said the policeman. "You can tell us all about it in court, on Monday."

"I shall certainly be in court," said Anthony.

"Here's the car," said the policeman. "Put the boys in the back." And to Anthony, "Personally, if I were you, I should go home and go to bed, and have a nice sleep."

Mr. and Mrs. Burgess undressed methodically. Just because he was on holiday, Mr. Burgess did not believe in being sloppy. He emptied everything out of the pockets of his blue blazer, and placed it on a hanger. Trees went into his brown and white shoes.

Mrs. Burgess said, not for the first time, "I shan't go back to *that* place again."

"Rowdyism," said Mr. Burgess, removing his top-set and placing it carefully in a glass of disinfectant. "It's something I can't tolerate."

"It's the last thing I should have expected in Barhaven," said Mrs. Burgess.

"I'll have a word with James Sudderby tomorrow. I'm told there's a sports club out at Splash Point. You need a bit of pull to get into it. But he'll be able to fix it for us."

"No reading in bed tonight," said Mrs. Burgess. "I'm tired."

Mr. Burgess climbed in beside her, and turned out the light. "What *did* happen?" he said. "I saw a lot of people fall down."

"Someone moved the floor. A girl fell through into the swimming-pool."

"*Not* what you expect in Barhaven," agreed Mr. Burgess.

Anthony's home was in one of the new building estates on the fringe of the town, and it took him ten minutes' fast walking to get there. There was a light in the downstairs room which had been turned into a bedroom for his father, to save him climbing the stairs. As he unlocked the garage doors, his father called out.

"It's all right," said Anthony. "A bit of trouble in the town. One of my clients."

"Are you going to see him now?"

"I'll have to, yes."

"A fine time to see a client," said his father.

Anthony backed the car out. He knew where Charlie Roper lived, having given him lifts home from cricket. It was in the area behind the station, an uninspiring egg-box of matching streets and mass-produced houses. As Anthony stopped his car outside the house he saw the curtain in the front room move, and Charlie had the front door open by the time he reached it. He put a finger to his lips.

"Wife's asleep," he said. "Evening, Mr. Brydon. Thought I recognised your car. Something up with Terry, isn't it?"

"That's right," said Anthony. "We can talk in the car, as we go."

"Where are we going?"

"To the police station."

"Silly young sod," said Charlie. "What's he done?"

"It's not only what he's done," said Anthony. "It's what's been done to him."

He told him, and Charlie listened in silence. At the end he said, "The other boy'll be Sam Mason. Sam and Terry's always around together. They sort of egg each other on. If they've run into real trouble this time it may bring 'em to their senses."

Anthony stopped the car.

"You don't understand," he said. "If they'd just been fooling about and been run in, I wouldn't have bothered. A night in a cell and a good fright is probably what they were asking for. But this wasn't anything like that. One of those men held Terry, and the other hit him, hard, in the face, twice. He's probably broken his nose. I don't know what they did to the other boy. As he was in the gutter being sick, they'd probably kicked him in the stomach. It was none of it necessary."

Charlie Roper looked at Anthony curiously. He had never seen him in that mood before.

He said, "They're a rough crowd at the Pleasuredrome. I heard they got two or three men down from London – professional chuckers-out. They were frightened of Mod an' Rocker trouble and didn't want to take chances. I expect that's it."

Anthony engaged gear and drove on. It had occurred to him that it was always stupid for a solicitor to get more worked up over a client's troubles than the client was himself.

The boys were sitting on a bench in the charge room. When Terry opened the remains of his mouth in a sickly smile, it was clear that one tooth, at least, was gone, and there was a long purple bruise across his face from left eye to right cheek. Sam Mason was chalk-white but otherwise seemed unharmed.

Anthony said to the desk sergeant, who was making entries in a ledger, "This is Mr. Roper. He's the father of that boy there. I'm their solicitor. If you've finished booking them, is there any reason they shouldn't be taken home?"

The desk sergeant finished what he was writing, blotted it deliberately, and said, "Can you identify yourselves?"

Anthony looked at Charlie Roper, who looked blankly back at him.

He said, "You could ring up my father. That is if you really think I'm an impostor. He's pretty well known in the town."

"I'll have to ask the Inspector."

"Where is he?"

"He'll be here in a moment—I think this is him now."

The newcomer, Anthony was glad to see, was Inspector Ashford, the head of Barhaven's small C.I.D. force. Anthony had met him, and, illogically, had liked him because he had played rugby football for Blackheath and Kent and had had a trial for England.

The Inspector acknowledged Anthony's existence with a tight smile, and said to Charlie Roper, "You ought to keep your son at home in the evenings, Mr. Roper."

"What's he been up to?"

"They seem to have caused a bit of trouble at the Pleasuredrome. They had the bright idea of pulling the lever that controls the dance floor over the swimming-bath. It's a sliding arrangement. When the bath's in use, they roll it back."

"Was anyone hurt?"

"A girl fell through into the pool. And two or three more got hurt in the stampede. And there's a question of damage to the machinery. When they tried to stop it, they put it into reverse and stripped a lot of cogs."

Anthony said, "First things first. This boy ought to be seen by a doctor. And they'd be better at home than here. Mr. Roper can stand surety for his son. I'll undertake to produce the other one."

"Hasn't he got a father?"

"He lives with his mother," said Anthony. "If you try to bring her out here at this time of night she'd have a fit."

Inspector Ashford considered the matter. The unshaded overhead light shining down on his head showed up a deep scar, which ran from his left temple to a point behind his left ear. It was more a fold than a scar.

Anthony remembered how Inspector Ashford had got this. It had been during the final England trial at Coventry. He had been kicked on the head, and had been unconscious for forty-eight hours. It had cost him his England cap, too.

"We shall want them in court on Monday, ten o'clock sharp," the Inspector said. "You can take them away."

Chapter Three

Anthony Appears in Court

Miss Barnes, the Chairman of the Barhaven Magistrates and Councillor for the East Marine Ward, was a dark, squat, taciturn woman with a large mole on one cheek. She had qualified, but never practised, as a barrister and ran a prosperous nursery garden specialising in miniature pot plants.

"Anything else you want to tell us, Mr. Marsh?" she said.

Mr. Marsh said that the damage to the machinery was not, fortunately, as serious as had at first been supposed, but, on the other hand, the damage to the good name and reputation of the Pleasuredrome was deplorable. "Once decent people get the idea it's a rowdy place," he said, "they won't come near it. I've heard from a lot of our patrons already. They're absolutely disgusted. One of them said to me, only this morning, 'We've been coming to the Pleasuredrome regularly since it opened, three years ago. We've never had any trouble there before, and now—'".

"We've got the point," said Miss Barnes. "Anything you want to ask him, Mr. Brydon?"

"Yes," Anthony said. "If you haven't had any trouble in the three years since you opened, Mr. Marsh, why do you need two chuckers-out?"

"I have two attendants. They're not employed as chuckers-out."

"What do they do? Hand round lemonade?"

"No."

"Look after hats and coats? Clean the brass? Compare the dances?"

"What I said. They're just attendants."

"All right," said Anthony. "Let's look at it this way. They're your employees. You must give them some instructions about what their duties are. What do you tell them to do?"

"I tell them to look after things—generally. See that the dancers behave themselves."

"And if they don't behave themselves?"

"They ask them to leave."

"Ask, or order?"

"Well—order, if you like."

"And if they won't leave?"

Mr. Marsh looked uncomfortable, and shot an appealing look at the bench.

"Then they can − in fact − use a degree of force − a reasonable degree − to evict them."

"And a reasonable degree of force includes punching boys in the face and kicking them in the stomach?"

"I don't quite see where this is leading us," said Mr. Lincoln-Bright, from his seat on the left of Miss Barnes. "It's the boys who've been charged, surely, not Mr. Marsh."

"It comes in this way," said Anthony. "That I hope to be able to show you that however reprehensible this prank by Roper and Mason was, the treatment which they received was out of all proportion to the offence."

Mr. Lincoln-Bright looked down his long and well-shaped nose, and then, sideways, at Miss Barnes, who said, "I'll give you a little more rope, Mr. Brydon, but not much."

"Thank you," said Anthony. And, to Mr. Marsh, "Did you, yourself, see either of the accused tampering with the handle of the mechanism which activates this floor?"

"It was Morris who saw them."

"One of your chuckers-out. I beg your pardon, attendants."

"Yes."

"That's all right then," said Anthony. "I shall have a chance of questioning him about it when he gives evidence?"

He waited invitingly, the question-mark hanging in the air like a wisp of smoke, until Inspector Ashford climbed to his feet and said, "We hadn't intended to call Morris."

"Then how were you going to prove the offence?" asked Miss Barnes. "Mr. Marsh says *he* didn't see 'em."

"Both boys made statements, on the night in question, admitting that they tampered with the mechanism."

"Statements," said Anthony, "which were obtained from them in a state of shock, before their legal adviser arrived, and which they now entirely withdraw."

Inspector Ashford said, "The statements have been made. I don't see how they can withdraw them."

"I think what's being suggested," said Tom Allerton, on Miss Barnes' right, "is that the statements weren't properly taken, and oughtn't to be admitted."

"That's what I am suggesting, sir," said Anthony. (If Lincoln-Bright was against you, you could count on Tom Allerton taking your side. It was a perfectly balanced bench, pivoting on the massive impartiality of Miss Barnes.)

The Chairman said, "Let's hear your reasons."

"I suggest you've only got to look at the two boys. Mason has recovered now, but at the time I saw him on Saturday night he was being sick in the gutter—."

"*You* saw him."

"That is correct. And if these proceedings develop, in a certain way – I can't say any more about that at the moment – it may be necessary for someone else to conduct the defence so that I can give evidence—"

"We're giving the press a real field day," said Miss Barnes. From where she sat, she could see their pencils jumping and skidding across the pages of their notebooks. Arthur Ambrose, editor and leader writer of the *Barhaven Gazette,* was looking quite pink with excitement.

"We'll deal with that when it arises," she added.

19

"Although I'm not on oath at the moment," said Anthony, "perhaps you will take it from me that both boys were very badly shaken. Roper's face speaks for itself."

"*Res ipsa loquitur,*" said Miss Barnes. She conferred for a moment, in undertones, with her two fellow magistrates, and then said, "For the moment, we're not going to decide about this statement, one way or the other. All that we're going to say is that we should prefer to have the case proved without it. This man Morris, who saw the boys tampering with the machinery, he can come here and tell us about it – I suppose."

"No difficulty about that," said Inspector Ashford. "I was simply trying to save the court's time."

"I'm sure you didn't act from any improper motive," said Miss Barnes. "I shall adjourn this case for seven days. Will that be enough for you, Mr. Brydon?"

"Certainly," said Anthony. "But before you finally adjourn the proceedings this morning, there is one other point I should like to raise. This is, in form, a Summons and Complaint by the injured party. It is not, in fact, a police prosecution."

"That's correct. The complainant is Mr. Marsh."

"If the matter is to be adjourned for a week, do you think the real complainant might be substituted?"

"Have you got any reason to suppose that Mr. Marsh *isn't* the real complainant?"

"I hardly think he can be," said Anthony. "After all, he's only an employee. He doesn't own the Pleasuredrome. If any damage has been done to it, it isn't Mr. Marsh's pocket that has suffered."

Miss Barnes said, "What about it, Mr. Marsh?"

Mr. Marsh looked blank.

"I'm afraid I didn't quite follow that," he said.

"*Are* you the owner of the Pleasuredrome?"

"No, no. I'm just the manager."

"Who does own it?"

"It's a company—I think."

"We don't want to make this any more complicated than it need be," said Miss Barnes, "but I think I agree with Mr. Brydon that the complaint ought to be in the name of the person who has been damnified. Particularly if these proceedings lead on to further, civil, proceedings, as I understand may be the case. The man, Morris, who saw the alleged offence must give evidence. We make no ruling as to the admissibility of the statements taken from the two boys. When we have heard Morris' evidence there may be no further need for them. Adjourned seven days, on parents' recognizances in twenty pounds each."

Chapter Four

Anthony Tries to do a Morning's Work

Outside the court room Anthony was buttonholed by Arthur Ambrose.

"Truly magnificent," he said. "Front-page stuff. I'll be doing the story myself. If you could give me a couple of minutes of your time, you could fill in a lot of background—"

"I've got a *very* busy morning—"

"Five minutes."

"Oh, all right."

"We can get a cup of coffee in here, and chat as we imbibe it."

"You realise this case is still *sub judice.*"

"It wasn't the case I wanted to talk about. Although, incidentally, I thought you handled old Ashford splendidly. You know what they call him in the force? Bull Ashford. I expect that's because he does his thinking with his—oh—two white coffees please, miss. Not too much milk in mine. No. It's the Pleasuredrome I wanted to talk about. The *Gazette's* had its eye on that place for some time now. Did you see Marsh's face?"

"Did I—?"

"Did you see his face? When you asked who the real owner of the place was? Owned by a company, he said. Ha! And now he's going to have to tell the court the name of that company. That's going to be good. I'm going to be there to listen to that. I'm looking forward to it."

"Why—"

"A company has shares," said Ambrose. He had the habit, common to newspapermen and schoolmasters, of speaking in short sentences, with the verb in the middle. "The shares have owners. There are ways of finding out who those owners are. True?"

"Oh, certainly," said Anthony. "Once you know the name of the company, you can make a search in the Companies Registry—"

"And I'll tell you what you'll find. You'll find that most of the shares are owned—" Mr. Ambrose leaned forward, although the cafe was entirely empty, and whispered in Anthony's ear— "by Hamish Macintyre."

"Really?" said Anthony. "Look, I must be going. I'd no idea it was as late as this. I've got a terribly busy day. I'm doing most of my father's work these days, whilst he's out of action. You'll have to drink my coffee for me—"

The office of Messrs. Brydon & Pincott, Solicitors and Commissioners for Oaths, was on the west side of Connaught Square opposite the Council building. Eleven o'clock was striking as Anthony ran up the steps, but the waiting-room was empty. Chris Sellinge was late; or quite possibly had forgotten his appointment.

His secretary was sitting beside his desk taking down a telephone message in shorthand.

He waited until she had put the receiver back.

"What's it all about?"

"Do you know a Mr. Raymond Southern? Isn't he someone on the Council?"

"He's Vice-Chairman. And next year's Mayor, provided he doesn't come a cropper at the elections next week."

"He's coming to see you. Twelve o'clock. Is that all right?"

"Our practice is looking up," said Anthony. "Certainly it's all right. Did he say what he wanted?"

"Something to do with forming a company."

"We ought to be able to do that for him, and talking about companies, that chap who runs the *Barhaven Gazette and East Surrey Advertiser*, Arthur someone—"

"Arthur Ambrose."

"He buttonholed me on the way back from court. He had some story about the Pleasuredrome being owned by a company and he hinted that the shares were held by a man called Hamish Macintyre. The way he told me about it, I could see I was meant to jump out of my skin."

"There's only one Hamish Macintyre in Barhaven as far as I know," said Ann, "and he's the Borough Engineer and Surveyor."

"Didn't we have some trouble with him over the drains in the Victoria Park building estate?"

"That's right. And we may be having some more trouble with him. That is, if you'll take on another new client. I've got you Colonel Barrow."

"How does Colonel Barrow come into your life?"

"He was a friend of my father's."

"I see."

Ann Weaver had been Anthony's secretary for a month now. He had already made a number of discoveries about her, and a few guesses. Her father, who was dead, had been a Captain in the Regular Army. It had puzzled him that a professional soldier should not have risen beyond the rank of Captain. When he met Mrs. Weaver, that piece of the puzzle had fallen into place.

Captain Weaver must have been commissioned from the ranks. And the studied gentility of Mrs. Weaver suggested that he had married before leaving the ranks. Ann, then, must have been born some time around the end of the War, and her father's improving rank and status would have ensured that she was sent to a boarding-school; probably a more expensive school than they could really afford.

"Isn't he head of that prep school? The one whose boys wear a scarlet cap?"

"Castle House School."

"What does *he* want?"

"He says they're trying to shut his school down."

"Who are?"

"The Borough Council. It's something about drains."

Anthony thought about this. It didn't seem to him to make a lot of sense. But he had a feeling that, added to one or two other things he had heard lately, it ought to mean something. He said, "Fix him an appointment for tomorrow morning."

"He says it's practically impossible for him to leave the school at the moment. One of the masters has got mumps, and another one's broken his leg playing cricket with the boys."

"You can't break your leg playing cricket."

"This one did."

"All right. Then telephone and say I'll try and get out after tea today. It's easier to look at drains than to talk about them. Yes?"

This was to an old man who had poked his head round the door.

"It's a Mr. Sellinge, Mr. Anthony. Says he's sorry he's late, he got tied up."

"Show him in, Bowler."

"Sorry to be late," said Sellinge. "I got stopped by Ambrose. Arthur means well, but he can't stop talking. If we could clear the top of this table, I could spread this map. Now – this is what I was trying to explain to you on Saturday. The red lines are proposed new roads. The green lines are main drainage. The purple are extensions of the grid. Everything comes in from the west, which is natural. The focus of development is always on the London side. That's the side the main roads and railway and grid come from.

In other words, if you develop west, you've got the services on your doorstep. If you develop east, you've got to extend them, and pull them out after you, as you go."

"Which is what the Council are doing."

"Exactly. And why? Because *if* they develop east, they won't have to buy so much land. They happen to own a lot of it already. When they extended the front towards Splash Point they picked up the marsh-land behind it for a song. They can close down the last nine holes of the Municipal Golf Course, which will ruin it, but what do they care? The Borough Councillors can still play on the Splash Point course, which isn't affected. And by turning us out of our cricket ground they can grab another six acres."

Anthony wasn't really listening. He was looking at the map. This was the twenty-four inch to the mile Ordnance Survey, and it was detailed enough to show private properties, buildings and field divisions.

He ran his finger down the secondary road which snaked out towards Splash Point.

"It's reclaimed marsh south of this road," he said. "North of Haven Road there are five or six little private properties – bungalows, I seem to remember. Castle House School here. But who owns this bit?" He outlined with his finger-tip a large, wedge-shaped piece of land bounded on the west by the school playing-fields, and on the north by farmland.

"I'm not dead sure," said Chris. "It's some farmer, I think."

"He's going to be a very rich farmer."

"And the best of British luck to him," said Chris. "I don't object to private citizens making a profit. It's when the Council makes a profit out of the private citizens that I get upset. And that's just what we're going to stop. Luckily, they've given us a handle. Mr. Shanklin – who owns this bungalow here, and who's a jobbing builder – has bought the strip along the other side of the road, and applied for permission to put up a terrace of four shops with living quarters over. He says there's a demand for the shops, and he may be right. The Council opposed it, because it didn't fit in with *their* development plans, and the planning authorities turned it down. Mr. Shanklin has asked for a local enquiry. The Council fought the idea tooth and nail. I think they'd even have supported his shop scheme, if he'd abandoned the enquiry, but I've got some backers on the Council too. People like Tom Allerton and Mike Viney, and we managed to scotch that one. So the enquiry's on. And *that* means that we're going to have a chance of thrashing the whole scheme out in public. Which is the last thing they want."

"It seems to me that there's a good deal to be said on both sides."

"You'd better not be too broad-minded about it. If we're going to fight the Council, we shan't have to pull our punches."

"I'm not sure that I am going to take it on."

Chris stared at him. Then he said, "There's nothing illegal about this, you know. We've got as much right to press for the development our side as they have on theirs."

"I know," said Anthony.

"If it's the costs you're worried about, my clients aren't exactly paupers."

"Don't be silly," said Anthony. "I know you, and I know a lot of the people who are behind you, and I'm perfectly certain that you're all sound as the Bank of England."

"What's the trouble then?"

"The trouble is," said Anthony, "that whichever way this comes out, it's going to cause a lot of ill-feeling. I don't need to tell you. You're on the Council yourself. You know that."

"There'll be a lot of dirt flung about, but why should any of it stick to you? You're a professional man. You'll just be doing a job."

"I know," said Anthony, unhappily. "I know. The trouble is, that once you start on a thing like this, you just can't help getting involved. Can I think it over and let you know?"

"We can't wait too long. The hearing's in less than three weeks. You'll have to brief Counsel, I expect."

"I'll let you know tonight," said Anthony. "Without fail."

He had ten minutes with his morning mail before his next client was due but his mind wasn't on his letters.

Nothing that Chris had told him was news to him. He had heard it all half-a-dozen times, from James Sudderby, from Charlie Roper, from Tom Allerton, from old General Crispen (who had been a Sapper, and knew more about roads and railways than the rest of the Council put together). Most of them were his friends. He thought that there was a lot to be said for a big, impersonal, London practice where clients were clients, and business stopped at the office door.

"Have I got a smut on my nose?" said Ann.

"No—why?"

"You were staring at me – opening and shutting your mouth – just like one of our goldfish."

"I'm sorry," said Anthony. "I was thinking."

"I'll get you a cup of tea," said Ann. "The stuff Bowler brews is guaranteed to take your mind off any problem. And your next client's due any moment now."

Raymond Southern was a small man with a pink face, blue eyes and white hair. He wore a pin-striped flannel suit with a double-breasted waistcoat. He was neat, from the top of his well-brushed hair to the tips of his shiny shoes; as neat as if he had been unwrapped from a cellophane wrapper a moment before; so neat that you might have started by thinking him effeminate, though the impression would not have lasted long.

"I've just sacked my accountant," he said. "I've had my suspicions of that man for some time."

"Davies dishonest?" said Anthony. "You really do surprise me. If you'd said incompetent—"

"He's not dishonest. He's too damned honest. Do you know what I caught him doing on Saturday? *Playing golf with the Inspector of Taxes.* I told him he's got no right to be friendly with the Inspector of Taxes. The Inspector's my enemy. If Davies worked for me, my enemies must be his enemies."

"What did he say?"

"He blethered about the personal touch, and how it was easier to arrange things on a friendly basis. I don't operate by being friendly with my enemies. I fight them."

"All right," said Anthony. "Who do you want to fight now?" He knew Raymond Southern too well to be afraid of him.

"At the moment, I'm not fighting anyone. I'm forming a company. Mentmores are the solicitors I usually go to, but now that Arthur Mentmore has been made Clerk to the Justices – a piece of nepotism, between you and me: Lincoln- Bright's his cousin, and Magda Barnes is related to his mother – and being on the Council myself, it might conceivably have made things a bit difficult. Are you willing to take me on?"

"I'll try," said Anthony.

"Good. I'm a great admirer of your father's. How is he, by the way?"

"As well as could be expected."

"Bad as that, is it? Poor old chap. We formed the first Home Guard platoon in Barhaven, in 1940. I expect he's told you? He was Platoon Commander and I was Platoon Sergeant. Now then—"

He pulled out a thick sheaf of typewritten documents, schedules and accounts.

"I've been picking up one or two quite promising little businesses lately—"

Not really a soft mouth, when you looked at it more closely. A predatory mouth.

"Hairdressers, sweet shops, newsagents, places like that. When a town grows, they are the sort of people who grow with it. And Barhaven is growing. You don't need statistics to tell you that. You can see it happening. We're God's gift to the Upper Middle Class. The sort of people who find Brighton too raffish and Eastbourne too stuffy. They're beginning to discover Barhaven. And what's more, with the south leg of the M2 and the doubling up of the railway to Maidstone, we're becoming accessible. Not much more than an hour from London either way. When I first came here it was a minor resort. Now it's on the map. It's growing, and nothing's going to stop it. Population's going up. Thirty per cent more visitors this summer than last. Land values sky-rocketing. Unfortunately, it's too late to get in on *that* racket. The Council's got all the land on one side and a gang of farmers under Gauleiter Sellinge have got a stranglehold on the other. Wasn't that Sellinge I passed in the corridor, by the way?"

"That's right," said Anthony, wishing he could cure himself of the weakness of blushing.

"Able chap, in his way. I believe he's planning to go to town at this enquiry. Did you know about that?"

"I had heard something about it," said Anthony.

"Ah." The blue, knowledgeable eyes rested on him for a fraction of a second. "Mustn't waste your time talking about other people's business. Now. My idea was this. Form a private company. The company holds all my properties, and it holds my ordinary business, too – insurance brokerage. That makes a reasonably steady profit every year. Nothing to get excited about. Four or five thousand. I can give you the exact figures later. The businesses – I've picked up five of them so far, and got options on two others – sometimes make a profit, sometimes make a loss. Obviously, if I can set the losses off against the brokerage profits—"

They descended into the mass of papers, and came up for breath half an hour later when Southern looked at his watch, and said, "Heavens, it's a quarter to one already. I've got to go and have lunch with the Lady Mayoress, to brief her for this afternoon's session. It's the report of the Lands Committee and she thinks we're in for trouble. So do I. We'll fix another appointment when you've digested all those figures and had a think about them."

Chapter Five

Anthony Lunches with his Father

Anthony went home to lunch.

He had made a habit of doing this since his father's second coronary had confined him to the house. He found the old man perched in his high-back chair, with a tray in front of him and the *Barhaven Gazette* propped up against the water jug. With his hooked nose and ruffled hair, he looked like a little eagle. But he was a little eagle in bondage.

"Blasted idiot," he said.

"Who's an idiot?"

"Ambrose. That man's got so many bees in his bonnet I wonder honey doesn't drip out of his ears."

"What's he on about now?"

"Parking."

"It's time someone did something about parking," said Anthony, sitting down to the hot-pot which, regardless of the weather, was Mrs. Stebbins' standard Monday offering. "It's all right in the winter, but from May to September you can't squeeze a car in anywhere."

"And how would *you* deal with it?" said his father in his cross-examining manner.

"For a start, it wouldn't do any harm if we had two or three more big underground garages like the East Pier Garage."

Mr. Brydon chuckled.

"Exactly," he said. "Exactly." He was back in court, luring an opponent into a trap. "And why does no one build these garages?"

"No money."

"For a profitable venture like that? You could borrow all the money you needed from the bank."

"Why then?"

"Because the Borough Council, and in particular, the Borough Engineer and Surveyor, Macintyre, won't let them. Whenever a project's put up to Macintyre he vetoes it. Structurally unsound, danger from infiltration of sea water, unsafe, insanitary."

"I'm not a surveyor," said Anthony, "but it sounds pretty good nonsense to me."

"It sounds nonsense to Mr. Ambrose," said his father. "But he always spoils a good case by going too far. He's now suggesting that an enquiry ought to be held to find out *who really owns the East Pier Garage.*"

"Does he suggest an answer?"

"He's not quite such a fool as that. There's a law of libel. But the implication is pretty clear, I think."

Anthony had been reading the article whilst his father was talking. Ambrose wrote well and forcibly. His talent was wasted in Barhaven. He would probably end up in Fleet Street. And he would certainly be unhappy there.

"Anything new at the office?"

"I had rather a busy morning, actually." He told his father about the police court proceedings.

"Silly young asses. They'd only got themselves to thank," said his father. "All the same, I'm glad to see us back in court. We lost a lot of that work when they made Mentmore Clerk to the Justices. A mistake to have a partner in a local firm doubling up that job. Bound to lead to discrimination."

Anthony grinned to himself. He was well aware that his father had angled for the job himself. Nor was he being insincere, now. He was exercising the prerogative of old age, of forgetting inconvenient facts.

He said, "Business is looking up all round. We had two new clients this morning."

"Good," said the old man. "That's very good."

He had started the practice from nothing when he came back from France in 1918. He had lived in it, and for it. It had been work and play, wife and family. In 1937, on doctor's orders, he had taken his first real holiday – a six weeks' cruise, down the west coast of Africa and across to South America. He had met Anthony's mother at dinner on the first night out, made up his mind to marry her at Freetown, proposed to her at Lagos and been finally accepted at Capetown.

Mr. Brydon, like most front-line soldiers, was an admirer of Earl Haig. Had not Haig met his future wife at a house-party on Friday, played golf with her on Saturday, and proposed on the ninth green? And when friends expressed their surprise at the speed of his wooing had he not said that "he had made his mind up on many more important matters more quickly than that?"

Mr. Brydon approved the sentiment. Marriage was something you went in for when more important business allowed. When he learned of Anthony's birth, he did sums on his fingers and said, "We'll have him through his Finals by 1960." When his wife died he mourned her genuinely and briefly. It had been an episode; satisfactory in itself, and doubly satisfactory because it had produced a junior partner for the firm of Brydon & Pincott.

To Anthony his mother was hardly even a memory.

"Who were these new clients?"

"There was Chris Sellinge."

"And who's he?"

"Shorter & Sellinge."

"Oh, those house agents. Yes."

"They don't call themselves house agents. They call themselves Surveyors, Auctioneers and Valuers."

Mr. Brydon snorted. He was not fond of house agents. They made difficulties over deposits, and charged more, in his view, for five minutes' work in selling a house than the solicitor did for two months' work transferring it to a purchaser.

"What did *he* want?"

Anthony explained, and his father listened in silence. At the end he said, "I suppose you'll have to take it on."

"I haven't made up my mind yet."

"You can't pick and choose. It's legitimate work. If you don't do it, someone else will."

"In this case, I'd rather someone else did."

"Why?"

"Whoever wins, it's going to antagonise about half the top people in Barhaven. The Council's split. By no means down the middle, I agree. The Sellinge gang are in a minority. But don't forget, the Council elections are coming on. Five retiring members, four of whom happen to be anti-Sellinge. And if one or two of them don't get back, it might be quite a different picture."

"That's politics. It's nothing to do with lawyers."

"I wish you were right," said Anthony. "But I'm afraid you aren't."

The old man shifted uncomfortably in his chair. It irked him that he couldn't get down to the office and grasp the complexities of matters like this one. Anthony was a clever boy. Cleverer than he had ever been himself. But had he got the tough, inner core which you needed if you were to come out top in the competitive world of a solicitor's practice?

"There's another snag," said Anthony. "My second new client this morning was your old friend Raymond Southern."

"Has he deserted Mentmores?"

"For the moment."

"That's very good. I've always wanted Raymond as a client."

"I've not had much to do with him before this morning."

Mr. Brydon chuckled.

"Raymond's a crook," he said. "But an honest crook. If you follow me. In a business deal he'll fight with every weapon in his hand, but he won't bear you any ill-will afterwards, even if you win. That's how he plays bridge, too. He'll open on nothing, double to scare you, bluff you out of game. But if you call his bluff and he goes down a couple of thousand points, he simply smiles like a crocodile."

"There's nothing illegal in what *he* wants us to do."

He explained the details to his father, who was only half-listening. He was thinking of his old companion-in-arms of Home Guard days, of nights spent on the cliff-top, of confidences shared.

"He's the sort of man the socialists hate. He's too hard for them. And too successful. And, in a way, too kind. He gives to charity, but he gives it on his own terms. If he works hard and makes money he doesn't see why a lot of parlour pinks should take three-quarters of it away and sprinkle it round among people who are too lazy to earn it for themselves. What are you laughing at?"

"I wasn't laughing," said Anthony. "I was just thinking what a pity it was you couldn't stand for the Borough Council at this election."

What he was really thinking was that there was no gap like the gap between twenty-five and sixty-five.

Chapter Six

"Take One"

"I have the honour," said Lincoln-Bright, "to present to the Council the report of the Lands Development Committee. As you will be aware—"

"A point of order, Madam Chairman."

"Yes, Mr. Viney?"

"I know that I am speaking for one or two others besides myself when I say that I question whether a matter of this importance should have been referred to a committee at all."

"You were here when that was agreed," said Jack Crawford.

"Wouldn't it be better if the member for the Marine East Ward observed the proprieties of debate and addressed his remarks to the Chair?"

"Hear hear," said Chris Sellinge.

Crawford, his brick-red face turning several shades darker, presented his back to Sellinge and addressed the Mayoress with elaborate formality.

"I merely wished to point out, Madam Chairman, that since the member for North Ward was present when this committee was appointed, it seems to me to be a bit late in the day to object to the committee presenting its report."

"My point has been misunderstood," said Mike Viney. He was a tiny figure, with a hunch-back, and a mop of grey hair. "When this committee was appointed, more than two years ago, the situation was very different from what it is now. The eastern extension of the Marine Parade was only a project. It is now nearly completed—"

"No thanks to you," said Crawford, loud enough for the speaker to hear, but not loud enough to constitute an official observation.

"—moreover we had not then had the reports of the Drainage Sub-Committee or the Roads Sub-Committee, both of which, I think it would not be unfair to say, leaned toward western rather than eastern development—"

"Madam Chairman—"

"If I might be allowed—"

"I have not yet concluded my remarks—" The Mayoress rotated her head slowly, her myopic gaze lighting on each speaker in turn. Finally the interruptions cancelled each other out, and a moment of silence ensued.

"It really does seem," she said, "that there are differences of opinion about this. Perhaps we ought to discuss the whole matter before we listen to the report "

"A debate of the whole Council—"

"On a point of order—"

"I don't think Madam Chairman—"

"If you all talk at once," said Raymond Southern, his high voice riding easily over the clamour, "we're going to be here all day, and get nowhere. So far as I know, the member for North Ward still has the floor. I think, Madam Chairman, he should be allowed to conclude his observations, and that you should then call on the next speaker—and so on. We may then preserve what have already been referred to this afternoon as the proprieties of debate."

"Hear hear," said General Crispen.

"I am obliged," said Mike Viney, who had not sat down through the whole of this. "I had, in fact, nearly finished what I wanted to say. We have none of us any objection to hearing the report of the Lands Development Committee who have, I am sure, done their work in a most thorough and conscientious way. As long as we all bear in mind that their conclusions are not binding on the Council, and that conditions have changed so radically since they were appointed that their terms of reference may well now be out of date."

He sat down, and no one seemed quite clear what to do next, until Southern whispered in Mrs. Lord's ear, and the Lady Mayoress first said, "What?" and then, after further whispering, "I now call on the member for Victoria Park to present the report of the committee."

Lincoln-Bright again rose to his feet.

"As you will be aware," he said, "this committee – which consists of myself, as Chairman, the senior member for the Liberties, Mr. Andrews, and the junior member for Connaught Ward, Mrs. Coverdale, who was, unfortunately, unable to be here today – was charged with a general survey of the development plans of this Council—"

"We're a mixed bag," Chris Sellinge had once said to Anthony.

Around the long, horseshoe-shaped Council table, itself reputedly five hundred years old, sat the elected representatives of the people of the Ancient Borough of Barhaven: Charlie Andrews and Willie Law from the "Liberties", the rich farmlands which had been the delta of the River Barr before it had been diverted, and which now formed a private green belt round the inland side of the town; Ian Lawrie, Tom Allerton and Mike Viney, the North Ward representatives, a solid Radical block who spoke for the station area and the slums which lay behind it; Miss Planche who (with the absent Mrs. Coverdale) represented the Connaught Ward, and who would vote Progressive as long as her *bête noire,* Miss Cable, supported the Independents; Raymond Southern and Lincoln-Bright for Victoria Park; Chris Sellinge and Miss Cable, for Marine West; Jack Crawford and the redoubtable Miss Barnes, J.P., for Marine East where the big hotels stood; General Crispen, the retired Sapper, who stood alone for Splash Point; George Gulland, an almost inarticulate fisherman, whose family had represented Dollington for centuries; and, in the centre, at the head of the horseshoe, looking as apprehensive as a mother who realises that her family has finally grown beyond parental control, Mrs. Lucy Lord, Mistress of the Tolls, inheritrix of Dollington Park, and three times Mayoress of Barhaven.

"—And we came, therefore, to the unanimous conclusion that the scheme prepared for us by our consultant surveyors, Messrs. Grey Dorfer & Co., involving a lay-out of the eastern area from the fringe of the present development, in three successive phases, up to the line of Splash Point and the old river outlet, was the optimum scheme, both in its planning and its economic aspects."

As he sat down three people tried to get to their feet together. Chris Sellinge, who had the advantage of sitting immediately opposite the Mayoress, caught her eye.

"I am not going to repeat what has been said by Mr. Viney—"

"I should hope not."

"—And if the member for Marine East would refrain from making puerile interruptions we could get on with our business a bit faster."

Jack Crawford glared at the speaker, and scribbled a note which he pushed across to Raymond Southern. The Vice-Chairman glanced at it, folded it, and put it into his pocket without looking at the sender. His face was tranquil.

"I would like, instead, to elaborate on the suggestions he has made. There seems to me to be a danger here that we ought to guard against. If the report we have just heard is put to the vote of this Council it will quite clearly be passed. It recommends what I should describe, briefly, as the eastern scheme. And this has always been the scheme favoured by the Independent Party on this Council—"

"Mr. Sellinge," said Southern. "I don't want to interrupt you, or usurp your right to free speech. We've had quite enough of that sort of thing this morning. But could I clear up this point before we go further? If the majority on the Council finds itself in favour of the report of this committee, why shouldn't the fact be recorded?"

"For two reasons, Mr. Vice-Chairman. The first is that any formal decision could prejudice a matter that is already *sub judice.*"

"You mean the public enquiry about Haven Road?"

"I do."

"I agree that we don't want to prejudice the enquiry. But we can easily avoid doing so. Approval of the report can be made without prejudice to our decision about the Haven Road Enquiry."

Sellinge looked thoughtfully at Southern. They were the two ablest men, and the two strongest characters in the room, and they were conscious of each other's strength.

"*If* the Council accepts the report, won't it mean that it is bound to oppose the appeal? The report specifically allocates Haven Road as residential."

"I don't think so. The Council can approve the report in principle without binding itself to support every detailed recommendation."

As Sellinge hesitated, Southern went on, "You said there were two reasons."

"My second reason isn't going to recommend itself to some of you, I know. But I have to remind you that we are less than three weeks from the Council elections."

"What of it?" growled Miss Barnes.

"I think that if a decision is going to be made which may dictate the whole development of our town, it might be better to defer it for a fortnight so that the new Council can decide on it."

Willie Law said, "I don't agree. We can't put off decisions just because an election's coming up. That's daft."

"I agree."

"I don't think—"

"Absolute nonsense—"

"The feeling of the meeting is against you on that point, Mr. Sellinge."

"I thought it might be."

"Is that all?"

"That's all."

"Then," said Southern, looking at the Mayoress, "I think—"

"You want me to put it to the vote."

"I think that is the general feeling, yes."

"You have heard the report of the Lands Development Committee, and have had an opportunity to comment on it. The proposal is, that the report be adopted. Those in favour?"

Eight hands went up.

"Those against."

Five hands went up.

The Mayoress looked baffled. Five and eight made thirteen. Excluding herself, there were surely fourteen people at the table.

"Could we do that again?"

Eight people. Andrews and Law, Southern and Lincoln-Bright, Clifford and Miss Barnes, Miss Cable and General Crispen. All staunch Independents.

"Those against."

Viney, Allerton and Lawrie, as expected. Sellinge of course, and that cuckoo, Amy Planche.

Of course – Gulland had abstained.

"Are you voting, Mr. Gulland?"

George Gulland came out of a dream. His face was as brown as one of his own lobster pots. "Oh, aye," he said. "I'm voting."

"For which side?"

"I'm with them."

"You mean that you're against the report."

"I'm with the last lot."

"But that means," said the Mayoress, patiently, "that you are *against* the report of Mr. Lincoln-Bright's committee."

"Don't twist his arm," said Chris Sellinge. "He's already said it twice."

"Very well," said the Mayoress. She would have to speak to George's father about this. George's father was over eighty, but had a lot more sense than George. "That makes eight votes in favour and six against. I declare the motion carried."

"I should like the actual voting recorded."

"Very well, Mr. Viney."

"And I would like to register a protest."

This unexpected attack baffled the Mayoress. She looked at each of the Councillors in turn. They all seemed as surprised as she was.

"I think it's an insult to democracy that a biased report should be forced through the Council on a party ticket—"

Good gracious! This was coming from the body of the hall. She peered into the misty dimness. No. It was from the press bench. Surely this was out of order? She looked round desperately for support.

"You're out of order, Mr. Ambrose," said Raymond Southern.

"I'm no more out of order than the Council is."

"You're being childish. The press and the public are admitted to these meetings on sufferance. If you can't behave yourself, you will have to leave."

"A fair example of the way discussion is stifled in this town."

Southern said something to the clerk, who scuttled round the table and disappeared.

"And before your hired bullies arrive to throw me out, I should like to ask a question. Who was the Chairman of the Lands Development Committee? Mr. Lincoln-Bright. And who's his chief supporter? Mr. Crawford. And who are members of the syndicate which run the hotels on the eastern side of Barhaven? Lincoln-Bright and Crawford."

"Will you sit down."

"And who's going to benefit most if the development comes on the eastern side? Lincoln-Bright and Crawford. And who's going to line their own pockets at the expense of the citizens of Barhaven—"

The clerk reappeared, accompanied by a constable and one of the Council employees.

"I must ask you," said Southern, his face still amiable, "either to sit down and undertake not to interrupt Council business further, or to leave."

"I shall do neither."

"In that case—Constable—"

"I protest."

"You'd better come along, sir."

"I refuse."

"Take his other arm, Waller."

At this moment a magnesium flash went off, as one of Mr. Ambrose's assistants, carefully stationed in the gallery, levelled his camera.

"Take one," said Sellinge.

Chapter Seven

Anthony Observes his Secretary out of Office

"Eight-six," said Anthony.

He held the soft black ball delicately in the tips of the fingers of his left hand, dropped it on to his racquet, and struck it in a high, gentle parabola into the backhand corner of the court. Chris Sellinge observed it suspiciously, decided it was going to come off the wall in time for him to hit it, swung hard and hit wall and ball simultaneously.

The ball rocketed across the court and smacked into Anthony. The head of the racquet snapped off, flew into the air, and bounced off the back wall. Sellinge swore.

"Game and set," said Anthony. "Sorry about your racquet."

"It doesn't matter about the racquet. It was an old one. What does worry me is why I can never beat you."

"You don't put your feet in the right place."

"I remember you telling me so before."

"Take that last shot. How can you expect to play a backhand shot if your left foot is almost up level with your right?"

"You can tell me about it in the shower."

They left the squash court and climbed up the wooden steps to the gallery to collect their towels and sweaters. Sellinge, who had strolled along to look at the other game, said, "There's some nice form in Court Two."

Anthony walked across to look. The sports club professional was having what was evidently an instructional game with a girl.

Anthony's first impression, foreshortened and from above, was of a pair of tapering legs in very short white sports-briefs.

"What a piece of home-work," breathed Sellinge. "Can't Bunny Davies pick 'em."

"Can he?"

"He's laid every layable girl in Barhaven."

Anthony said nothing. He was examining the girl.

On his visits to London he had sometimes strolled down Greek Street and studied the photographs which hung outside the Strip Clubs. He had come to the conclusion that there must be something wrong, either with the photographs or with himself. Presumably they were hung there to attract and stimulate customers? They had filled him only with nausea. Those breasts like children's balloons after a party – enormously inflated, but now sagging very slightly in the heat; the nipples like bell-pushes; the coat-hanger hips, the soft, feather-bed bottoms.

As this girl swung half-round to play a backhand shot he noticed with appreciation that her top half, covered but not concealed by a clinging sports vest, was constructed on infinitely more satisfactory lines than the odalisques of Soho. The small firm breasts seemed to be forward extensions of an integrated system which started somewhere up at her shoulders and shoulder blades, not disassociated flabs slapped on to the front of the body like lumps of plasticine. The stomach was flat and the hips, though wide, were unexaggerated.

The professional stopped the rally by catching the ball in his hand.

"You're holding your racquet all wrong," he said. "Let me show you."

"Here we go," murmured Sellinge.

"Like this." He stood behind her, holding her right wrist lightly, and laying his left hand on her bare arm. "Drop the head a bit. Bring the left foot forward. If you try and keep that position in relation to the flight of the ball you'll hit it easily enough."

"Thank you," said the girl politely.

Anthony found himself blushing. He moved away.

"Do you think it's wise to leave 'em without a chaperone?" said Sellinge.

"I wouldn't trust Bunny," said Anthony, "but the girl's quite reliable. I'm going to have a shower before I get cold."

"Do you know her?"

"Certainly. You've met her too. She's my secretary."

"Knock me down," said Sellinge. "I thought I'd seen that bottom before. She looks quite different in her office clothes, doesn't she?"

"Oh, quite," said Anthony.

"Did you know she was a member here?"

"I didn't. But there's no reason she shouldn't be. She's quite—I mean, her father was a Captain in the Army."

"My father was a film actor," said Sellinge. "And look at me." He stepped under the shower, turned on the hot tap by mistake, swore, and jumped out again. "If you should get a chance of seeing the first version they ever made of *Ben Hur,* you'll notice him rowing. He's in the second galley, on the third bench."

They got dressed, and strolled across to the clubhouse.

The Splash Point Country Club was built on a shelf in the shoulder of the downs overlooking the former estuary of the River Barr. Some six hundred years ago the river had circled the tiny fishing village of Barhaven to the east, and run out to sea through a network of marshy channels. Then an enterprising group of inhabitants, whose names were preserved in the Wool-market (Anthony had got most of this from James Sudderby during their walks over the downs) had decided to divert the river, and to drive it straight out to sea through the Chine on the west of the town. From that date Barhaven had flourished.

Its long, slow decline had then started, like the gentle, untroubled years of a man who has been too successful in youth. By the middle of the nineteenth century, when wool was coming from Australia and corn from Canada and shipbuilding was being done on the Tyne, and it looked as though Barhaven might drop off to sleep altogether, it was rescued for a second time by royal favour. Queen Victoria, who spent a number of enjoyable weekends at Ditchling House, was much taken by the quiet and decorous charm of the little fishing village. When her Paulet Commission was reorganising county boundaries in 1880, and Barhaven was unceremoniously detached from Sussex and incorporated into Kent, its privileges as an ancient and independent borough were reserved to it by a fresh royal charter.

In gratitude Barhaven had named a confusing number of streets, avenues, crescents, terraces and squares after members of the royal family. A statue of the queen, erected outside the railway station, and paid for by public subscription, had proved a convenient resting-place ever since for stormbound seagulls.

As Anthony strolled with Sellinge along the asphalt path which led from the squash courts to the main clubhouse the town lay spread out at his feet in the evening sun. It was framed on one side by the cobalt blue of the sea and on the other by the green and brown of the fields. If you looked closely, you could see the thin red lines of town development forcing their way outwards, through a network of narrow streets.

"Just like an aneurism, getting ready to burst," he said.

"What a disgusting metaphor. All the same, I wish I knew which way it was going. Someone's going to make a packet out of it."

"Money isn't everything."

"And that's such a bloody silly remark," said Sellinge, "that you can buy the first round of drinks."

The early evening crowd was already in the club room. It was mostly men, who would drive out to Splash Point on their way home from work, postponing for half an hour the moment when they would have to be husbands and fathers again. Wives came out with them at weekends but were discouraged at other times.

Anthony pushed his way to the bar. Jack Crawford was there, talking to Lincoln-Bright and Raymond Southern. Southern said, "Hullo, young Anthony. How's your father?"

"He was in good form at lunch," said Anthony. "Sitting up and taking nourishment and damning the younger generation. Two ginger beer shandies, please."

"Ice, sir?"

"No. Just stir them."

"You've been well brought up, I can see," said Southern. "Never put ice in, or near, beer. Terrible American habit."

"Your father is a great lawyer, and a credit to this town," said Crawford, swinging suddenly round to face Anthony, and bringing a blast of whisky-sweetened breath with him.

This was the sort of remark that Anthony found it difficult to deal with. The first part, he knew, was wrong. His father was a very competent solicitor, but had no pretensions to being a great lawyer, and would have laughed if he had been accused of it.

"Well, that's very good of you," he said.

"Get it in writing," said Southern. "You'll be able to put your charges up."

"I'm serious," said Crawford, putting on his serious face. "I wasn't a client of your father myself, but I'd have trusted him—implicitly. And why I should have trusted him implicitly was because he put the town first."

"Four-and-eightpence please, sir."

"Some of us," said Lincoln-Bright, "*are* prepared to put the community above our private interests." He had the thin, incisive voice of a man who has few opinions but has memorised them thoroughly.

Anthony pocketed his change with some difficulty, picked up the two pint glasses, and started to edge his way out.

"Grab one of them, will you," he said to Sellinge, who had come up to help him.

Sellinge stretched out a hand, and at that moment Crawford swung round, holding a full whisky glass. A lot of the whisky went on to the floor, some of it slopped down the front of Crawford's coat.

"Sorry," said Sellinge.

"Handkerchief," said Southern.

Crawford went very red, and said, "Would you bloody well mind out what you're doing."

"Don't think it was entirely his fault," said Southern. "Mop it off before it stains your coat, and I'll buy you another."

Crawford took no notice of this. His mouth was working, framing something ugly. He said, "This Club was intended for gentlemen. It seems to have got clattered up with estate agents."

There was a pool of silence in the little crowd in front of the bar. Then Sellinge said, "Either you apologise for that, or I shall report the remark to the committee and ask them to cancel your membership."

"You can report it to your Aunt Fanny," said Crawford. "I'm not taking orders from a jumped-up land profiteer."

Sellinge raised his glass of shandy and tipped it down the front of Crawford's shirt.

Spluttering an obscenity, Crawford swung a low short arm jab which, if it had landed where he meant it to would have done some damage, but Sellinge turned and caught it on the hip. By this time, Anthony and Raymond Southern had manoeuvred themselves between the two men.

They were the centre of an embarrassed crowd. The only person who seemed to retain a grasp of the situation was Southern. He said, "Better come and change your shirt, Jack. I've got a spare one in the locker room," and to the barman, "There's been some drink spilled, Bob. Clear it up, would you."

Before Crawford could protest he had grabbed him by the arm and steered him out of the room.

Sellinge said to Anthony, "I'm going home."

"Me too," said Anthony.

As they left the room they heard the pent-up comment burst into spate behind them.

Chapter Eight

Anthony Encounters Opposition on All Sides

"Quite a shemozzle at the sports club yesterday evening," said Ann, as she brought in Anthony's post and proceeded to slit it open for him. "Did you see it all?"

One of the differences between Ann and other secretaries he had had was that she seemed to have no idea that she should wait for him to speak to her. If she wished to introduce a topic she did so, boldly and forthwith.

"I was there," said Anthony.

"*Did* Chris Sellinge empty a pint tankard over Crawford's head?"

"Down his front."

"Because Crawford called him a Communist."

"He called him an estate agent, actually."

"I missed it by five minutes. It's always the way. If anything exciting happens, I'm in the next room. The only morning I came down late for breakfast was when my aunt threw the electric toaster at my uncle. She hadn't bothered to unplug it, either."

"When I saw you," said Anthony, "you seemed to be having quite an exciting time yourself."

Ann looked puzzled.

"In the court with Bunny Davies."

"Oh, that was you in the gallery was it. He's certainly a trier. When he put his arm right round my waist to demonstrate a drop shot, I asked him if he was teaching me to waltz or play squash. That cooled him off a bit."

"He's got a very bad reputation."

"Can you be warning me against him?"

"Er—yes."

"I expect you mean it kindly," said Ann, "but you ought to know that it's absolutely fatal – warning girls about men. You might just as well say to a wasp, there's jam in that there jar. Steer clear."

The telephone saved Anthony from having to answer this. It was Charlie Roper, speaking from a call-box. It took Anthony a moment to grasp what was being said.

"They've *dropped* the charge," he said. "Against your son and the other boy. *Who's* dropped it?"

"The police, I suppose."

"Why?"

"Search me. They just dropped it. Lack of evidence was what they said."

"They can't do that to us."

"It means the boy gets off, doesn't it?"

"He gets off, yes. But what about his reputation? It's been in all the papers. If they just say, 'the case was dropped for lack of evidence,' everyone's going to say they did it, but it can't be proved."

"I hadn't thought about that," said Roper. "Look here, I've got to get back now. I just slipped out from work for five minutes to tell you." Anthony thought quickly.

"When do you get out for lunch," he said, "and where?"

"I usually have it in the canteen. Sometimes I go to the Duke of Clarence."

"At the top of Leydon Avenue?"

"That's right."

"Can you be there at a quarter to one?" said Anthony. "I'll have a word with the police and find out what's happening."

"All right," said Roper. He sounded doubtful.

Anthony dealt with the rest of his letters as quickly as he could. What he had told his father was quite true. Brydon & Pincott was experiencing one of those little surges of new work which occur from time to time in professional practices. When this happened, it meant overwork at the top; which was better than underwork, but could be difficult just the same.

If Ellis Pincott had pulled his weight in the office the burden would have been tolerable. But Ellis seemed to spend more and more of his time on outside duties. He was Secretary to the Barhaven Chamber of Commerce, Convenor to the Archdeaconry of East Sussex, and clerk to the Foreshore Commissioner. They were posts of much honour and small remuneration. In theory they were a good connection, but in practice they meant that Ellis spent half his working day outside the office, leaving such mundane but necessary duties as conveyancing, litigation and probate to Anthony and two managing clerks.

One of the advantages of having a secretary like Ann had been that he got through his letters much quicker. When she first came he had dictated each answer solemnly through from beginning to end. She had put up with this for a week, and had then said, "If this is just to be a 'thank-you-very- much-and-I'll-attend-to-it-as-soon-as-I-can-get-round-to-it' letter, I can write it. There's no need to dictate it." In an increasing number of cases, now, Anthony found himself pushing the letter across to Ann and saying, "The usual, please." He sometimes suspected that the work would get done even quicker if he wasn't there at all.

Inspector Ashford was a big man; not tall, but wide through the shoulders, barrel-chested, and with a lowish centre of gravity; a textbook lock forward. He had a thick crop of black hair, which he wore unusually long, partly concealing the ugly scar down the left side of his head.

He said, "And what can we do for the law today, Mr. Brydon?"

"I heard a rumour," said Anthony, "that the case against Roper and Mason was being dropped."

"Roper and Mason? Who—oh—those two young tearabouts who made nuisances of themselves in the Pleasuredrome."

That was nicely done, thought Anthony, but not really convincing.

You'd been told I was coming to see you. So you must have known what I wanted to talk about.

"I believe that's right. What are you planning to do about it? Ask for costs against the prosecution?"

"I might do that," said Anthony. "But it's not the real point. What I want to know is, are the police going to take over the case? Even if Pleasuredrome won't prosecute, the police can."

"Certainly."

"Are you going on with it?"

"I think I can set your mind at rest on that score. If the owners of the property don't wish to proceed, the police aren't going to fight their battles for them. If the disturbance had taken place in public, it might have been different—"

"Then you won't go on with it?"

"You must rest on your laurels, Mr. Brydon."

"I'm not going to do any such thing."

"If the prosecution won't prosecute, I hardly see how you can defend."

"You seem to forget that there's a counter-charge. Unnecessary brutality by the two chuckers-out. That's something we want the court to hear about."

"I don't fancy you'd find a great deal of sympathy for that sort of action. This town doesn't like teen-aged rowdies."

Anthony nearly said, "I don't want sympathy, I want justice." It was a good line, too. But it would have been wasted on Inspector Ashford. Instead, he said, "There's another thing. If we can get the case on its feet, we shall at least find out who owns the Pleasuredrome. And that's something a lot of people in Barhaven are beginning to be curious about."

"I don't follow you."

"If the boys sue the manager, he'll be bound to join the owners. He's not going to take the rap personally. Even if he wanted to, we wouldn't let him. Then we should see who the owner is."

Whilst Anthony was speaking, Inspector Ashford had sat still. The only change was in his eyes, which had gone opaque, as though he was looking inwards. When he spoke his voice, too, was abstracted.

"Why would a thing like that interest you?"

"Someone must be making a lot of money out of that place if he can keep two whole-time professional bullies on his pay-roll."

"I still don't see how you come into it. You were briefed to defend the two boys. Your defence has been successful."

"You haven't answered my question," said Anthony. "Why aren't the police taking this matter any further?"

"I've told you."

"Was it your decision?"

"Not entirely."

"Then whose decision was it?"

Inspector Ashford was getting angry now. The blood was swelling the veins in his neck and engorging his scar so that it showed up scarlet against the white of his skin. He lowered his head as a bull will do when it is going to charge.

"So far as you're concerned," he said, "it *is* my decision."

"It was a silly question," agreed Anthony, "because I know the answer. The only people who could give you any orders are the Watch Committee. If I want the truth, I shall have to go to them."

The Inspector said nothing. His eyes had gone blank again. Anthony went out quickly, and shut the door behind him.

As the third quarter after twelve was striking from the Victoria Memorial Clock tower he squeezed his car alongside a delivery van at the edge of the Duke of Clarence car park. He found Charlie Roper in the Saloon Bar drinking beer and eating bread and cheese and pickled onions.

Anthony accepted a half-pint, said "No" to the pickled onions, which he considered an unattractive form of food, and started to talk. He found himself up against some unexpectedly solid resistance.

"'Tisn't that I don't appreciate what you've done for us, Mr. Brydon. The wife and I both appreciate it a lot. But if this case is dropped, and the boys get an apology, that'll be in the papers, too, won't it? And then everyone'll know they're in the clear. And that'll be an end of it."

"Will it?" said Anthony.

"How d'you mean?"

"An apology won't mend Terry's nose for him."

"The doctor says it isn't broken. Just bent. And suppose it had been broken—" Mr. Roper speared an enormous onion, balanced it on top of a wedge of cheese, and placed the cheese on a segment of roll and butter— "I'm not sure it wouldn't have served him right. If he's going to arse around, he's got to learn to take the rough with the smooth."

He added an effective full stop to this sentence by inserting the whole forkful into his mouth.

"If it's the expense you're worrying about," said Anthony, "forget it. I'll fight this thing for you free, and enjoy doing it."

Roper chewed on this for a bit. Then he shook his head.

"It's not the money," he said. "Not that I'm keen on throwing my money away, but if I thought it'd do a mite of good, I'd pay up and be glad to do it. The thing is, I'm not keen to make any more trouble. I got my job to think about."

"How on earth does your job come into it?"

"I'm with Collyers, the transport people – they're a good firm to work for, too. But they're sticky. They don't like trouble. My boy gets involved in a bit of trouble, that's all right. Boys will be boys. But if I start going to law about it – stir up more trouble – get a lot of publicity, I've got a feeling I might be looking for another job."

"All right," said Anthony. "If that's how you feel. I suppose Mrs. Mason doesn't want to start anything either."

"You seen her," said Roper with a grin. "What do you think?"

"She didn't look like a very willing litigant," agreed Anthony. "By the way, that firm you work for – Collyers – I'm always seeing their lorries up and down the front. They do a lot of work for the Corporation, don't they?"

"That's right," said Roper. Anthony thought he was avoiding his eye.

When he got outside, a policeman was standing beside his car.

"You're outside the parking area," he said.

"I'm sorry," said Anthony. "There was a big lorry parked just there, and it must have been obscuring the white line."

"We've had a lot of complaints about obstruction of this street. I'll have to take your name and address."

Anthony gave them.

"And might I see your driving licence and insurance certificate?"

"You might if I had them on me. But I haven't."

"Then you'll have to produce them at the police station within twenty-four hours."

Anthony drove home to lunch.

He found his father finishing his meal, and reading a typewritten sheet which had come to him in the midday post. Looking over his shoulder he saw that it was addressed from the Splash Point Country Club.

"I can't make head or tail of this," he said. "A special committee meeting. As an ex-Chairman of the Club my attendance is particularly requested. I can't get to committee meetings now. Commander Sathwatt must know that."

"I suppose it's about the row yesterday evening."

"What happened?"

Anthony told him. His father said, "Two grown men behaving like children. No need for a special committee meeting. They want their bottoms kicked."

"It was Crawford who started it."

"Every stupid quarrel is always started by someone."

"He was pretty high, too."

His father said, "Well, I'm not going. But I'll write a letter to Sathwatt and tell him what I recommend."

"Which is what?"

"Suspend both memberships for a year. Give them time to cool off."

"It might be the best thing," said Anthony. "But don't forget, they're both Councillors. And they're both up for re-election next week. It's not going to do their chances much good if it gets about they've been thrown out of the Country Club for brawling."

"They might have thought of that before they started. I hope you didn't get involved."

"Well, as a matter of fact, I didn't, but if it had come to the point I'd have stuck up for Chris. He was absolutely in the right—this time. And anyway, he's my client."

"Only in office hours," said his father. "Ask Mrs. Stebbins to clear away my lunch, and give me the writing paper."

After lunch Anthony drove out to see Colonel Barrow. Castle House School occupied a broad ledge of ground overlooking the road from the town to Splash Point. The building, originally designed either as a large private residence or a small and superior hotel, was of scarified red brick with a frontage of thrown stucco topped off with curly tiles. Over the years the expanding fortunes of the school had led to additions. From one side straggled a long, low classroom block with a flat roof designed to support extra dormitories which no one had got round to building. At some distance from the other side there had, at some time, been erected a wooden hut of first World War vintage, which the main building had then reached out and engulfed, as a boa constrictor will eat, but not at once succeed in digesting, its prey.

The playing-fields were wonderful. Ten acres of green downland turf, mowed and rolled to perfection, girdled by a belt of trees which had been planted when the building was first put up, and by a much older wall of knapped Sussex flint.

Colonel Barrow, a long, brown, thin, sad, weathered man, was keeping an eye on two games of cricket. He said to Anthony, "Good of you to come out to see me. I'm afraid I'm almost single-handed, as usual. Matron's taking the third game. I don't think she knows a lot about cricket. Luckily the third game know even less. Keep your left elbow up, Ferguson."

"I believe you've been having trouble with Macintyre, the Borough Surveyor."

"He certainly seems to have his knife into me."

"What's he been up to?"

"Two years ago it was fire escapes. He made me put up that iron monstrosity – between the fives court and the new games hut. I pointed out at the time – hands, Piatt, hands – there's no need to fall on the ball to stop it. This isn't rugby football – I pointed out that there were two internal staircases, one at either end, and it was most improbable that both would be on fire at once. He quoted some regulation to me. Then there was the entrance to the drive. That had to be widened, and the gate-posts set back, in order to expedite the flow of traffic in the road outside. I said that the very last thing I wanted was the traffic outside ray gates going faster—"

"Reasonable," said Anthony.

"And anyway, why should *I* pay for it!"

"He made you pay for it?"

"In the end. Yes. There was some bye-law. I didn't understand it."

"I wish you'd come to me about it at the time."

"I wish I had too." Colonel Barrow stretched out a leathery hand, caught a ball from the second game which had been skied in his direction, and returned it to the small, white-clad fieldsman.

"No. It's not out. I'm not fielding for your side. All the same, O'Regan, you will get out if you try a straight drive without getting your left foot far enough down the pitch. Ann tells me you're a cricketer, Brydon."

"I play when I can," said Anthony. The boy who was batting in the first game had a good eye, and some natural aptitude, and with a bit of proper coaching could have been a useful cricketer.

"It's shortage of staff," said Colonel Barrow, apparently reading his thoughts. "Before the War we had a resident staff of eight – two or three of them useful school and university cricketers – *and* a professional. Now I have to do the whole thing almost single-handed. It's getting too much for me. I shall have to give up soon."

He cast an eye round his green kingdom, the private fortress he had built for himself against a world he disliked and distrusted. It would be slow death to him to give it up.

"Tell me about these drains," said Anthony.

"Apparently main drainage is being brought down Castle Road. I've had a paper about it. I've got it somewhere." Colonel Barrow pulled a wad of papers out of a bulging side pocket and found the one he wanted.

"Order under Section 9 (1) of the Private Street Works Act 1892," said Anthony. "Being a householder with premises fronting on the said private street—yes—I see. Where's the new pipe actually coming?"

"Along Castle Road."

"And you don't want to join up."

"I'm perfectly happy with my existing septic tank."

"How much will it cost—if you have to join up?"

"About eight hundred pounds. Which is a lot more than I can afford. If they'd wanted to close me down, they couldn't have chosen a more effective way. Be a good chap, and see if you can do something about it will you? I'll have to bowl Ferguson out myself. No one else seems capable of doing it."

The letter was written in a firm, round, boyish hand.

"Dear Mr. Sudderby,
It was very kind of you to suggest that some of our Sunshine Boys Club came down for a week at Barhaven, and forward the money for the fares. Would it be all right if we used the money for camp kit and petrol and stuff like that because we've been able to borrow a car and trailer big enough to take all of us and our stuff and now that I have passed my driving test it will be cheaper all round to do it that way. The old Roman Camp should suit us fine. We can get water from the farm at the end of the track.
Yours faithfully (crossed out) Sincerely, Eric."

The Town Clerk read this twice, smiling at the occasional crudities of grammar and phrasing. He had picked up his pen to answer it, when his buzzer went.

"Who?" he said. "Oh, all right. Send him up." He folded the letter carefully away, and was studying a report on the new refuse collection system when Anthony was shown in.

"Hullo, Tony. What can I do for you?"

"I'm not sure," said Anthony. "And I'm not sure if even you can help me. But I couldn't think of anyone else."

"You've known me long enough to ask me anything you want."

"Yes," said Anthony. "But this is something quite out of the ordinary. Look here – can you forget, for a moment, that you're the Town Clerk."

Mr. Sudderby smiled, stroked his short, greying beard, and said, "Try me."

"I think one of the senior Council employees is a crook."

"Am I allowed to know his name?"

"If I have your absolute promise that nothing I say will go outside this room."

"You shall have it."

"I'm talking about your Borough Engineer and Surveyor."

"Hamish Macintyre? A difficult man to deal with. I should hardly have said a crook. Have you got any proof?"

"Nothing concrete. He seems to be trying to drive Colonel Barrow out of business." He repeated what he had been told that afternoon.

"The law's the law," said Mr. Sudderby. "It's hard on a private householder, but if those really are the regulations, he's got to enforce them."

"It was the drainage line that stuck in my throat. It looks as if he's persuaded the Council to proceed under the Private Street Works Act so that Colonel Barrow will have to pay for it."

"What would be the object of a manoeuvre like that?"

"If the school was forced to sell up," said Anthony, slowly, "someone could get their hands on a very valuable bit of building land, right in the middle of the new town development—*if* the development goes out that way."

"And you think that Macintyre might be going in for land speculation."

What was missing in Mr. Sudderby's reactions, thought Anthony, was any sense of outrage. His lips were framing the right sentences, but there was nothing behind them. It was running like a good scene played by a bad actor.

He said, "There have been hints – in the local press – that Macintyre had a personal interest in the new underground car park on the front. It's got a very profitable monopoly. And it's helped by the fact that there's no municipal car park within easy walking distance of the sea."

"I should say, myself, that that was just newspaper speculation."

"I thought so too when I read it," said Anthony. "Now, I'm not so sure. Who told the police not to press the case against Roper and Mason?"

"Roper and Mason?" Mr. Sudderby looked blank for a moment. "Oh—those two boys. I don't know. I suppose they weren't worth powder and shot."

"If they can prosecute me for parking six inches outside a white line, surely they can do something about boys who break up a dance hall."

"But I thought you were defending them."

"I was. And I want to. But I can't. If the case had gone on, I might have been able to find out who owns the Pleasuredrome."

Mr. Sudderby remained silent for so long that Anthony looked up. When he had put the same point to Inspector Ashford it had kindled a slow anger. Fear was an even more surprising reaction.

When Anthony had gone, Mr. Sudderby took out his pen and started to answer his letter.

"Dear Eric," he wrote. "It was nice—"

But his hand was shaking so much that he had to stop.

Chapter Nine

The Independent Caucus Holds a Meeting

All the windows in the small committee room behind the Council building were open, but it was still too hot. The Independent Party was assembled in nearly full strength.

At one side of the table sat Raymond Southern, dapper and at ease; Lincoln-Bright looking important, Jack Crawford sulky, and Miss Cable bemused.

Opposite them, General Crispen, with the neat army look which had been stamped on him at Woolwich and which had not worn out in more than half a century; Miss Barnes, adjusting her new hearing-aid; Mrs. Coverdale, in all her many satin-covered inches a parson's widow, and Willie Law, brown of face, slow of speech and rooted in the soil of the Liberties. Miss Cable, proprietrix of the Marine Hotel, was at the far end. At the head of the table sat Mrs. Lord, fragile, inconsequent, and yet, in her own indefinable way, more secure than any of them.

"I think that's the lot, Madam Chairman," said Southern. "George Gulland, I know, can't get here, and I have an apology for absence from Mr. Andrews. Would you like to start the proceedings?"

Mrs. Lord considered the matter. It was clear that something was expected of her. A prayer? Perhaps not. A vote of thanks? But that usually came at the end. To gain time, she switched on her smile of womanly helplessness.

"You do these things so much better than I do, Mr. Southern," she said. "I abdicate in your favour."

"You flatter me," said Southern. "Then if the meeting has no objection—?"

The meeting had none.

"Our object this morning is to consider our tactics, as a party, in the forthcoming elections. As you know, by the ancient constitution of this Council, one-third of its members retire each year. This year five of us go out. We are, of course, all eligible for re-election—if we wish to stand again."

He paused for a moment, as if inviting comment, but got no more than a cough from Mrs. Coverdale.

"This year, the five longest in office are myself, my colleague in the Victoria Park Ward, Mr. Lincoln-Bright, Mr. Crawford, Mr. Law and Mr. Sellinge."

"You must add me to your list," sighed Mrs. Lord. "I have done my duty – and more than my duty – to Barhaven. It is time that age and experience yielded place to youth and new ideas."

There was a murmur round the table which might equally have been dissent or applause.

"This isn't the time for *any* of us to back down," said Crawford sharply.

"I'm not talking of backing down, Mr. Crawford. I'm talking of yielding my seat to another who will support the Independent code."

There was a sharp click. Miss Barnes had at last got her hearing apparatus in working order. She said, "I think it's a great pity we have any party divisions on the Council at all."

"*I* think it's a pity," said Southern. "But since we've got them, we have to operate that way."

"*We* didn't start it," said Lincoln-Bright. "It was only when those left-wingers got together and started calling themselves Progressives and voting as a bloc that the rest of us – the Conservative element – had to protect themselves."

"I still think it's a lot of nonsense," said Miss Barnes.

"When I first went to my preparatory school," observed General Crispen, "a large boy grabbed hold of me and said, 'Are you Oxford or Cambridge?' I hadn't the faintest idea what he was talking about, so I said, 'Which are you?' and he said, 'Oxford' so I said, 'So am I'. I've supported Oxford ever since, with undiminished partisanship."

"What I take it you're saying," said Southern, "– and if it is, I agree with you – is that all you really need is two sides. It doesn't matter what you call them, Conservative and Socialist, Republican and Democrat, Black and White. Once you've got two sides, all questions can be argued out between them."

"Surely," said Mrs. Coverdale, "you are ignoring the question of Right and Wrong."

"Right and Left, you mean," said Crawford.

"You can talk till next Tuesday," said Miss Barnes, "you won't persuade me that there's any God-given reason why Barhaven should extend east rather than west. We, as Independents – stupid name – why not be honest and call ourselves Tories?– we happen to have sponsored a plan to go east. All right. It's a plan. Let's stick to it. But don't let's pretend it's a judgement from Mount Sinai."

"Do we have to listen to all this guff," muttered Crawford.

"I beg your pardon," said Miss Barnes, slewing round.

"Really, Crawford—"

"I think," said Mrs. Lord, "that that might have been expressed more tastefully."

"Hear hear," said Willie Law.

"All right, all right," said Crawford. "I'm sorry. This isn't a formal meeting. Perhaps I used informal language. If it gave offence, I apologise."

"I'm far from certain," said Miss Barnes, with a face like stone, "that I accept your apology. And might I suggest, that if there's one thing more likely than another to harm the Independent cause, it's the behaviour, in public, of the senior member for Marine East."

Crawford turned scarlet and there was a moment of silence.

"And I've no intention of apologising for *that,*" added Miss Barnes.

Southern got up, went across to the door, and switched on an electric fan. Then he came back, sat down and said, "If we might take it that the preliminaries are concluded, should we get down to business?"

Mrs. Lord, who had watched the scene with bright, birdlike eyes, said, "If we don't, all the shops will be shut, and I have a piece of lace I particularly want to match."

Southern glanced round the table. No one else seemed to have anything to say.

"The real object of our meeting seems to have been in danger of being overlooked," he said. "By an unhappy coincidence, at this most urgent moment in the municipal history of Barhaven, no fewer than four out of the eleven members of our Independent group are due for re-election. And only one of the so-called Progressive opposition. I suggest we don't waste our time arguing about the merits of the party system in local politics. Let's just face the mathematics of it. If three out of the four of us fail to appeal to the voters of Barhaven" —his eyes rested for a moment on Crawford— "and three of the opposition get in, our numbers in Council will, by my calculation, be equal. But since one of us has, at the moment, the honour of being Lady Mayoress, and therefore, ex officio Chairman, we would, in that case, have the benefit of her casting vote which I am bold enough to assume would be exercised in our favour. Nevertheless, as I think you'd agree, the situation would be too tight to be comfortable."

"That's an extra, very strong argument, Madam Chairman," said Lincoln-Bright, with a gallant gleam of his well-fitting dentures, "against your depriving us of your support and advice at this critical moment."

"I'm not sure," said Mrs. Lord. She was drawing a dog on the pad in front of her. It looked as if it was going to turn out to be a long-haired dachshund. "Do you realise that simply by being a councillor, I am depriving the town of one representative. We have sixteen elective seats. Even if I resigned my seat in the Dollington Ward, as Mayoress, I should still, ex officio, be a member of the Council. And," she added with a sweet smile at Lincoln-Bright, "entitled to the casting vote on which you set such store."

"That's true," said Mrs. Coverdale, "*but suppose a Progressive got your seat.* The votes would then be nine eight and there wouldn't be any question of a casting vote."

"That's true enough," said Southern. "And it underlines the fact which I've been trying to rub into all of you – and which, I repeat, is the purpose of this meeting. We have to fight this election, and we have to fight damned hard. We don't want to lose *any* seats."

"You and Lincoln-Bright should be safe enough," said General Crispen. "The Victoria Park Ward is business. And businessmen mostly vote Conservative."

"I hope you're right," said Southern, "because neither Jack nor I have had much time for canvassing."

"And I don't see Mr. Law coming unstuck."

"I wouldn't be so sure about that," said Law. "We've got a lot of new smallholders in the Liberties these days. And don't forget the caravan site. When you put those people up there last year, I warned you."

"Do *they* get a vote?"

"Certainly. A caravan's a house, for voting purposes. And they've put up a candidate of their own. Will Stitchley."

"In that case," said Crawford, "we might as well write the seat off. They're bolshies to a man. And they can outvote the farmers two to one."

"I think it's scandalous," said Mrs. Coverdale, "that a man with a van – here today, gone tomorrow – can vote equally with a man who has farmed five hundred acres for a generation."

"Scandal or not," said Southern, "it's a fact. It looks as though we've got to regard Willie Law's seat as doubtful. Then we come to you, Jack."

"Don't bother about me," said Crawford. "I can take a hint. If my face doesn't fit, I'm quite prepared to stand down."

There was a murmur of dissent.

"If you stand down now, Jack," said Southern, "there'll be no time to nominate another candidate. That means that your opponent gets a walk-over."

"Who is standing against Mr. Crawford in Marine East?" asked the General.

"My opponent," said Crawford, "is that eminent journalist and crackpot, Mr. Arthur Ambrose."

"We can't have *him*," said Lincoln-Bright.

"Terrible man," said Miss Cable.

"He would no doubt enliven our proceedings," said Southern, "but I think, on the whole, we should get on better without him."

"Do I take it, then," said Crawford, with a sour smile, "that it is the general feeling of the meeting that I should not stand down?" He directed a venomous look at Miss Barnes, who ignored it.

"My dear Jack," said Southern, "we none of us want you to withdraw. The idea was entirely your own. Now then – to details. First, the usual eve-of-poll meetings—"

Chapter Ten

Anthony's First Visit to London

Anthony caught the Commuters' Special to London and at ten o'clock was entering the offices of Messrs. Moule, Mainwaring & Co. in Bedford Row. He was shown straight into Dudley Powell's room. Dudley was a few years older than Anthony and had a wife, two small boys, and a passion for boats. Photographs of all of these were arranged on his mantelpiece, the wife smiling, the boys scowling, and the boats heeling over at improbable angles.

"I've fixed a con with Martin Hiscoe for half-past ten," he said. "That'll give us plenty of time to stroll down. How's Barhaven?"

"Pretty crowded, just at this moment."

"I often wish that I lived in a proper town. I've a feeling I should enjoy local politics."

"Come to Barhaven. We've got plenty of them."

"It's an idea," said Dudley. "No, seriously, I mean it. Now that the boys are growing up we shall have to think of getting out of London. I'd get some sailing, too."

"If I see a house, I'll let you know. Incidentally, your best chance of getting one is probably on this very development we're opposing."

They talked about this as they walked along Bedford Row, across High Holborn, and through Lincoln's Inn on their way to the Middle Temple.

"This *is* local politics," said Anthony. "The Independent Party on the Council – they're the Tories really – want to go east. The Progressives – who are Radicals – want to go west."

"Unusual, that," said Dudley. "Reds usually seem to be drawn to the east. We can take a short-cut through the courts here."

"The eastern development's logical enough," said Anthony. "But it happens to be the wrong side of the town. And it'll mean putting up the wrong sort of house. Nice, expensive, detached residences for the idle rich."

"Like me."

"Quite so. But if the town went west, on to its existing roads and drains and services, we could put up a lot of economical little houses – maybe even a few blocks of council flats – and then we might manage to start rehousing the people who live in the slums."

"*Do* seaside towns have slums?"

"They have them," said Anthony, "but they keep them behind the main line railway station, so that visitors will have their backs to them when they arrive."

As they crossed the Strand and plunged down Middle Temple Lane Anthony added, "Another thing against going east is that we shall lose our cricket ground."

"That's the strongest argument I've heard so far," said Powell.

Mr. Martin Hiscoe, of Counsel, was a very tall man and his clothes seemed to have been specially designed to accentuate his length. He wore tight, well-creased, striped trousers, a black coat, cut long in the tail, and a high old-fashioned collar. On top of the collar was balanced an incongruous, round, pink babyish face.

"Come in," he said. "Come along. Good morning, Mr. Powell. Nice to see you again. This is—oh, yes—Mr. Brydon. I've met your father. A fine man. I met him at Sandwich in 1935 in the Halford-Hewitt Cup. He was playing for Tonbridge. I was for Charterhouse. We both lost our matches."

Anthony gazed round the agreeable book-lined room, more a study than an office, with its view across the Temple Gardens of the Embankment and the river. Like most busy solicitors, he envied

Counsel their dignity, their power to pick and choose their clients, their opportunity to specialise, their soft path upwards to the dignity of the Bench.

"An interesting case," Mr. Hiscoe was saying, as he untied the red tape from the fat bundle of papers. "But not without its difficulties. On the face of it, this is simply an appeal by Mr. Shanklin, a householder of Haven Road, Barhaven, against the refusal of the Kent County Council as planning authority to allow the building of a terrace of four shops with accommodation over. He was advised that his best course was to make an application to develop, knowing that it was likely to be turned down, since it conflicted with the plans of the Borough Council – quite so. He then appealed against the refusal, and has succeeded in forcing a local enquiry."

"That's right."

"And where exactly is this development going?"

"It falls into three parts. There's the piece which belongs to the Council already, behind the promenade extension. They salvaged that, and no one disputes that they're entitled to do what they like with it. And there's the southern nine holes of the Municipal Golf Course."

"I've had many a game on it," said Mr. Hiscoe, a real spark of enthusiasm warming his voice for the first time. "Many a game – it must be one of the best municipal courses in the south of England."

"It won't be if they cut off the last nine holes," said Powell.

"I suppose not. But I interrupted you."

"That's typical of the whole scheme. It'll take away the cheap, public course from the local inhabitants and leave the expensive one – that's the Splash Point Country Club – for wealthy visitors and a few local residents who've got enough pull or money to get into the Country Club."

Mr. Hiscoe looked at Anthony for a moment, with his head on one side, and then said "Deplorable," in a neutral sort of voice. "But proceed."

"There's the field that's let to the cricket club. Well, that's not so important, as we're getting another one. That makes up what you might call the municipal slice of the cake."

Mr. Hiscoe had picked up a blue pencil and was gently hatching in the areas as Anthony mentioned them.

"Next?"

"The next bit's Castle House School. It's a boys' prep school. And its headmaster is being oppressed by the local authorities."

Anthony launched into that part of the story. Mr. Hiscoe's pink face had grown serious.

"Do you suggest," he said at the end, "that the Borough Engineer and Surveyor is corrupt?"

"I think Macintyre's been feathering his nest in half-a-dozen ways. The local gossip is that he has a share in the big underground garage. It's the only one in Barhaven."

"Local gossip?"

"I can't prove it."

"I see," said Mr. Hiscoe. He sounded sadder than ever. As Anthony was speaking he had shaded, in yellow, the grounds of Castle House School. Between the yellow and the blue lay a long, wedge-shaped area of white. "You said *three* parts?"

"Yes," said Anthony. "And that last piece is really rather a mystery. It's bang in the middle of the development, and is obviously going to be terrifically valuable – if they go that way. But nobody knows who owns it."

"Nobody knows?"

"I expect somebody does. I mean, that it isn't public knowledge, and it's difficult to find out. It's three large fields. Willie Law – he's one of our local farmers – keeps a few animals on it. He has a periodical grazing agreement, which can be terminated at any time—"

"Who does he pay his rent to?"

"An accountant in London."

"I see."

Mr. Hiscoe had got to work with another pencil, and was colouring the wedge-shaped piece red. He said, "By the way, Mr. Brydon, I was intrigued, when I first read your instructions, to note that Barhaven was a Borough. It had not occurred to me that it could be large enough."

"We may not be big," said Anthony. "But only Canterbury is older than us. Our charter as a Borough was given to us by Edward the Fourth, and it was confirmed by Queen Victoria. And I don't see anyone taking it away from us in a hurry."

"Antiquity is still valued in this country," agreed Mr. Hiscoe. "But it may, in this case, operate against you. As a Borough, you control a great many matters which would otherwise be outside your scope. Roads, education, police—"

"Yes," said Anthony. If he spoke shortly, it was because Mr. Hiscoe was voicing uncomfortable thoughts which, until now, he had kept at the back of his mind.

"But not planning, of course."

"No. That's delegated to the County Council, fortunately."

"I'm not sure about that, either," said Mr. Hiscoe. "If the Borough Council were the planning authority, they would be so obviously being judges in their own case that a Ministry Inspector would lean against them. As it is, they're in a very strong position. Very strong indeed."

"Are you saying," said Anthony, "that this appeal has no chance of success."

"There's always a chance," said Mr. Hiscoe. If he noticed Anthony's irritation he seemed quite unaffected by it. "But you must appreciate what your clients are trying to do is to use the processes of law for their own ends. As I said, I can probably show good cause, on planning grounds, why Barhaven should be developed west, rather than east. But your clients, as I understand it, want me to go a good deal further. They want me to show that the people who are planning the eastern development are doing so for improper reasons. Possibly for corrupt reasons. If we are to do that, we shall need something more cogent than local gossip."

"Is he always like that?" said Anthony as he and Powell walked back up Middle Temple Lane.

"Like what?"

"He seemed to see nothing but the difficulties."

"Better now, than later."

"I shouldn't think he's much use in court."

"You don't want to judge by appearances," said Powell. "What about a cup of coffee? I usually have one at this time in the morning." He steered Anthony into a cafeteria, where they sat on stools like outsize drawing-pins, and balanced their coffee cups on shelves. "As a matter of fact, when he gets into court, he's very effective. I heard him take on the South London Construction Group *and* the L.C.C. single-handed in that Battersea case, and talk them out of court. Give him good ammunition and he'll fire it off for us."

Anthony's heart warmed to Powell. So many people would have said, "He'll fire it off for *you.*"

"What do you suggest?" he said.

"The strongest card would be to find out that that piece of land in the middle belongs to one of your Councillors – or to that Borough Surveyor fellow – Macintyre. They wouldn't be able to talk their way out of *that* very easily."

"It seems a stupid question for one lawyer to ask another," said Anthony, "but just how *does* one find out who land belongs to?"

"I was thinking about it as we walked up," said Powell. "Oddly enough, it isn't at all easy. One way would be to squat on it. Park a caravan there, or something. Then the owner would be bound to take some action to turn you out."

"Wouldn't it be more logical for the tenant to do it? Willie Law's a friend of mine, but he wouldn't want a caravan parked among his cattle."

"Law's the farmer who owns the ground on the far side?"

"That's right. The main part of his farm is up in the Liberties. That's the land which was won when the River Barr was diverted, and it's Green Belt, and untouchable for building. Last year he bought a second strip, farther south—" Anthony unfolded the map with difficulty on to the shelf— "it's that bit north-east of the school. And this year he made this arrangement about keeping his animals on the red land. But he doesn't own it. He just rents it."

"Is Law one of your clients?"

"No. Mentmores acted for him. Incidentally, we're not on very good terms with them."

"Pity." Powell stirred his coffee without taking his eyes off the map which seemed to fascinate him.

"Would Law let you look at his title deeds?"

"I should think so. What was in your mind?"

"Rights of way, drainage, obligations to erect fences. Even acknowledgement of earlier title deeds."

"That's right. Of course. There might be. I hadn't thought of that. I'll tackle Law as soon as I get back. I had a rather simpler idea. I'm not sure if it'd work, though. I was going to have a word with the Greyslates people. They're the people who are going to do the development. Do you know them?"

"Yes," said Powell. "I know them."

"You don't sound as if you like them."

"One of our clients had a bit of trouble with them. I expect they're all right really. How were you proposing to tackle them?"

"I hadn't worked out anything elaborate. I thought I'd just go along and do a bit of sounding."

"I see," said Powell. He paid for the coffee, overruling Anthony's protests, and they walked out into Fleet Street. It was a beautiful summer morning, with enough breeze to take the edge off the heat.

"If you want Greyslates, you'd better take a bus to the Bank. Anything from here except a thirteen. They go up Cannon Street."

"Thanks for all your help," said Anthony.

There was no bus in sight, and they stood for a few moments in silence. Then Powell said, "There's just one thing. I shouldn't show too much of your hand at Greyslates. They're a tough crowd. And there's an awful lot of money involved in this. Have you thought just how much may turn on this decision?"

"I hadn't got as far as working it out."

"Do the arithmetic some time. I think it might surprise you. If a man buys a hundred-acre field at agricultural prices – that's about £200 an acre nowadays – and happens to be able to sell it, as building land, for £5,000 an acre, how much profit does he make?"

Anthony was working this out as his bus crawled towards the City. The Greyslates Property and Development Company Ltd. occupied one of the new buildings on the south side of Tower Wall. It was constructed of grey, pre-cast, interlocking slabs with synthetic marble insets, oxydized bronzine strip and self-coloured glass.

Anthony pushed open the door, which hissed back at him, and walked up the long entrance lobby. He passed what he took to be the model of a submarine, but which turned out to be a reclining female nude, of strange proportions, carved in basalt, and balanced on one buttock on a chromium pedestal.

"Mr. Morgan?" said the white-haired man at the desk. "Might I have your name, sir?"

"It's Brydon. I don't expect Mr. Morgan will know it. But if you say it's in connection with the Barhaven development he'll probably see me."

"Let's try, shall we?" said the man.

He put down the *Directory of Directors* which he was studying, and picked up the receiver. A one-sided conversation ensued, which ended with the white-haired man saying, "If you'd take the lift to the third floor and ask for Mrs. Horseburgh she'll look after you."

He dismissed Anthony from his mind and returned to his study of the *Directory*. Anthony thought he was probably choosing another firm. The basalt girl had got him down.

When the lift came to rest with a bobbing motion at the third floor and the bronze doors clanged open, Mrs. Horseburgh was waiting for him. She was middle-aged and wore glasses and an air of absent-minded efficiency. She said, "Mr. Morgan can see you now. You're lucky, you know. He's usually busy in the mornings."

Anthony followed her down the passage. It was panelled in imitation rosewood, close-carpeted, and lit by indirect lighting from the cornices. They passed a great number of doors.

"This is a very splendid office you have here," said Anthony.

"Isn't it," said Mrs. Horseburgh. She seemed as pleased by the compliment as if it had been directed at her. "The door fittings are phosphor bronze. They were specially cast for us by a firm in Wolverhampton. Here we are."

The man who rose to greet him had iron-grey hair cut *en brosse,* a pale face, and eyes of neutral colour behind rimless glasses. He smiled briefly, showing teeth which were as great a credit to his dentist as his grey suit was to his tailor.

He said, "Please sit down, Mr. Brydon. You're lucky to find me free."

"So your secretary told me. I'll keep it as short as I can. I'm a solicitor—"

"Brydon and Pincott, 12 Connaught Square, Barhaven. And you must, I fancy, be Mr. Anthony Brydon. It's all right—I'm not psychic. I looked you up in the *Law List.* You wanted to talk about our Barhaven development." He reached into the bookcase behind him and brought out a folder, bound in Cambridge blue.

"Your proposed Barhaven development."

Mr. Morgan looked mildly surprised, and said, "I thought it had got rather further than a proposition."

"That's what I wanted to talk about," said Anthony. "I imagine that you can't be certain of going ahead until you've got the land to build on."

"True," said Mr. Morgan. His hand moved, fractionally, under the desk, felt for the button concealed there, and pressed it twice.

"Have you got it yet?"

"I don't really think—"

"I appreciate," said Anthony, "that I'm asking an impertinent question, and one that, very possibly, you won't feel inclined to answer. But bear with me for a moment. The land you want is on the east of the town. Roughly half of it is Council property, and *if* the Council supports the development, you'll get the use of it. The other half is private property. I imagine you've got some sort of option on it."

He paused, invitingly, but Mr. Morgan said nothing.

"But even so," Anthony went on, "one-half will be no use to you without the other."

"Since, according to you," said Mr. Morgan, "we have both halves, why should we worry?"

"Because, if the Independents lose control of the Council at the next election you won't get the Council land."

"Do you think there's any likelihood of that happening?"

"A fortnight ago, I should have said 'No'. Now I'm not so sure."

"I see. Is this just a friendly warning, Mr. Brydon, or were you going to suggest, perhaps, that if we employed you as an agent, you could secure a happy result in the forthcoming elections?"

"You're joking," said Anthony. "I'm not the boss of Tammany Hall. No. What I had in mind was this. Wouldn't it be a good idea, from your point of view, if you backed yourself to win both ways? I feel sure you don't want to drop this proposition. I've no doubt you've drawn up a lot of plans. Perhaps even signed a few sub-contracts. If the election goes against you, you could carry out your development – with a few very minor modifications – on the west side of the town."

A deep silence fell on Mr. Morgan's office. In it, Anthony could hear the ticking of a clock. Since there was no clock visible, he assumed that it must come from somewhere else. He noticed, for the first time, that what he had thought was continuous panelling had, in fact, a door in it, and that this door was very slightly ajar. It was interesting, because he was tolerably certain that it had been shut when he came into the room. He noticed, too, that when Mr. Morgan spoke, he raised his voice very slightly.

"That is a very remarkable proposition, Mr. Brydon," he said. "Do I understand that you represent the owners of the land lying west of the town, and that you are in a position to offer us an alternative site if the eastern one falls through?"

"That's it," said Anthony.

"And you would make us a formal offer? Give us some sort of option?"

"The option my clients would give you, and the price they'd ask for it, would depend on one thing. How far you had got with the owners on the other side."

"I don't entirely follow."

"Oh, come," said Anthony. "If you've got binding agreements there, with all the existing owners, and a fair chance of getting the

Corporation sites, then you're obviously in a strong position. If not, it's equally clear that it would pay you to take up my offer."

"And you expect me to show you our hand."

"Certainly. This is the sort of deal which will only work with all cards down on the table."

"It's an interesting idea. I can't give you an immediate answer—you appreciate that—"

"Don't wait too long," said Anthony. "There's another firm very interested in the project."

"Would you care to tell me their name?"

"All cards will be placed face up on the table—simultaneously."

Mr. Morgan smiled. It was a cold smile.

"You're wasted as a lawyer, Mr. Brydon," he said. "You ought to be in the property business yourself."

When Mrs. Horseburgh had removed his visitor, he walked across to the communicating door and went through.

Mr. Grey, Chairman and controlling shareholder of the Greyslates Company, was a tiny man. He sat, perched on a thick foam-rubber cushion, on his chair. His right eye was a blank screen, the iris fused into the cornea in the milky whiteness of advanced traucoma. His left eye glittered coldly.

"Impertinent bluff," he said.

"I agree," said Mr. Morgan.

"All the same, it wants watching. We don't want to lose this job. There's too much money sunk in it already."

"I don't think there's any real danger of that."

Mr. Grey said, "I've seen a lot of deals slip up, because people thought there was no chance of them going astray. In a large property transaction, you're dealing with a lot of people. Each one of them represents a chance of human error. I think you'd better go down to Barhaven, and do a little checking up."

Chapter Eleven

The Sunshine Boys Arrive

In the hot but stimulating summer of 1940, when German fighters were swarming like black bees across the South Coast of England, when the Home Guard was mustering with high spirits and few weapons and Winston Churchill was adding a robust chapter to English martial mythology, an observation post had been set up on Roman Camp looking down over Barhaven and the estuary of the River Barr. From it, with a good pair of glasses, could be seen nearly twenty miles of coast line from Dungeness Point in the east to the outskirts of Hastings in the west.

The post, now long abandoned, had never consisted of anything more than a hut of railway sleepers with a corrugated iron roof built on the forward edge of a knot of beech trees, with a concrete platform in front of it and a water point beside it. From it the Sussex turf, short and springy, ran down to the hedge and gate which marked the top of the sunken lane leading to Charlie Andrews' farm.

It was a good spot for a camp; and the Sunshine Boys had settled down into it with the speed and dexterity of old soldiers. Two army tents had been put up beside the hut. From a pole in front of the tents hung their flag, green with a golden sun on it and, underneath it, the Club motto *"Labor Vincit Omnia"*.

A hearth of bricks had been built and a blow-lamp, of the type used by house painters, was directing a blue flame on to a dixie of water.

The two smallest boys were still unloading stores from the old motor-car and trailer, which had been backed into the gate at the lower corner of the field and covered by a pegged-down nylon sheet. The other five boys were sitting in a semi-circle, cross-legged, round the hearth waiting for the dixie to boil.

All of them were smoking. Eric, the troop leader, a stout, well-muscled boy with blond hair and placid, oriental features, was smoking a cheroot. He surveyed the scene with satisfaction. Below them the hard outlines of Barhaven were blurring as the gold of day softened to the grey of evening. Behind Barhaven was the sea, an unruffled palette of grey-green and blue. A line of clouds on the horizon marked the Pas de Calais.

"We ought to go to France next year," Eric said, breaking a long silence.

"'Tisn't much when you do get there." This was Dennis, a thin, bitter boy, with black hair. "I went with a crowd last summer. We went over for the day. It wasn't any different from England, not that I could see. Tea shops, fish and chips."

"What about the girls?"

"You're joking. You can pick up all the girls you want in the Borough High Street, can't you? You don't need to go to France to pick up a girl, do you?"

"If you wanted to date up a French girl, what'd you say to her, eh Denny?"

"Better ask Trev, he talks French."

"That's right, Trev. You tell us."

Trevor, who was polishing his horn-rimmed glasses with a folded silk handkerchief, considered the matter.

"What you'd want to say to her would be *Je t'adore.*"

The other four boys dissolved in laughter.

"Shut the door," said Colin. "That's all right. You got the right ideas, Trev."

"You're exposing your ignorance," said Trevor. "What I gave you just then was the French for '*I love you*'."

"That's not what I'd say to a girl if I was trying to date her," said Dennis. "It's the last thing I'd say. You don't want to go round telling 'em you love 'em. That gets you nowhere. But fast."

"What's your technique then, Denny?"

"The best thing I've found is to start off by insulting them. You get talking to a girl and you say something like, 'Why don't you buy your own clothes? You ought to stop borrowing 'em from your elder sister.' Then she gets mad, and says, 'I haven't *got* an elder sister. And I *do* buy my own clothes'. And you say, 'Well, that dress looks as if it was made for someone a bit bigger round the top than you', and, boy, does *that* start them off."

"It's a fact," said Colin, his brown, monkey face wrinkled in thought. "You can say anything you like about a girl, like she's dead stupid, or mean, or she smells, but you tell her she isn't as big round the top as the next girl, and whammo."

"I don't follow that," said Trevor. "I don't mean about girls being bust-conscious. Any idiot knows that. I mean about this technique of insulting them. If you want to get along with a girl, what's the object of insulting her?"

"You set up a love-hate relationship," said Dennis.

Eric knocked the ash off the tip of his cigar, shouted to the smaller of the two small boys to hurry up with the grub, they were all bleeding well starving, couldn't he carry two boxes at once, ignored the answer, which sounded distinctly mutinous, and said, "We've got serious things to talk about, so take your minds off girls for a moment, if you please, and let's discuss something a bit more to the point."

His four companions fell silent. It was clear that Eric was leader of the Sunshine Boys, in fact as well as in name. Authority shone from his pose and his accent, and was reflected back by the deference with which the others listened to him.

"What you've got to grasp," he said, "is that what really matters in this life is money. If you haven't got money, everyone treads on you. If you have got money, everything else follows."

Lord Baden Powell himself could not have been listened to with closer attention.

"What we're down here for is to lay our hands on a bit of money. Some of you kids may think Barhaven's a stupid place to come to, but that's where you're wrong. There's more money to be picked up in a place like Barhaven than there is in London or Southend or Brighton. And why? Simple. Because there's less competition. All you've got to do is keep your eyes open, and play it quiet. That's what people forget when they're young – play it quiet."

Eric paused to draw on his cheroot, and his face looked at the same time charming and ageless.

"When you're young you like to go round in crowds and make a noise. It's natural. I'm not saying it's wrong. But it's a stupid way of trying to make money."

"What about pop groups?" said Dennis.

"You feel you've got a talent in that direction, Denny?" asked Fred. He was the biggest of the boys, a full-blooded eighteen-year-old with curly black hair and the shoulders of a boxer.

The two small boys had opened a cardboard box, and were handing out sandwiches. Trevor took a packet of tea and emptied about a quarter of it into the dixie, which was now boiling.

"You want to put a chip of wood in, too," said the smaller of the small boys. "It stops the tea getting smokey."

"Who taught you that?"

"A Scoutmaster."

"Was that the only thing he taught you?" said Dennis.

"You've got a horrible mind," said Eric. "Get that tin of condensed milk open. You can put it all in. Thicken it up nicely."

Conversation was suspended, whilst seven pairs of jaws munched contentedly. When the meal was finished, Eric said, "What we were talking about before. If any of you have got any ideas, I'd like to hear 'em."

Colin said, "There was a thing we did at Southend. Four or five of you go into one of those amusement arcades. One of you keeps the attendant busy. Best way is to give him a quid and ask for the change in pennies. The other four pick up one of the fruit machines and bounce it. Sometimes you can get the jackpot out that way."

"Another thing we did," said Fred, "was stopping up telephones. All you have to do is push a lump of rag, or something like that, up the return coin hole. Then when people press Button B, they don't get their money back. You come back later with a bit of wire and pull the stopper out. I got four and tenpence out of one telephone that way."

"If we could get hold of a couple of arm-bands," said Trevor, "—or we could make them – something like 'Corporation of Barhaven' – we could collect money hiring out deckchairs. All you've got to do is keep ahead of the man who's meant to be doing it."

"Pennies," said Eric, with benevolent contempt. "Pennies and sixpences. You'll never get rich on pennies and sixpences. If you're going to get on in this life, you've got to think big, lads. You've got to dig down to fundamentals."

"Such as what?" said Dennis.

"Sex," said Eric. "And you two kids can get on with the washing-up."

"Don't be soft," said Ernest, the larger of the small boys. "We know all about sex. Don't we, Arthur?"

"In this troop," said Eric, "washing-up comes before talk. If you two don't do what you're told, and quick, you'll be on jankers for a week."

When the washers-up had departed, muttering, Eric lit another cheroot.

"Now take sex—" he said.

They took sex in all its fascinating aspects, whilst the sky paled, and the sun descended, a huge ball of crimson fire, into the waters of the English Channel.

Chapter Twelve

Arthur Ambrose Writes a Leading Article

"Mr. William Law to see you," said Ann. "He's got a big parcel under his arm. It could easily be title deeds."

"Tell Arnold to bring him in at once," said Anthony. "And what's this you've put in my diary for eleven o'clock? It looks like apple sauce."

"Hand-writing was never my strong point. It's meant to be Ambrose."

"What does *he* want?"

"He rang up, in a flap, about five minutes before you got here. It's something about an article in the *Barhaven Gazette* this morning."

"For God's sake! Who's he libelled this time?"

"The police."

When Anthony said nothing, she looked at him. The smile which she had expected to see was not there.

"Nip out to the stationer's at the corner," he said, "and buy me a copy of the *Gazette*. Buy two whilst you're at it. Come in, Mr. Law."

Willie Law laid a brown paper parcel on Anthony's desk and unfastened the string. Inside were three bulky envelopes.

"That's the lot," he said. "The big packet's the farm and farmhouse. I bought it off Scranton at auction – way back in the thirties. I misremember the date. It'll be on the papers. That's the upper fields

– I had them just after the War. The little one's the fields I bought off old Colonel Kidd, last year. I paid him too much, but I needed 'em."

Anthony ignored the first two packets, and opened the third. It contained, he saw, an 'abstract' of title consisting of twenty or thirty closely typed pages of brief, a few old local search certificates, and a solitary conveyance.

"There aren't any more deeds," said Law. "Just that one. Mr. Mentmore explained it to me at the time, but I've forgotten what he said."

"You bought a small piece of the Kidd Estate. The earlier deeds refer to the whole estate. You wouldn't get them. Just an acknowledgement of your right to their production."

"That's correct. He said I could see them any time I wanted to."

Anthony was unfolding the parchment. He looked first at the plan. The property conveyed was a long, roughly rectangular plot, comprising six or seven different Ordnance Survey numbers, and, sure enough, it ran right along the northern edge of that wedge-shaped piece which Counsel had called "the red land".

Anthony ran his finger along the boundary.

"What about that bit to the south of your property? Those three fields, between you and Castle House School—"

"I only rent that. It doesn't belong to me."

"It was Kidd property too, wasn't it?"

"That's right. The old Colonel and his family had everything down to the road."

"And when was that particular bit sold? Do you know?"

Willie Law scratched his crop of sun-bleached auburn hair, and said, "It was some time before I bought my last piece. It was sold to a London company, so I heard."

Anthony was skimming through the body of the deed. He gave a little sigh of satisfaction. "That's *just* what I was hoping for," he said. "Do you see? There's an easement reserved for water-pipes over your land in favour of your neighbour's."

"That'll be to the ram in the top corner of my field. He'd take all his water from there. Is that all you wanted to know? I could have told you that, without bothering to get all the deeds out of the bank."

"What I wanted to know," said Anthony, "was in whose favour the easement was reserved." He scribbled something on a note-pad, and started packing the deeds back into their long manilla envelope.

"And now you do know?"

"That's right."

"What good's it going to do you?"

"Not a great deal, by itself, but it's a step in the right direction."

Law stretched out a big brown hand as Anthony was about to put the conveyance back with the other papers.

"Show me," he said. Anthony placed the tip of his pencil on a line of typing about halfway down the second page— "Reserving therefrom the running of water through the two-inch pipe indicated by the blue dotted line on the said plan as at present enjoyed by Carlmont Property Limited their assigns and successors in title." Law spelled out the words slowly.

"And *that's* what you wanted to see."

"That's it."

"It doesn't look much to get excited about."

"It may be only a two-inch pipe," said Anthony, "but there's no saying how far it'll lead."

Willie Law thought about this for a moment, then he said, "Wherever it leads you, don't you go pulling me into it."

"Now I know the name of the Company there won't be any need to mention you at all."

"I'll be obliged if you don't."

"But why?"

Willie Law said, "When I stand on Long Bank, at the top of my fields, and I see a lot of that thick cloud – it's got a scientific name – what do you call it?"

"Cumulus."

"That's it. When I see this cloud coming up from the east. I don't bother to read weather reports. I just go home and make sure I've got everything lashed down tight. I'll take the deeds with me, if you've finished with 'em. My bank manager gets fussed if they're out of his sight too long."

When Law had gone Anthony asked for a Holborn number and found Dudley Powell at his desk.

"Could you do a personal search in the Companies Registry for me," he said. "The name of the Company is Carlmont Property Limited. Carlmont. I'll spell it for you—that's right. Would you see what you can find out about it."

"You shall have anything that's in the Register," said Powell, "but you realise it mayn't be a lot. If this is a Trojan horse company, you can be sure it'll be pretty well camouflaged – nominee shareholders and so on."

"What about the directors?"

"Nominee directors, too, probably."

"What about their other directorships? Mightn't that give us a line?"

"It's a thought," said Powell.

"And another thing. I'd like to know the name of the solicitors who formed the company. Their name'll be on the file somewhere, won't it?"

"If it is, you shall have it."

The internal telephone burped at him.

"Arthur Ambrose," said his secretary, "has arrived. He is ten minutes early, and pregnant with great, unspoken troubles. Would you fancy him or your coffee first?"

"My coffee."

"If we don't see him immediately, do you think he'll burst all over last year's *Tatlers?*"

"We'll have to risk it," said Anthony. "And is that the *Gazette?* Good girl. Give me five minutes."

Ambrose started talking as soon as he got inside the door.

"We stand," he announced, "on the edge of a volcano. If a match lit by me can start the eruption, I shall be a proud man. I'm aware that that is a mixed metaphor. Journalists are encouraged to mix their metaphors. I'll put my hat here, if I might. The papers are in my brief-case. Before you read them—"

"I've read the only paper that matters," said Anthony. He nodded towards the copy of the *Gazette* on his desk. A headline set in great pica said *"A Call to Men of Conscience"*. *"It is said that a nation gets the government it deserves. This is no less true of a town—"*

"I wrote it myself," said Ambrose.

"It's good, rousing stuff," said Anthony, "and unless you can justify it to the hilt, you're going to get into very serious trouble."

"Naturally I can justify it."

"With witnesses?"

"With any number of witnesses."

Anthony turned back to the article, and read: *"The most serious responsibility placed on a Borough Council is the control of its own police force, through its Watch Committee. How many people know this? How many citizens of Barhaven could tell you, if challenged, the names of their own Watch Committee. Let the Gazette enlighten you. They are, ex officio, the Mayoress, Mrs. Lord, Mr. Raymond Southern, the member for Victoria Park, Miss Planche, Member for the Connaught Ward, General Crispen, Member for Splash Point, and, last but not least, Jolly Jack Crawford, the member for Marine East.*

These are the five people in whose hands, in the last analysis, the responsibility for law and order in Barhaven rests."

"Nothing wrong with that."

"All right so far," said Anthony.

"I was going to say something about Crawford getting tight and kicking up a row in the Country Club – and setting a good example, etcetera."

"But you thought it wiser not to?"

"I'd have done it like a shot, but it didn't fit in very well with the rest of my article."

Anthony returned to his reading.

"And what of the force that these ladies and gentlemen control? We in this country are apt to assume, as an article of faith, that our police are wonderful.

It follows that any reflection on them is heresy. But is this true of Barhaven? And if you really think it is true, ask yourself a few questions.

"Why do motorists regularly get booked for parking offences on the front except *when they are using the Pleasuredrome?*

"Why were five licensees in the town prosecuted for serving alcoholic drinks after hours – in one case, the Victoria Tavern, the alleged offence was serving a drink *two* minutes *after the legal closing hour – when it is common knowledge that the bar at the Splash Point Country Club is open to* non-members *until one o'clock in the morning? Could this be in any way connected with the fact that three of the five members of the Watch Committee are members of this Club?"*

"Can you prove that bit about the bar?"

"Certainly."

"How?"

"A junior member of the *Gazette* staff – he isn't yet eighteen, by the way – walked in at half-past midnight, and got served without difficulty."

"He did it on purpose I suppose?"

"Of course. On my instructions."

"Courts aren't very fond of *agent provocateur* evidence. But it might stand up. It's this last paragraph I'm nervous about. It reads like a personal attack on Inspector Ashford."

"If it reads like that," said Ambrose, with satisfaction, "it shows that my hand has not lost its cunning, because that's *precisely* what it's meant to be."

"We are quick to condemn other countries, America in particular, where we see the police force subordinated to its political masters. As the Bible pointed out, we perceive a splinter in the eye of another, and ignore a sizeable beam in our own. When you see a police force which appears to protect certain private commercial enterprises at the expense of their rivals; when you see a force which represses certain types of wrong-doings and turns a blind eye to others; when, in short, you see a force which operates one law for one section of the community and a different law for another section, you are bound to take a second look at the people controlling that force. Our Chief Constable, Mr. Davy, is a genial and popular character. He is also, incidentally, within one year of his compulsory

retirement age; and it may be that his recent devotion to culture and the arts has not left him sufficient time for active oversight of his force—"

"What on earth are you talking about?"

"He's taken up painting. Didn't you know? He's having a one-man exhibition in the Town Hall in the autumn. He said if Churchill could do it, so could he."

"I see," said Anthony.

"This necessarily leaves much of the day-by-day control to his subordinates, of whom the most notable is Inspector Ashford, head of the Barhaven Criminal Investigation Department. Inspector Ashford is also a popular character – in certain quarters. In his youth he was a highly skilled rugby football player. And he is the proud owner of a very beautiful Aston Martin car, which he drives very fast; in pursuit of wrongdoers, no doubt. But however fast he drives, can he outstrip that inner voice which says, 'Quis custodiet ipsos custodes?'"

"You're practically accusing him of being a crook."

"I *am* accusing him."

"Have you got any evidence?"

"I've got plenty of evidence. If I have to justify it, I'll produce a dozen witnesses. Small shop-keepers – who've served customers after hours, or committed some technical offence under the Food and Drink Acts – who've been threatened with proceedings and bought them off by a cash payment to Ashford. Stall-keepers on the front, who've had their licences withdrawn and bought them back again. Motorists who've squared the police over traffic offences. Organisers of dances, who want a late licence and know the police will oppose it, automatically, unless the right people are squared."

"Is this hard fact?"

"Hard as the rock."

"And these people will actually come forward and give evidence in court?"

"Certainly."

"You're sure of that? It puts *them* in a bad light, too."

"I'm pretty certain. Anyway, we have even better evidence soon. Official action."

Anthony waited, watching the excited little man in front of his desk. He guessed what was coming.

"When I first got to hear about this, I reported it to Holford – our M.P. He was a bit nervous of it. It was close to election time. His reactions were the same as yours. He wanted more definite proof. I gave him more proof. He still stalled."

"So—?"

"About a fortnight ago," said Ambrose, "I sent my whole dossier up to the Director of Public Prosecutions."

"And what did he do?"

"He sent me a printed card, acknowledging it."

There was a short silence. Ambrose seemed to have run out of words and Anthony had nothing to say. He heard Ann's typewriter being belted in the next room and, farther away, the querulous voice of Mr. Pincott speaking on the telephone.

He said, "Has anyone done anything yet? About this article, I mean."

"I had a telephone call from Mentmore. He was very angry about it. He talked about getting an injunction, and I said, what was the point? It was too late to try and stop the publication, and he said something about further proceedings, and rang off."

"Was he being angry in his official capacity as clerk to the Barhaven Bench or as Inspector Ashford's solicitor, or what?"

"I wasn't at all clear, and I doubt if he was. It's been sprung on him rather suddenly."

"You've sprung it on everyone rather suddenly," said Anthony, trying to keep the resentment out of his voice. "How do I come into it? And what do you want me to do?"

"When I saw how you dealt with that case of the boys down at the Pleasuredrome," said Ambrose, "I knew that you were the man for us. We need a fighter, and you *are* a fighter. You'll take this on, won't you?"

"If anyone starts anything – I mean, if they issue a writ – I'll enter an appearance for you. But anything more than that—I'm not sure."

"The price of liberty," said Ambrose, "is eternal vigilance."

"The price of a solicitor's practice," said Anthony, "is keeping on good terms with a great many people, and not annoying anyone unnecessarily. No. Don't say anything more now. I'll let you know. Goodbye."

When Ambrose had gone, Anthony sat for a few minutes, thinking.

It was going to mean fighting; fighting a lot of people, some of whom he liked, some of whom he had no desire at all to antagonise; people like Raymond Southern and General Crispen, and the Lady Mayoress. The firm would lose clients; the cricket club would lose its new cricket ground. And for what? To support a tiresome little man like Ambrose. It was all very well for *him*. He had no intention of spending the rest of his working life in Barhaven. He was going to climb, on the carcass of the *Gazette*, to higher things; Fleet Street and the national dailies.

"Mrs. Parnell, to make a new will," said Ann, putting her head round the door.

Chapter Thirteen

Mr. Morgan Surveys Barhaven

Mr. Morgan alighted from the train at Barhaven, and walked out of the station yard. The 12.40 was not a much- used train, and there were no taxis on the rank. A seagull, balancing on Queen Victoria's right shoulder, stared at Mr. Morgan with a predatory yellow eye. Mr. Morgan, not unlike a foraging gull himself, stared back. It was a beautiful day. His first appointment was not until half-past one. He decided to walk.

The length of Grand Avenue lay ahead of him, running downhill in a gentle slope towards the sea. He sauntered down it, passing, in turn, Victoria Park, Consort Gardens, Connaught Square, Albert Terrace and Stockmar Crescent.

As he went he cast a shrewd eye over the passers-by. The visitors, who carried cameras, wore bright clothes and walked slowly; the residents who dressed soberly and walked at a normal pace. It was the first time Mr. Morgan had been to Barhaven although, directly or indirectly, he owned a sizeable fraction of it. He thought it was a nice town; a good-class place, attracting good-class people. He thought it was a cake ready for the knife.

Grand Avenue joined the Marine Parade at a point opposite the Municipal Band Stand, halfway between West and East Pier. To his right he could see the steel and glass bulk of the Pleasuredrome, one of Greyslates' more profitable investments. To his left, the garage, motor show-rooms and underground car park. "We service your car whilst you wait."

Had they been a little weak over that? They needed the pull that Macintyre could give them, but was that any reason for giving away a 51 per cent interest? Mistaken generosity rarely paid dividends.

Mr. Morgan turned east, and made his way along the Parade. The beaches were full, but not over-crowded. Most of the visitors seemed to be children, splashing in the shallow water and digging holes in the fine, well-packed white sand which was one of Barhaven's main attractions. And there were elderly people who were happy to sit in deckchairs, watching the children digging. This seemed to Mr. Morgan to be right. The British seaside was no place for anyone between the ages of fourteen and forty. They got bored, and caused trouble.

At the eastern end of the front he stopped to look at the extension to the Marine Parade. It was just ready for its public opening (three weeks ahead of contract date, Mr. Morgan noted with satisfaction). They had been in danger, at one time, of a heavy penalty payment, but the sacking of one foreman and the payment of an unofficial bonus to another had worked wonders.

Under the lee of the old parade, and forming a full stop to a row of original fishermen's cottages which had somehow survived the modernisation of Barhaven, was a small public house, with whitewashed rough-cast walls and blue check curtains in its windows. Mr. Morgan glanced at it casually and then, with the air of a man making up his mind, descended the concrete steps at the back of the Parade, crossed the narrow road and pushed open the door of the Private Bar.

This was a tiny, panelled room with a bulkhead light over the bar, a ship in a bottle on the mantelpiece, an advertisement for Guinness Milk Stout on the wall and three battered wooden settles round a table whose top was polished to black glass by jerseyed elbows and spilt beer.

The only other occupant of the room was a tall and quite remarkably ugly-looking man. He had a head like a reversed and elongated pear topped with a scattering of sandy hair. A short, thick nose divided two unequal battlefields of seamed flesh and ended in a hedge of moustache which partly concealed a mouth of yellowing tusks.

"Hullo, Mac," said Morgan. "You got here first, I see. How are things?"

"Bloody awful," said Hamish Macintyre, Barhaven's Borough Engineer and Surveyor. "What are you drinking? Whisky I don't doubt."

He raised his voice in a shout and an old man appeared at the bulkhead hatch, and took their orders.

"Sandwiches," said Macintyre. "Beef if you can. Cheese if you can't. Ham if you must."

The old man grinned and departed. Morgan took a quick pull at his whisky and said, "You're having some trouble, I hear."

"You've heard bloody right."

"Mr. Grey thought I ought to come down and have a look round."

"Is *he* getting worried?"

"I wouldn't have said that Mr. Grey ever really got worried. He's not the worrying sort. But he did think there might be a situation here that wanted looking into."

Macintyre grunted. He really was quite astonishingly ugly, thought Morgan. Hadn't there been a general, in the first World War – Henry Wilson, was it? – who claimed to be the ugliest man in the British Army. If they had a competition for the ugliest man in Barhaven, Hamish Macintyre would have been a long-odds favourite. And not only ugly of appearance, but deliberately ugly of speech and manner. Mr. Morgan who was, when off duty, a person of some refinement and intellectual accomplishment, felt sorry that he should be forced to have anything to do with him.

"It's mostly that screaming pansy, Ambrose, stirring up trouble. He's in with Sellinge, and they've got a bit of backing on the Council. Bolshie sods like Viney and Lawrie and Tom Allerton. Luckily they're only a minority. They can talk themselves sick, but they can't carry a vote."

"Not at the moment."

"What are you thinking about. The elections? Ach, forget it. They're in the bag. Open and shut."

"You're sure about that."

Macintyre emphasised his certainty with two obscenities that made Mr. Morgan wince. He said, "I hope you are right about this. We've got a lot of money tied up in the eastern extension. More money than we'd care to lose." He turned his rimless glasses full on his companion. "A great deal more."

Macintyre shifted uneasily.

"I don't know what you're wetting your pants for," he said. "We've always had a Tory majority on the Council here, and we always will."

"As long as they don't behave stupidly."

"Meaning anyone in particular?"

"I was talking about Mr. Crawford."

"You heard about him getting pissed at the Club?"

"There is very little happens in Barhaven that Mr. Grey doesn't hear about, sooner or later. Another thing, we had a visit a couple of days ago from a young solicitor, called Brydon. Do you know him?"

"Tony Brydon? Yes, I know him. I should have said he knew more about cricket than he did about law."

"He seemed to know quite a lot about our affairs," said Mr. Morgan. "He seemed to us to be a keen and enterprising young man. We might be able to put some work in his way."

Macintyre said, "You're a shifty lot of bastards up there in the Metropolis, aren't you."

Mr. Morgan got up. He felt that he had had enough of Macintyre for one day. He said smoothly, "Thank you for the drink. I won't have another. Remember what I said, won't you. Mr. Grey isn't a man who likes to fail. And you can have my share of the sandwiches."

He went out, leaving Macintyre staring after him with a mixture of irritation, greed and apprehension in his rhinoceros eyes.

Chapter Fourteen

Ann Recites Poetry

Ann, who was a bit late herself at the office on Thursday morning, was relieved to find that her employer was later still. By the time she had opened his letters, sorted out the ones that went to the two managing clerks, thrown away the insurance circulars and advertisements and answered three telephone calls, it was a good deal later and she was beginning to get worried.

It was the first time since she had been there that this had happened and she had no idea what she was supposed to do about it, if anything.

She looked at the desk diary. The first appointment was at eleven-thirty – "Mrs. Messenger about a dog" – and there was a sale due to be completed in Hastings at twelve-fifteen. Suppose he had overslept? (She had a momentary picture of him, in blue pyjamas, his hair tousled and his eyes gummy.) On the other hand, why shouldn't he be late if he wanted to? He was his own boss.

At a quarter to eleven her resolution weakened. His father would be at home, and would know the form. As his secretary it was surely her duty – her hand was on the telephone when Anthony came in.

"Hullo," said Ann, "this is a nice time for a hard-working solicitor to turn up."

Anthony said, "I beg your pardon."

"It's a quarter to eleven, and I've had three people asking for you already."

"I take it you've made notes of what they wanted."

"The notes are on your desk. Typed out, since you can't read my hand-writing."

Even this didn't raise a smile. Anthony said, "Thank you. I'll be wanting you in about five minutes. I must try to get some of these letters answered before Mrs. Messenger arrives."

Ann departed and went to look for Mr. Bowler, who was a source of information on every topic in the office from where to find probate forms to what biscuits Mr. Pincott liked with his tea.

"What's biting Mr. Anthony?" she said.

"I was wondering about that myself," said Mr. Bowler. "He came in very early, about twenty to nine. He was here about five minutes – took one telephone call – and went off."

"Where to?"

"No idea. He didn't take his car, so he can't have gone far. I thought he might have been doing some shopping."

"He didn't look like someone who has been on a shopping spree," said Ann. "He looked like someone who's had his toes trodden on in a bus queue. Polite on top, but furious underneath. Hullo. There's the bell. Hurry up with the coffee, Arnold. I've a feeling it's going to be one of those mornings."

When she got back Anthony was reading one of the letters which had arrived that morning and started dictating as soon as she had got her book open.

It was a complicated letter, about the redemption of a mortgage and the release of a life insurance policy and Anthony was dictating at twice his normal speed. Ann was a competent shorthand-typist, but she felt herself slipping slowly, but inexorably behind the flow of his words. It was like trying to go up a moving staircase that was moving down. Any moment now she was going to have to say, "Slower, please." Her wrist was aching. She shifted the book slightly and the movement caught Anthony's eye.

He stopped in the middle of a long sentence and said, "Sorry. Something happened this morning. It upset me rather. But that's no reason why I should take it out on you."

"That's what secretaries are for," said Ann, "or so I'd always understood."

"In the old days of slavery and indentured labour, maybe. Not now. They have to be wooed with bonuses and cosseted with luncheon vouchers."

He sat for a moment in silence and Ann wondered if he was going to go on dictating. It was always difficult when you stopped in the middle of a sentence and lost the thread. The last symbol in her book might have been "monetary" or "mortgage" or even "mortuary" although that was hardly likely in the context.

"I had to go round to the police station," said Anthony, "about that 'ticket' I got for parking the other day. Inspector Ashford wanted to see me about it. He said that he realised that it wouldn't do me much good – me being a local solicitor, and so on – to be hauled up in front of the bench, even for a trivial offence like parking. He said that no Summons had been issued yet, and no Summons need be issued, if—"

"Do you mean," said Ann, turning pink, "that he had the nerve to ask for money."

"No. It took him quite a long time to get round to what he actually wanted, but I picked it up in the end. He wanted me to stop supporting Sellinge. And, particularly, he wanted me to stop acting for him in the planning enquiry."

"But Sellinge would just get someone else."

"At this late hour? He might find it a bit difficult."

"You refused, of course."

"Yes," said Anthony. "I refused."

"What did he say?"

"Oh, he gave me a lecture, on co-operation with the authorities and civic pride."

He couldn't tell her what Ashford had actually said, his big face flushing, his scar flaring out like a warning shout. It had been an unnerving experience, to see a man he had previously respected behaving in such an illogical and stupid and utterly undignified way; like a child, who can't get what he wants with cajolery and suddenly flies into a temper, beating with his hands and screaming.

"When I got away, I felt I wanted to wash my mouth out."

"There was some story about Ashford, before he came here," said Ann. "He's too senior, really, for a potty little job like bossing the Barhaven C.I.D. He started in the Metropolitan Police. Did you know?"

"I'd never heard that. Where did you get it from?"

"I heard daddy talking to mummy about it. He didn't know I was there, and when he found out, he told me I was never to repeat it. He pretended he was only joking, anyway."

"How would your father have known about it?"

"He had a job in the War Office after the War. In the section that deals with Courts Martials. He got to know a lot of policemen. Military ones, and ordinary ones."

"Have you ever said anything about this, to anyone?"

"Not until this moment."

Anthony tried to fit in this new piece of the jigsaw. If Ashford was not only dishonest, but had a previous history of dishonesty, it suggested a number of possibilities, all of them alarming.

One of the typewritten slips on the desk caught his eye. He said, "What did Powell want?"

"He wanted you to ring him back."

"Let's do that," said Anthony.

"You're halfway through a letter."

"I'll finish it whilst we're waiting for the call."

When Dudley Powell came through he said, "I went down to the Companies Registry yesterday to have a look at the file of that Carlmont outfit. As I feared, it's fairly un-revealing. The secretary's a partner in Michaelsons, the City accountants, and they're the company's auditors, and registered office too, which doesn't tell you anything, because they act as registered office for hundreds of companies. The directors are a Mr. Heffer and a Mr. Hill, who are both, incidentally, directors of a dozen other small private companies. The majority of them seem to have something to do with building and property; although it's difficult to say on what sort of scale they operate, as they're all exempt companies, and don't have to file their accounts."

"Did you find any connection between any of these other companies and Greyslates?"

"They're not subsidiaries of Greyslates, if that's what you mean. They could easily have trade connections. But that wouldn't show on the records."

"It all seems to be pretty tightly wrapped up."

"It's a cocoon," agreed Powell. "As soon as you strip off one layer, you find another inside. There was one thing that might help you, though. I noticed from the Articles that the company was incorporated about five years ago, by a firm from your part of the world – Mentmores. And the subscribers were Arthur Mentmore and James Sudderby – both described as solicitors."

Anthony's scurrying pencil checked for a moment; then he said, "Thank you. I'll follow that one up."

"Let me know what happens," said Powell. "I'm getting interested in this paper-chase."

"Mentmore and Sudderby," said Ann, who had been looking over his shoulder.

"They were partners until Sudderby was made Town Clerk, and had to get out of private work altogether. Mentmore was made Clerk to the Justices about the same time – but kept on his practice. He was entitled to do it, of course, but father never forgave him for it."

"There was some sort of row, wasn't there?"

"There was a stand-up fight," said Anthony. "Father was appearing for a motorist, and Mentmore kept interrupting him – or that was father's version of it. Finally he lost his temper and called Mentmore a legal Himmler."

"Lovely," said Ann. "I think he's a horrible man."

"Do you know him?"

"I don't know him myself, but one of my oldest friends, Molly Quist – I was at school with her, and we used to go everywhere together – she works in his office, and she says he's an absolute brute. Luckily she doesn't have anything to do with him herself. I say—"

"What?"

"If you really want to find out something about this company, why don't I ask Molly to help us?"

"Help us?"

"If Mentmores formed the company, there must be a file in the office. That would show who was really behind it, wouldn't it?"

"I suppose so."

"I mean, *someone* must have written to them in the first place. And told them to do it. And what it was for. And to be careful to keep his name out of it. It'll all be in the letters. And that's about the only place it will be."

"Are you suggesting," said Anthony," that she *steals* the file?"

"No need. All she's got to do is look at the first few letters on it, and see who they come from, and what it's all about."

"I don't like it," said Anthony.

"Why not?"

"I'd hate to think of anyone looking into my files."

"Can you think of any other way of finding out who's behind this company?"

"It would be a short cut, but I still don't like it."

"It seems to me," said Ann, "that when you're fighting a battle like this, you can't be too scrupulous about the methods you use."

"Why," said Anthony, in tones of exasperation, "should everyone assume that I'm fighting a battle? First it was Sellinge, then Ambrose, and now you. Solicitors don't fight personal battles. They represent their clients. If one of them wants me to do something, and provided it's legal, and within my powers and he'll pay for it, I'll tackle it. But that doesn't mean that I have to turn the thing into a crusade."

"If you see a mess, it's your job to clear it up."

"Why *my* job?"

"It's nothing to do with being a solicitor. It's a thing every decent person ought to do."

Anthony was dimly aware that this was not the way in which secretaries ought to speak to their employers, but that wasn't what was worrying him. It was the look in Ann's eye. The awful, remorseless, unarguing, unarguable look of a woman who knows that she is right; who sees her courses in clearest black and white, no blurring at the edges, no shading of grey, no permissible compromise; the look of Boadicea, Joan of Arc, and Florence Nightingale; the look which makes the strongest men dive for cover.

She said, "There's something going on in Barhaven which has to be stopped. You read about it in other places. It's always hard to realise that you're living with it. Though what happened to you at the police station this morning might have opened your eyes. I think the trouble is that Barhaven's such a jolly sort of place – sunshine and sand and ice-cream and kids in rompers – not like Soho or Glasgow, or somewhere like that where you naturally think crime might happen. Do you want me to finish that letter?"

"No," said Anthony. "I don't. I want you to finish what you're saying. You think Barhaven is all right on the surface, but rotten underneath, is that it?"

"There was a thing I read, when I was at school. It always gave me the creeps. 'The glacier knocks in the cupboard, the desert sighs in the bed, and the crack in the teacup opens a lane to the land of the dead.'"

"The crack in the teacup," said Anthony. "How very odd." He had suddenly remembered, less than a week before, taking tea with the Lady Mayoress out of her priceless Royal Worcester china cups.

"What's your idea?" he said at last.

"Well," said Ann. "I think the first thing will be to find out who *does* own the 'red' land. I've got a pretty shrewd suspicion, haven't you?"

"Macintyre."

"I should think so. He's obviously trying to drive Colonel Barrow out of Castle House School so that he can pick it up cheap. He'd probably make an offer through Carlmont Property Ltd."

"He must have a good deal of money, if he's going to do that."

"If he's got a share in Pleasuredrome and the East Pier Garage, he *has* got a lot of money."

"All the same," said Anthony, "it seems a big project for one man to handle. Particularly a man in Macintyre's position. After all, he's only a paid employee of the Council."

"I don't suppose he's in it alone. If I had to guess who's behind him, I'd put Crawford near the top of the list. And that toothsome wonder, Lincoln-Bright. And don't forget, they're both members of the Watch Committee, which ties them in with Inspector Ashford."

"I wonder," said Anthony. He sat for a moment, drawing a pyramid of equilateral triangles on his blotting paper. "Suppose you're right— suppose all the guesses you've made are bang on target—it's still going to be devilish tricky to prove. And almost impossible to prove in time."

He looked at his calendar.

"Today's Thursday. The public hearing is on Wednesday and Thursday fortnight. Polling day for the Council elections is the day after. That doesn't give us much time."

"Then the sooner we get busy the better," said Ann. "I'll have a word with Molly in the lunch-hour. If there's anything on the Carlmont file, she can let me know this evening."

"All right," said Anthony. "But for God's sake, tell her to be careful."

In fact, his mind wasn't on the Carlmont Property Company and its problems. He was wondering at exactly what point he had allowed the initiative to pass to Ann; and whether it was wise of him to have done so; and whether he ought to make some attempt to assert himself.

They were important questions, since he had made up his mind, five minutes before, to marry her.

Chapter Fifteen

Sudderby Visits the Sunshine Boys

"It's called Roman Camp," said James Sudderby, as he drove his old car along the flinty secondary road running north out of Barhaven, "because, according to tradition, it's the place where Caesar spent his first night ashore after his crossing from Gaul."

"Ah ha," said Mr. Burgess. *"Veni, vidi, vici."*

"Isn't it a pretty spot," said Doris Burgess. "Oops, that was a nasty bump."

"It's not a very good road," agreed Sudderby. "But being outside the municipal boundaries, it's the County Council who are supposed to look after it. Not us. We turn right at this farm and up the lane."

"It's quite an adventure," said Mrs. Burgess.

"Who are these boys, Sudderby?"

"They're a group of boys who live in South-East London — the Elephant and Castle and the Old Kent Road, and places like that — they've organised this troop, on Boy Scout lines, and they like to go out camping at Easter, and during the summer holidays."

"Good for them."

"I thought it deserved encouraging. I got in touch with them through their vicar, and they were down here two years ago. A nice set of lads, I thought. The boy who organises them, is a cut above the rest. He wrote a very nice letter to thank me, and I sent him a set of the natural history stamps. We've kept up our correspondence ever since.

Through this gateway, and you have to get out and walk the rest of the way."

"We'll stop in the car," said Mr. Burgess. "We've done enough walking for one day."

A small sentry had seen the car turn into the lane and when James Sudderby reached the encampment area, he found the boys sitting, cross-legged, in a circle round Eric, who was demonstrating something with a length of rope and a stick.

"I didn't mean to interrupt," said Mr. Sudderby. "I just came up to see how you were getting on."

"Meet the gang," said Eric. "From left to right, Denny, Fred, Trev, Colin, young Ernie and Arthur. I was just running through a few useful knots."

"What was that last one called?" said Dennis. "It sounded very useful."

"It was a running bowline with a half hitch," said Eric smoothly.

"Ah, I *thought* that was it," said Dennis.

"You seem to be well settled in here," said Mr. Sudderby. "I can see you're old hands at the game. I asked Charlie Andrews – that's his farm down at the bottom of the lane – to keep an eye open for you. You can get fresh milk and eggs from him."

"He's been very kind, too," said Eric.

"You don't want to spend *all* your time up here. You must come down and see the town. There's plenty to do."

"The thing is," said Eric, "we live in town, all the rest of the year. What we come out into the country for, really, is to see nature. Trees, flowers—"

"Birds," said Dennis.

"Bees," said Arthur.

"If you're keen on that sort of thing," said Mr. Sudderby, "I expect I could help you. There's a lot of interesting wild life on the down. Two years ago I found a new sub-variety of yellow brimstone butterfly. Perhaps we could organise a ramble."

"That'd be very nice," said Eric.

"Tomorrow's Friday. I'd be quite free in the afternoon if you're keen on the idea."

"I'll find out who wants to come," said Eric. He showed Mr. Sudderby round the camp, whilst Dennis, assuming his role of instructor, started to tie Arthur and young Eric together. When he had seen all there was to see, they walked down towards the gate.

"I don't like to feel," said Sudderby, his gentle, bearded face breaking into a shy smile, "that the real reason that keeps you out of the town is lack of funds. Would you take this—" he slipped something into Eric's hand— "and divide it out among the troop."

"Well, that is kind of you," said Eric. He was staring down the lane at the parked car. He could just see the backs of Mr. and Mrs. Burgess' heads. "You mustn't keep your friends waiting."

As the car drove back towards Barhaven, Sudderby said, "One can't help wishing one saw more of that sort of thing, and less of these gangs of long-haired hooligans with knives."

"Absolutely," said Mr. Burgess.

"I'm sure Prince Philip would approve," said Mrs. Burgess.

Eric walked slowly back to the camp. He seemed to be thoughtful.

"I say," said Dennis, "I bet that bearded pal of yours is a queer."

"Of course he is," said Eric. "Queer as a three-speed walking stick. I've known that for years."

Chapter Sixteen

Anthony is Guilty of a Breach of Professional Etiquette

It is said that there are underground passages running the length of Whitehall, from the Admiralty Arch to the Treasury on one side, and from the Defence Ministry to New Scotland Yard on the other, the keys of which are entrusted only to senior civil servants and police officers, who can thus conduct their conferences without coming under the eye of the national press. Certainly no hint appeared in the papers of a meeting, that Friday morning, of three very important officials.

One was the Senior Permanent Under-Secretary at the Home Office. The second was the Assistant Commissioner of 'A' Branch at Scotland Yard, who is responsible, among other matters, for discipline; and the third was the Director of Public Prosecutions. They had in front of them a red-tabbed dossier which contained a couple of dozen sheets of paper, and it was clear that all three men had read it, since, although it was frequently referred to it was never, in fact, opened.

At the conclusion of the conference the Assistant Commissioner said, "It's badly put together. The work of an amateur, not of a lawyer, I mean."

"Agreed," said the Director. "There's a good deal of hearsay in it, and second-hand stuff that a lawyer would have left out. All the same—"

"All the same, I don't think we can ignore it," said the Under-Secretary. "It's too detailed, and too circumstantial. If half the people on that list were prepared to get up in a court of law and repeat what they've said here, we should be in for trouble."

The Director said, "Hasn't Inspector Ashford got some sort of record already? It's in the back of my mind—"

"Barking, in 1949," said the Assistant Commissioner. "It was youths, damaging a building site. Inspector Ashford was a Sergeant in 'Q' Division at the time. He caught them at it, and got rough with them. Very rough indeed. One had a number of cracked ribs, and one fell into the well of the building site and broke both his legs. He said that Ashford threw him. There was a conflict of evidence. In fact, there was a good deal to be said on Ashford's side. There was a lot of vandalism going on, and it had to be stopped, somehow."

"Only—?"

"Only it happened to come to light that Ashford was being paid a private retainer by the developers to keep an eye on the site."

"What did you do?"

"Ashford was reprimanded, and given a chance to change forces. He transferred to Kent, and was posted to Barhaven. We thought he'd settled down quite well. This is the first we've heard to the contrary." He tapped the file.

The D.P.P. said, "I saw him play for Kent in the county semi-finals. He got the ball ten yards out, and instead of passing, he put his head down and went for the line. Straight through the opposition. Like a runaway tank."

The Under-Secretary coughed. It seemed to him that they were straying from the point.

"What do you suggest we do about this?" he said.

"We'll have to send someone down, quietly, to have a look round. Brennan will be best. It's never a nice job."

"I think I've met him," said the Director. "He looks like a tired businessman."

"He's a very shrewd operator," said the Assistant Commissioner.

As the conference was breaking up the Director said, "By the way, do you happen to remember the name of those contractors?"

"Which contractors?"

"The ones who had Ashford on their pay-roll."

"It was a curious name," said the Assistant Commissioner. Greyfriars—Greyslates—something like that."

The back of the Dolly Varden tea shop was a cavern of comfortable obscurity. In its shadows, Molly Quist and Ann Weaver sat, with their heads together. The tea which they had ordered stood cold and neglected on the table in front of them.

"It was rather tricky," said Molly. "Most of our old files are stowed away in shelves in the basement. There's a sort of register which tells you the number of shelf a file's meant to be on, but it isn't always there; people take them out and forget to put them back in the right place. So I had to look through all the shelves. It took about an hour."

"You're an angel to do it," said Ann.

"Mr. Parsons – he's the partner I work for – was out, so that bit was all right. When I couldn't find the file, I remembered that Mr. Mentmore kept some of them in a cupboard in his room. I asked his secretary, and she said it would be all right for me to go and have a look – old Mental was at a meeting."

"Is that what they call him?" said Ann, with a giggle. It seems a singularly inappropriate nickname. She had seen Arthur Mentmore in court. He had iron-grey hair, bushy eyebrows, and a long grey face, and looked a formidable and extremely wide awake character.

"I found the file straight away, because it was on top of the pile. He must have had it out himself. And when I got it open, I could see he hadn't only had it out, he'd been through it. Or someone had. It could only have been him or his secretary, really, and she swore she hadn't touched it."

"How do you know someone had been through it?"

"Because they'd taken a lot of the letters out."

"Are you sure?"

"Absolutely sure. We number our letters as we file them. All the earlier ones were missing – the personal ones, I guess. What was left was just the official ones, from the printers, and our London agents, who did the registration."

"And from what was left," said Ann, slowly, "you couldn't get any idea who had actually formed the company?"

"As a matter of fact, I wasn't able to look all that closely. Just as I was getting started, he came back."

"Mr. Mentmore came in?"

"Yes. Just had time to stuff the file back. Of course I had a story ready for him, about Mr. Parsons wanting a file and thinking it might be in his cupboard, etcetera."

"What did he say?"

"He just grunted."

"I think you did brilliantly," said Ann, but she said it in such abstracted tones that her companion looked up sharply.

"You don't think there's going to be trouble over this, do you?" she said.

"No, of course not," said Ann. "And if anyone does get into trouble, it mustn't be you. You must say that I talked you into it. I'll take the blame."

"I wouldn't like to get the sack over it," agreed Molly.

At about this time, Morgan was summoned by buzzer into Mr. Grey's presence. He found the Chairman of Greyslates dissolving a fat white tablet in a glass of water.

"My stomach," he explained. "It's been playing hell with me lately. When my doctor gave me these tablets he said, 'I don't suppose they'll do you much good, but they may take your mind off things.'"

"I should get a better doctor," said Morgan.

"There aren't any. The National Health Service has killed medicine in this country. To get proper attention you have to go to Germany or America. They understand insides there." He finished his drink, made a face, and said, "We've got to do something about the Barhaven project."

"What's happening now?"

"There's a local press campaign. It's getting up a lot of steam."

"I don't reckon much by local newspapers."

"Local newspapers can be very effective in local elections. It only needs a very small swing in public opinion. The *Barhaven Gazette* has got a circulation of around twenty thousand. That's a fleabite by Fleet Street standards, but it goes into the homes of a few thousand voters at this particular election, and if it sways a quarter of them, the Independents will be out of power, and the Progressives will be in."

"We can't take any chances on that," agreed Morgan.

"There was a man who was very useful to us, when we had the same sort of trouble – do you remember – in that Walthamstow development."

"I remember him."

"It was you who got in touch with him."

"Yes," said Morgan. He didn't sound very happy about it.

"It occurred to me that he might be useful here."

"It's a long time since I've had anything to do with him."

"But I expect you could locate him again." Mr. Grey looked sharply up at Morgan.

"I could try. The only thing is, I seem to remember that he was a bit rough."

"I don't remember being told anything about that."

"There was no official report. It was just—"

"I thought he was most co-operative."

"Yes," said Morgan. "He was certainly co-operative."

He had shot his bolt, and knew it.

"There's not a lot of time," said Mr. Grey. A small drop of moisture had escaped from the corner of his dead eye, and was running down his cheek.

"I'll do some telephoning this evening," said Morgan.

"The file had been tampered with?" said Anthony.

"That's right."

"By Mentmore?"

"Presumably."

"And fairly recently."

"I should guess so. It was an old file, and by rights it should have been stowed away down in the basement, but Mr. Mentmore had brought it up and put it in his own cupboard. And seeing it was still on top of the files there, it can't have been there long. You know how quickly things sink to the bottom – in an office when they're not looked at."

"It's extraordinary," said Anthony.

"He must have a guilty conscience, don't you think, if he goes to the trouble of tearing all the letters out of one of his own files, just in case someone happens to look inside—"

"I think he must."

"Isn't there any other way – I mean – it doesn't seem right. Here's this bit of land, right in the middle of the development. Someone's sitting pretty. They ought to be forced to tell us who it belongs to."

"*Who* ought to be forced?"

"These Carlmont people. The ones whose names are on the Register."

"They're only nominees."

"Isn't there some way we could force them to come out into the open?"

"I suppose," said Anthony, slowly, "that if we could show some legal cause, we might get an order of the court directing the nominees to disclose the true names—"

"Oh, order of the court! I didn't mean anything legal. That'd take donkey's years, and they'd block it every time. I meant some other short cut."

"Had you any ideas—?"

"Well, someone must have typed those letters that old Mental threw away—"

"I beg your pardon."

"It hardly seems possible, but that's what they call Mentmore in the office. As I was saying, if we could get hold of his secretary – Molly'd know who she is – and loosen her up – stand her a few gins—"

"I don't really think—" said Anthony.

"We've put our hand to the plough, now. We can't turn back."

"There's a limit," said Anthony, "and getting the secretary of the senior partner of another firm of solicitors drunk in order to learn his secrets is beyond the limit. A long way beyond. Yes, Arnold? What is it?"

"It's Mr. Mentmore to see you, sir. And he says it's urgent."

Anthony looked at Ann, who looked back at him.

"You'd better clear out," he said. "I've got a feeling we're in for trouble."

Arthur Mentmore was angry, but it was a controlled and dishonest anger, which had been stoked up to prearranged temperature, and kept there, with intent to hurt.

"Yesterday afternoon," he said, "I found one of the girls in my office rummaging among my private files. She said that one of my partners had asked her to look for a document.

"I happened to speak to that partner, and he denied it, completely. So I had another word with the girl. I questioned her—closely." Mentmore's formidable eyebrows came together in a frown. "In the end, she told me an extraordinary story. So extraordinary that I could hardly believe it."

He's worked this all out, thought Anthony. It's exactly like a closing speech for the prosecution.

"—She said that she was examining one of my files at the suggestion of *your* secretary." When Anthony said nothing at all, he repeated, "At the suggestion of *your* secretary. Would you care to comment on that?"

"Why should I?"

"It calls for some comment, surely."

"I don't see it," said Anthony. "All you've done is to pass on to me something your secretary said to you about my secretary. It's kind of you to take the trouble but I don't really see that I'm called on to say anything."

Mr. Mentmore's face darkened. He was getting really angry now, not pretending.

"I don't imagine," he said, "that your secretary would do this on her own initiative."

"That shows you haven't met her. She's an extraordinarily independent girl."

"If you insist on treating this outrageous breach of professional etiquette as a joke, I shall have no alternative but to report it to the Law Society."

"I don't think the Law Society has any jurisdiction over secretaries, but by all means try it, if you like."

Mr. Mentmore drew in a hissing breath.

"I am only too well aware," he said, "that there is bad blood between your firm and ours. If I may say so, the fault for that lies more with your father than with me."

"W—will you kindly leave my father out of it." Anthony was annoyed to find the stutter coming back.

"Some of the remarks he has addressed to me in open court exceeded the bounds of civility usual among professional men."

"Perhaps you didn't hear me," said Anthony, getting to his feet, his glasses glinting dangerously. "I told you to leave my father out of it—"

"Nothing personal—"

"You can say what you like about me, or my secretary. We're here, and we can take care of ourselves. But if you mention my father again, I shall have the personal pleasure—" he advanced towards Mr. Mentmore, who shuffled a pace or two backwards— "of kicking you downstairs."

"I don't think there's any point in prolonging this discussion."

"I don't think there is. Good day to you."

"My goodness, you were splendid," said Ann. Her eyes were shining. "Old Mental looked as if he was going to swallow his false teeth."

"Do you mean you were eavesdropping?"

"I can always hear anything you say in here."

"Can you, indeed," said Anthony. He felt strong, masterful and confident. He took half a step towards her, and said, "There's something

I've been meaning to tell you, and now seems as good a time as any. Blast you, Bowler. What do you want?"

"It's a telephone message, sir, from the doctor. It's your father. He's dead."

The old man's eyes were full of tears.

Chapter Seventeen

After the Funeral

When he tried to think about it afterwards, Anthony could recall very little of the period between his father's death and the funeral on Monday afternoon. The weather broke. It was the only wet spell in that hot, dry summer. He remembered the slanting rain outside the windows, as he talked to the undertaker, the wet laurels in the vicarage garden when he walked round to discuss the funeral arrangements with the vicar and the great drops of rain which hung from the points of umbrellas as they stood at the graveside. He remembered a feeling of outrage that strangers should be treating his father like that, and a feeling of astonishment that he should have possessed so many unknown relatives, mostly female and elderly, and all distressingly kind. But nothing was distinct. It was like the time when he had fallen off his bicycle at the age of eight and had concussion. Time marched erratically, sometimes very fast, sometimes very slowly. Reality was enshrouded in a damp mist.

On Monday evening Doctor Rogers, who had been looking after his father and had called to pay his condolences, took one glance at Anthony, and went out into the hall to fetch something from his bag.

"Have you been sleeping?" he said.

"Not very well," Anthony admitted.

"You're going to sleep tonight," said Doctor Rogers. "Take three of these, in warm milk, when you're actually in bed."

When Anthony woke up on Tuesday morning the sky was blue and life was back to its normal pace and colour. He could still feel a dull ache, where a vital piece of his past life had been amputated, but it was the sort of ache which he would learn to put up with. He decided to go to the office.

Ann was standing beside the desk slitting open envelopes. She said, "A lot of these are about your father. I've answered yesterday's batch in your name. I don't suppose you want to look at them, do you? There wasn't a grain of genuine sympathy in a bushel of wish-wash. Oh, and there was one particularly nauseating one from old Mental. I tore that one up."

"Thank you," said Anthony. "You deal with all that sort of thing. If there's anything really personal, let me see it." He turned gratefully to the other pile and started dictating an answer to a mortgagee bank which was getting uppish about unpaid interest.

After half an hour of this he said, "The town seems to be covered with posters this morning. I didn't stop to read them."

"It's a rash of electioneering. It burst out all over on Monday morning. 'Vote for Honest Jack Crawford. The man you can Trust.' 'Lincoln-Bright Washes White.'"

"When's polling day?"

"Friday week. The Progressives are having a monster meeting in the Winter Garden on Saturday, and the Independents are holding an open-air rally on the West Pier on Sunday. Life won't be worth living until it's over. Sit tight, and I'll get you some coffee."

As she got up to leave the room the sunlight from the window turned her hair into a coronet of gold and she looked so young and untroubled that he wanted very much to get up and put his arms right round her and say, "I love you, I love you, will you marry me?" only at this moment Mr. Pincott wandered into the room and sat down in her chair.

"I haven't bothered you before this," he said, "but I think there are one or two things we shall have to settle."

"I suppose so," said Anthony.

"You realise," said Mr. Pincott, unconscious of the sacrilege he had committed by depositing his shiny sponge-bag trousers and baggy black coat in a chair recently consecrated by radiant youth and innocence, "you realise that you are now the controlling partner in this firm."

"I hadn't thought much about it."

"Your father held 40 per cent of the shares. I had thirty-five and you had twenty-five. Under your father's will, all his property goes to you."

"I suppose that's right," said Anthony. "I can't see that it'll make any practical difference. We're still partners."

"It won't make any difference to the running of the firm," agreed Mr. Pincott, removing his glasses and polishing them with a clean white handkerchief from his top pocket. "It will simply mean that a larger share of the profits will go to you."

"If you think that's unfair, we could always rearrange it."

"That wasn't in my mind at all," said Mr. Pincott with a slight smile. "I should think very poorly of myself if I tried to take advantage of a sad occasion like this to cajole more money out of you. My intentions were the reverse. I have long felt that general practice was not my line. I should like you to consider releasing me from the terms of our partnership deed. Not immediately, of course. Say, at the end of the year."

"You want to retire at the end of the year?" said Anthony, blankly.

"Not retire altogether. I have my clerkship to the Foreshore Commission, my Archidiaconal work, and my secretaryship of the Chamber of Commerce. Those are personal appointments, and I should hope you would have no objection to my continuing with them."

"Of course not."

"I realise it will mean a great deal of added work and responsibility for you. You will have to think seriously of taking in a partner. Possibly two. There is scope for three working partners in this practice."

"How does one set about finding a partner?"

"One can always advertise in the Law Society's *Gazette*. I have noticed a section there, 'Partnerships Required'. Mostly they seem to be looking for partnerships with prospects. I should have thought there were any amount of prospects in Barhaven."

"I couldn't agree with you more," said Anthony.

The surprises of the morning were not over. Mr. Pincott had scarcely departed when Ann poked her head round the door and said, "Mr. Southern's in the waiting-room. He says, not to worry if you're busy. He'll go away and make a proper appointment. But as he was passing—"

"No. Ask him in," said Anthony.

"I didn't mean to butt in," said Southern. "I imagine you're up to the eyes in work. I didn't come to the funeral. I'm sorry. I couldn't face it. Particularly in the rain."

"I wish I could have dodged it," said Anthony. "All those terrible women."

"We're all frightened of death," said Southern. "That's why we dress it up. To try and propitiate it. However, I didn't come in here to philosophise. I came in to pass on a piece of news. James Sudderby, so my spies tell me, has hinted that he'd like to give up his job as Town Clerk."

"Why on earth—?"

"He says he's getting too old for it. Which is nonsense. He's younger than me. He also says he wants to give more time to his archaeological and natural history studies. But that, I suspect, is an excuse."

"Why do you think, then?"

"He was looking a very worried man when I saw him yesterday. And when someone in their middle fifties looks worried, I usually jump to the conclusion that they've had some bad news from their doctor."

"I suppose that might be it."

"That's only surmise. What I really came in to say was that if Sudderby does mean to give the job up, quite a few people think that you would be in line for it."

"Me!" said Anthony. "Really—I hardly—it's very good of you, but—"

"It'd mean leaving private practice, I agree. But it's quite a well-paid job. And it wouldn't end there. If you made a success of it, as I'm sure you would, you could move on after a few years to a bigger place. Experienced Town Clerks are in short supply. There's no saying where you might finish. The Town Clerk of Birmingham gets a higher salary than the Lord Chief Justice. Did you know that?"

"It isn't just money," said Anthony. "There are personal complications. I won't bore you with them—"

"Think it over."

"I'll do that," said Anthony. "Before you go, there is one thing—"

He opened the drawer of his desk and took out a jeweller's box with an elastic band round it.

"That's for you," he said. "Father left it to you in his will. Strictly, I suppose, I ought to wait for probate before handing it over, but since you're here—"

"What is it?"

"It's his medals. Three from the First War, and one from this. I think it's a sort of memento, really, of the good times you and he had in the Home Guard together."

Southern slipped the box, unopened, into his pocket. "What a very nice thought," he said. His voice was light, almost amused, and he took his departure with the same neat and unruffled grace as he had entered the room. Anthony thought, nevertheless, that it was the first time he had ever seen Southern thrown off balance.

Chapter Eighteen

Anthony has an Interrupted Morning

When Anthony arrived at the office on Wednesday morning he found Arthur Ambrose waiting for him.

"I know how busy you are," said Ambrose, "and my only chance was to get at you before you got *immersed* in your morning's work—"

Anthony looked at the pile of letters on his desk and sighed. Behind Ambrose's back Ann was making faces. He guessed that she had put up a fight to keep him out.

"All right," said Anthony. "Five minutes. Is someone else suing you for libel?"

"Not this time. I did have another letter from Mentmore. A lot of huffing and puffing. I am to publish 'a full retraction of my scurrilous and unfounded attack on the head of the Barhaven C.I.D.'. If I do this, he *may* be instructed to let the matter drop. Ha ha!"

"What *are* you going to do?"

"I thought of publishing his letter with an editorial footnote saying that the *Gazette* cannot be gagged."

"No," said Anthony.

"Why not?"

"You can't start publishing solicitors' letters in the newspaper."

"If you say so," said Ambrose, regretfully. "These two issues of the *Gazette* – the one that comes out this Friday, and next week's one. They're going to be pretty vital issues. You realise that?"

"I suppose they are."

"It's no exaggeration to say that they could settle the Council election. And this Council election could decide the future of the town. Barhaven has never, in the six hundred years of its corporate existence, had a more important decision to make. It must decide, once and for all—"

"This sounds like your next editorial."

"As a matter of fact, it is. I've got a proof of it here. And I want you to cast an eye over it—"

"To see whether it's libellous or not."

"I'd welcome your views on it generally."

"I'm not a politician," said Anthony. "But push it across."

He read it through carefully whilst Ambrose, who found it very difficult to sit still for any length of time, prowled round the room, read the titles on the backs of the law books, the names on the deed boxes, and, when he had exhausted these, the names under a photograph of the school cricket team which Anthony had captained in its Lord's match in his last term at Tonbridge.

"As far as libel goes," said Anthony, "I'd be inclined to give it a clearance. It's certainly a lot less scurrilous than your last effort."

"We learn," said Ambrose. "We learn."

"As a matter of fact, I think it's rather good stuff. I like the idea of appealing to the voters to elect a 'balanced' Council, so that politics can be kept out of local government. A lot of people will go for that."

"We must concentrate on kicking out Crawford and Lincoln-Bright. The Progressive candidates, Masters and Hopper, are both sound men. If people started to think about them as people, and didn't just vote the colour of their own convictions, they'd get in by a mile."

"If anything could make them stop and think," said Anthony, "I should think your editorial will."

Ambrose turned pink with pleasure.

When he had got rid of him, Anthony turned to his heaped-up in-basket, and started to sort it through. It seemed incredible that so much could have accumulated in two or three days. There was a lot of routine conveyancing and one or two county court matters which could be handed over to their two unqualified managing clerks, although Anthony was aware that they were neither of them really experienced enough to be working on their own. That was the way a lot of solicitor's firms got into trouble. An ageing or overworked principal left more and more of the work to the managing clerks—

"What's up?" said Ann, who had come back into the room after seeing Ambrose off.

"Why?"

"You're looking like a hanging judge. Has Mr. Ambrose been making a fool of himself again?"

"I wasn't thinking about Ambrose at all," said Anthony, and explained to Ann what was worrying him. It seemed a natural thing to do.

"It's the sort of thing that happens in solicitors' offices," agreed Ann. "Look at Uriah Heep and that silly old ass, Mr. Wickfield. I never had any patience with him. If he was so overworked, why didn't he get another partner?"

"Easier said than done," said Anthony. "Now—what are we going to tackle first?"

"There's a letter from Moule Mainwaring & Co.," said Ann. "It came in yesterday afternoon after you'd gone. It's got a further opinion from Counsel on the planning appeal, and Powell suggests you ought to go up – tomorrow if you can – and have a talk with Counsel about witnesses. There's nothing in your diary for tomorrow that can't be put off."

When he said nothing she looked up and found him staring out of the window.

"I'm sorry," he said, apologetically, "a sudden thought." And to himself, "I wonder if it would work out. It'd be rather fun if it did."

"This is a fine moment for the Town Clerk to be walking out on us," said Jack Crawford.

"Not until after the elections, I trust," said the Lady Mayoress.

"What's wrong with him?" said Lincoln-Bright. "Don't we pay him enough?"

Southern said, "I don't think money comes into this. He's a bachelor, and although he's not rolling in wealth, I imagine he's got enough to get by on."

"Then why's he doing it?"

"When we were discussing it, he said he was a keen naturalist and antiquarian, and wanted more time to pursue those hobbies."

"Can't blame him, really," said General Crispen. "If the alternatives were watching wild birds and listening to us, I know which *I'd* choose."

"All right," said Southern. He cast an eye round the table in the small committee room. Except for the inarticulate George Gulland, the Independent caucus was there in full strength. "We're not here to talk about the Town Clerk, or his successor. In fact, unless we pull our socks up, we may not have any interest in the question of his successor."

"I don't see any reason for defeatist talk myself," said Lincoln-Bright. "The voters in the Victoria Park Ward whom I've spoken to have all assured me of their continuing support. They realise that Masters and Hopper, whatever they may call themselves, are a pair of left-wing socialists. Hopper, I believe, once belonged to the Communist Party for a short time."

"Who *are* these people you've spoken to?" said Miss Barnes abruptly.

Lincoln-Bright looked put out.

"If you want a list of their names," he said, "I dare say I could supply you with it."

"What I mean is," said Miss Barnes, "that if you've just been chatting to your own cronies, of course they'll say they're going to support you. They always do. Have you done any actual canvassing—?"

"I've—well—yes, a certain amount."

"Because I hope you've had a look at the new Register. There're a lot of little shop-keepers on it, from Paston Street and Park Street and Marine Square. Leaseholders mostly. And Hopper and Masters have been calling on *all* of them. I've seen them at it."

Raymond Southern said, "Well I *have* done some canvassing in the Ward. And I think we shall get both seats. I don't say it's going to be a walk-over, though. And we shall have to keep hard at it from now till next Friday."

"And how are things going in Marine East, Mr. Crawford?" enquired the Lady Mayoress.

"It should be a push-over," said Crawford. "If the town extension goes east, as we plan it, they'll all benefit. If it goes the other way, they'll lose. Simple as that."

"It may be simple, but do they appreciate it?" said General Crispen. He found it difficult to keep the distaste out of his voice when he spoke to Crawford.

"They will when they get my election circular on Saturday," said Crawford. "It's hot stuff."

They started talking about circulars.

When Mrs. Lord left the Council offices she hesitated for a moment at the bottom of the steps, then crossed the road and entered the Memorial Garden. Several people nodded to her as she passed, moving like a frail boat drifting on the setting tide. Friends who were walking with Mr. and Mrs. Burgess pointed her out to them. "A fine old lady," they said. "Three times Mayoress. You don't see them like that nowadays."

At the western end of the gardens she paused. She seemed to be in such a mood of indecision that a puff of wind would have served to divert her course. Then she crossed the road, very slightly quickening her pace as if she had come, at last, to some conclusion.

"Who?" said Anthony.

"Mrs. Lord," said Ann. "It's gospel truth. I saw her myself. In the waiting-room."

"Show her up," said Anthony. "We don't often get visits from royalty."

He swept a clutter of papers and an empty coffee cup from his desk, straightened his tie, smoothed down an untidy lock of hair, and was seated behind his desk looking serious and professional when Ann showed Mrs. Lord into the room. He got up and placed a chair for her.

"I have come to consult you professionally, Mr. Brydon. I thought it right to make that clear at the beginning. Our family solicitor, for a

great many years now, has been Mr. Shard – I expect you know
him—"

Anthony did indeed know Samuel Shard, who was the doyen of
Barhaven solicitors, and almost as venerable as Mrs. Lord herself. He
had flabbergasted Barhaven six months previously by marrying a
nineteen-year-old assistant in a tobacconist's shop and had then gone
quietly off his head.

"Since he had his misfortunes, I have found no occasion for legal
advice, but it has been in my mind that I should look for a new
solicitor. I could not approve of either of Mr. Shard's partners. One is
a Presbyterian, and the other wears a woollen waistcoat at the office."

"I'd be very pleased to help you," said Anthony. "I think anyone in
Barhaven would."

"You are all too kind." She opened her black alligator handbag, and
produced a letter, written on familiar buff paper. "I received this
communication two days ago. My first indication was to ignore it. On
reflection, I was not sure that that would be wise."

Anthony read the letter slowly. It was from the Special Commissioners
of Inland Revenue and was couched in their familiar tones; half-
subservient, half-arrogant, the voice of the servant turned master.

"Our attention has been drawn," said the letter, "to the wording of
Section Three of the Barhaven (Toll Bridge) Private Act of 1829 and
the effect on Section Three of the Finance Act 1946 read in
conjunction with the Municipal Offices Act of 1888—"

"This isn't going to be very easy," said Anthony, "when the Revenue
starts talking about the effect of one section on another. And have you
got a copy of the Toll Bridge Act?"

"Mr. Shard's firm had one, I know."

"I'll see if I can borrow it," said Anthony. He turned to the end of
the letter. "What they seem to be saying is that your receipts from the
toll bridge would stop being a return of capital and would become
taxable if you happened to be occupying a *paid* municipal office in
Barhaven. I bet some busy bee in the Special Commissioners' Office
had fun working *that* one out."

"But is it true?"

"If they say so there's probably an arguable case. I'd have to look at all three Acts to see."

"Then it's just as well," said Mrs. Lord, "that I have always refused all emoluments for acting as Mayoress."

"You have?"

"It was the only condition on which my late husband would allow me to accept office. I remember him saying, 'The honour is enough. The pay will tarnish it.'"

"It's extremely fortunate that he did."Anthony could just remember the late Colonel Lord, a stringy little man with a face like a well-fed weasel. Was it possible that he had realised the effect of the Income Tax Act of 1946 on the Toll Bridge Act of 1829? Improbable. It had simply been snobbishness. Very lucky though. If the tolls *were* taxed, they would clearly be unearned income, and Mrs. Lord would be lucky if she got a quarter of them.

"I was paid my expenses, of course."

"Expenses would be all right—I think."

"You'll look into it, and tell me what I have to say to them."

"I'll draft an answer for you," said Anthony.

When Mrs. Lord had gone, he dispatched Bowler to see if he could borrow a copy of the Toll Bridge Act from Mr. Shard's junior partner, whom he happened to know, having once played cricket with him. He then sat staring at the irreducible pile of unanswered letters which cluttered his desk, sighed, and rang his bell. Three minutes later, when nothing had happened, he rang it again. Ann arrived looking flustered.

"I told him it was a busy morning," she said, "and that you were miles behind with your letters, and couldn't he make a proper appointment, but he didn't take any notice. He just sat there, looking at me, and saying that he had to see you."

"You've left out the subject of the sentence."

"I'm talking about Mr. Sudderby."

"What on earth does *he* want?"

"The same as everyone else in Barhaven this bright morning," said Ann. "You."

"Well, I suppose—"

"Couldn't you be firm for once?"

"Now that he's here—"

"Look at those letters."

"Anyone else," said Anthony. "But not James Sudderby. He took me out on my sixth birthday, on to the downs, to show me the nest of a red-backed shrike. It had a secret larder, with bumble bees impaled on thorns—"

"All right," said Ann.

"I really am most terribly sorry to disturb you," said Sudderby. "Your young lady told me how busy you were. I'm glad of that, by the way. It's splendid to be busy, when you're young—"

He smiled the smile which had always captivated Anthony's heart.

"What can I do for you?" he said. "In ten minutes," he added, hastily.

"It'll hardly take that long. I have to raise some money. Not a great deal. Five hundred pounds would do. Or I could get by with three hundred."

Anthony had acquired sufficient professional aplomb not to ask, "What do you want it for?" or even, "Why are you so hard up?" He said, "That oughtn't to be too difficult. I imagine your bank would oblige. They might need some extra security. How do you stand with them?"

"I saw my bank manager yesterday. He said the same thing. They'd need some security."

"How about your house?"

"There's a mortgage on that. With a building society."

"How much for?"

"I'm not quite sure. I took it out when I bought the house, about twelve years ago."

"How much was it?"

"Two thousand pounds."

"In that case," said Anthony, "there's really no problem at all. There can't be more than about eight hundred pounds of the old mortgage outstanding. And your house – it's freehold isn't it? – then it can't be worth less than four thousand. More probably you could either get a second mortgage, or you could pay off this one—"

Anthony spoke quickly, and cheerfully, to conceal a sense of distress. His visitor was sitting full in the light of the window, and the signs of collapse and defeat were clear.

Mr. Sudderby looked as though he had not slept for a long time. His eyes were red-rimmed with weariness and the flesh on either side of his face had fallen away, pulling down the corners of his mouth and leaving his cheeks hollow. Anthony wanted to say, "Please, tell me what it's all about, and let me see if I can't help." If he had been a little older, he might have done it, too.

Mr. Sudderby hardly seemed to be listening to him. In the end he said, "Will it take long?"

"Not too long. Two or three weeks to get it all fixed up."

"Oh dear—then I'm afraid—"

"When do you want the money?"

"I must have it by the end of the week."

Chapter Nineteen

Anthony's Second Visit to London

"You got a copy of Mr. Hiscoe's opinion," said Powell. "Don't let it put you off. He really is better on his feet than he sounds on paper."

"Well, I'm glad of that," said Anthony, "because when I read his opinion I thought he meant that we were chucking our money away fighting the case at all."

"Counsel always back themselves both ways. If they lose, they can say, 'I told you so', and if they win, you think they're jolly good chaps. Let's walk down and see what he's got to tell us."

As they went, Anthony broached the idea which had come to him the day before. Powell heard him out in silence.

"It's a serious offer," he said. "I'm badly in need of help. Pincott, who's the only other partner, wants to get out and look after his private appointments, and there's more work than I can possibly cope with. If you took a half share, and we did as well this year as we did last, it'd bring you in nearly five thousand. I could show you the accounts if you're interested."

"I'm very interested," said Powell. "As a matter of fact, I've been thinking of making a move for some time. I'm perfectly happy with Moules, but there's not much future in it. The other partners aren't a lot older than me, and two of them have got sons, anyway."

"How will they take it?"

"They won't lose any sleep. I'm only a salaried partner. It's always been understood that if I got offered a full partnership they wouldn't stand in my way. I should have to buy out Pincott, I suppose."

"Yes. We'd have to fix that. He'd probably take it in instalments. I'll send you the accounts as soon as I get home tonight. I am glad you like the idea."

"I like the idea of being able to do some sailing. Our two boys are growing up, too. And Barhaven sounds a nice quiet sort of place to grow up in."

"I don't know about quiet," said Anthony, with a grin. "We've got municipal elections on, and a first-class municipal row blowing up. And in mid-summer it's chock-a-block. But come the autumn, when the crowds have all gone home, and the storms come roaring down the Channel and blow the smell of hot dogs and fish and chips clean out of the place, it's a wonderful spot to be in."

They dodged across Fleet Street and into the calm of Middle Temple Lane.

Mr. Hiscoe smoothed out the papers on the table in front of him with a long finger and said, "What it comes to is this. We've got to convince the Ministry Inspector that our client's proposed development of shops with residential accommodation over is sound planning, so far as the neighbourhood in particular is concerned, and is generally in accordance with the needs of the area as a whole. You appreciate that the two considerations might conflict? The immediate neighbourhood might want shops. People usually do like having a few shops on their doorstep. The town as a whole – having regard to its proper lay-out – might not want shops in that particular place. You follow me?"

"Yes," said Anthony.

"I've read your surveyor's report. I think he'll make a good witness. And we've got the evidence of—" Counsel flicked over the pile of papers rapidly— "Mrs. Tuffin and Mr. Porteous that they find it difficult to get into the centre of Barhaven to do their shopping. Mr. Porteous is crippled, I understand—"

"He was seriously wounded in the last War."

"Excellent," said Mr. Hiscoe. "And Mrs. Tuffin?"

"Rheumatoid arthritis in both hips and one ankle."

"Couldn't be better. In fact, I should say that on the local issue we had a good chance of success." Feeling that this might be over-enthusiastic he added hastily, "A reasonable chance, anyway. What I am less confident about is the wider issue. Are the Borough Council being represented?"

"I understand they've got Paradine."

"A very sound man," said Mr. Hiscoe. "A little emotional for a planning appeal, but a fighter, and very sound on the legal aspects."

Anthony said, "There's a great deal more than law involved here."

"More than law?"

"Politics, and personalities, and prestige. And pounds shillings and pence."

(And the shifty Hamish Macintyre and the corrupt Inspector Ashford and the frightened James Sudderby. And the Lady Mayoress and Jack Crawford and Lincoln-Bright and Raymond Southern. And an estate agent called Sellinge and a journalist called Ambrose and a headmaster called Colonel Barrow. And, though less directly, the obnoxious Mr. Mentmore; and his own father's reputation; and the shadowy, but formidable Greyslates Company.)

Hiscoe heard him out. By the end he had stopped even fidgeting with his pencil and was staring dreamily at the ceiling.

"Every time our politicians create a new heaven and a new earth," he said, "they create a new bench of gods as well. The gods of today are the planners. Their power is prodigious. They say 'No' and your field is worth five hundred pounds. They say 'Yes' and the very same field is worth ten thousand."

"Which means that people look for some method of influencing their decisions."

"Oh, certainly," said Hiscoe. "All power leads to corruption. That is inevitable. The only question is, can it be stopped?"

"I know one thing," said Anthony. "The Council – or, to be more accurate, the Independent caucus on the Council – was utterly opposed to this enquiry. They even suggested, at one time, that if the appellant would drop it, they would use their influence with the planning authority, in the County Council, to push through what he wanted to do. In other words, they'd have been prepared to alter the municipal plan and fit our chap in, *to avoid having a public hearing.*"

"But your client wouldn't agree?"

"He wasn't given a chance of agreeing. The opposition on the Council managed to scotch it."

"What it amounts to, then, is this. That we have got to demonstrate that the Council, in opposing this application, is acting in bad faith."

"Right."

"And the simplest way of doing so would be to show that some member, or members of the Council, or their senior officials, had a personal interest in the eastern scheme of development."

"Right again."

"Which brings us back to the ownership of the 'red' land. Have you made any progress in your investigations there?"

"A little. But not enough. It was bought, about three years ago, by a company called Carlmont Properties. It's clear from the Register that this company has a tie-up with property developers in the City. And it's probable that the first initiative for its formation came from Barhaven. It was certainly formed by Barhaven solicitors. But unless we can break down the nominee shareholdings, I don't know how we can find out who really started it."

"I did have a thought about that," said Powell. "You remember we found out that the subscribers were Mentmore and Sudderby. Obviously you won't get anything out of Mentmore, but didn't you tell me Sudderby was a friend of yours? Mightn't you be able to get something out of him?"

"It's worth thinking about," said Anthony.

He was still thinking about it as he walked on to the platform at Victoria. Sudderby was no longer a member of Mentmores, and had, as Anthony knew, little liking for his former partner. Also, Sudderby was a badly worried man. Was it possible that there was a connection between these worries and what he knew, or suspected, about the land ramp?

The mid-afternoon train for Barhaven was never crowded. There were quite a few people in the second-class carriages, but the first-class was practically unused. It was a good train which ran non-stop to Swanley. Anthony chose a section of three empty first-class carriages in the middle of the train and settled down to read his papers.

A few minutes before the train moved off a tall thin man swung open the door and jumped in. He didn't come into the carriage, but remained standing in the corridor.

Anthony was mildly curious. It was common enough for passengers with second-class tickets to stand in the corridors of first-class sections when there were no seats for them anywhere else. It had happened on the way up that morning. But why should anyone bother to stand when there were dozens of seats for him to sit in?

He could see the man's face reflected in the glass of the window. It was a striking face, tanned, the nose hooked like a beak, the eyes puckered as if from staring into the sun, the black hair cut into an exaggerated peak in front and worn long behind. It reminded Anthony of something and it was a moment or two before he realised that what he was looking at was the face of a Red Indian.

He discovered, with a small shock, that as he was examining the stranger the stranger's dark brown eyes were studying him.

As the whistle blew, the man in the corridor turned, slid back the carriage door, and came in. He was smiling broadly, showing a set of very white teeth.

"Nothing to disturb us now – not till we get to Swanley," he said.

Anthony grunted. If the man wanted to cheat, and travel first-class on a second-class ticket, he might at least have chosen one of the other two carriages. As far as he knew they were both empty.

The man, who was still standing, steadied himself by gripping the luggage rack on either side, drew back one foot, and kicked Anthony hard on the shin.

The shock of it choked the cry that Anthony gave. As he was gasping for breath the man kicked him again in the same place. It was brutally done. He was wearing heavy, steel-tipped shoes and if he had more room to swing his leg he would probably have cracked Anthony's shin.

Through waves of pain Anthony saw the man swing his leg again. He had to get up. He had to get out of the corner. He half-rose in his seat. The man steadied himself, swaying with the gathering speed of the train. A long, hard finger shot out. The tip caught Anthony square in the throat, knocking him back into the corner seat and driving all the breath out of him.

The man sat down in the seat opposite him and lit a cigarette.

The waves of multi-coloured pain and sickness lessened in intensity and Anthony, blinking the tears out of his eyes, leaned forward to rub his leg. The man raised one arm, Anthony sank back in his seat.

"You move when I tell you, not before," said the man. "Next time, I might kick you where it really hurts."

"What—" the word came out like a croak from Anthony's throat. "What do you want?"

The man drew evenly on his cigarette. The train rocked over the points as it gathered speed.

"There's things you find out," said the man at last. "For instance, I'll tell you what you're thinking right now. You're thinking that when the train stops, you'll jump out and scream blue murder, and where are the police, and this man assaulted me, and all that caper. Here's the first thing you've got to learn. Don't try it."

A faint smile touched the man's thin lips. "Or perhaps you ought to try it. Then you'd find out. That's the only way to learn, in this life. Do things, and find out. You go to the police, and say I attacked you. I admit it. I say, I was standing quietly in the corridor. As soon as the train started, you invite me into the carriage, and make an improper suggestion, and I get mad, and hit you. Maybe they believe me. Why shouldn't they? I've got no reason for attacking you. I haven't tried to rob you. I don't even know you. Do I?"

"No," croaked Anthony. He would wake up soon. When he had been a child and had had a nightmare he used to think: if I keep very still, nothing can hurt me.

"Any old way, it'll get in the papers. That won't hurt me. I been in the papers plenty of times. And when it's all over, you'll be waiting for next time. Because there'll be a next time. In a month, or six months, or a year. You'll be coming home late one night, perhaps. Putting your car away. There'll be two or three of us there, waiting for you, and next thing you know, you'll be on the ground, and we'll be putting the boot in. Next morning, they'll pick you up. You won't be in very good shape. And that'll only be the start—"

"What—" said Anthony. He seemed to be getting his voice back as the pain in his throat died down. "What have I done to you? Or your friends?"

"You've been a little thoughtless. Or put it another way. You haven't been thinking hard enough."

"What do you want me to do?"

"That's up to you, really. But now you're being reasonable—" the man leaned forward, bringing his face close to Anthony's, so close that Anthony could smell his curious mixture of sweat and hair cream and savagery— "I'll give you a tip. What you need's a holiday. Pack up, and go away. Right away. Say for a fortnight."

"But—" said Anthony.

"If you don't like my advice, of course, you needn't take it. You can always take a chance—"

The man sat back suddenly in his seat. For the first time a change of expression had passed across his face. He wasn't looking at Anthony. He was looking past him. Anthony forced his head round.

A second man was standing in the corridor.

Seeming to sense that they were looking at him the man turned, surveyed the carriage deliberately and, after a moment's hesitation and to Anthony's unspeakable relief, opened the door, came in, and sat quietly down in the corner.

He looked at first sight like any other businessman, filling out the well-cut blue suit with a rose in the buttonhole. At second sight he looked different, but it was hard to say exactly how. Perhaps it was the eyes, deep set, above pouches of flesh, in a pale face. They were tired eyes, eyes which had seen everything, had forgotten nothing, and were surprised by nothing. They rested, for a moment, on Anthony and for another moment on his assailant, who was smiling quietly to himself, as if in enjoyment of a private joke. Then the newcomer appeared to lose interest in them altogether. He opened up a copy of the evening paper and settled down to read. All Anthony could see of him now was his hands. They were large, plump, white hands with a shading of black hair on the back, and they ended in a very thick pair of wrists.

So much he had observed when the train drew up at Swanley, and, with a single smooth movement, his assailant had opened the door and was gone.

The man in the corner never moved.

"Now," thought Anthony. "Now is the time. If I am ever going to do it, it must be now."

The guard blew his whistle. Carriage doors slammed. The tall man had disappeared. He was probably clear of the station by now. He couldn't hurt him any more.

The train jerked into motion. Anthony opened his mouth to speak, and shut it again.

Half an hour later, as they were swinging south to cross the River Barr and the red roofs of Barhaven were in sight, it was the man in the corner who put down his paper and said, "You hurt your leg?"

Anthony looked down. Blood had soaked through his trouser leg and formed a dark patch in front.

Chapter Twenty

Two Visitors to Barhaven

The thin man with the Red Indian face, whose name was Sturrock, had not, in fact, left the train at Swanley. He had mixed with the crowd moving towards the exit, and, as they reached it, had jumped back into an empty carriage in the end coach.

Since Barhaven was the terminus there was no hurry about getting out. He sat, well back in the carriage and watched the passengers go past. He saw the thickset man, the red rose flamboyant in his buttonhole, and he smiled sourly. He wondered just how the old bastard had managed to get on to the train unnoticed. He must have been tailing him, and must have nipped in at the very last moment, when the train was actually moving, at the moment he had turned round to go into the carriage. Smart work. And typical of him to stand by and not interfere too soon. He wondered how much he *had* seen and heard.

When the last of the crowd had gone Sturrock left the carriage and sauntered towards the exit. The ticket collector had disappeared. Sturrock returned his unclipped ticket to his pocket. No sense in wasting it.

The square outside the station was sleeping in the late afternoon sun. On her pedestal, Queen Victoria stared disagreeably out to sea. Sturrock walked slowly along the pavement. He was looking for a blue suit and a red rose.

He completed his tour of the square, coming back to the place he had started from. A lone taxi was waiting on the rank. Sturrock said, "You know a place called Caesar's Camp?"

"Up on the downs. About a mile. You want to go there?"

"That's where I want to go."

The taxi man hesitated. It was impossible to be a taxi-driver, even in a quiet place like Barhaven, without acquiring an instinct for judging people by appearance, and he said, "I can't get the car right up there. You'll have to walk the last bit."

"It won't kill me."

"What about getting back?"

"You wait and take me back."

Still the driver hesitated. Then he said, "It'll be a pound. The round trip."

"Fine," said Sturrock. "Fine." He opened the door, and jumped in. The car drove off.

From a vantage point in a near-by cafe the man with the red rose watched it go. He was quite happy. He had the number of the taxi. It shouldn't be difficult to find out where Sturrock had gone to. He was pleased with his observations so far. They had little connection with the job that had brought him to Barhaven, but they were interesting.

He finished his tea slowly, paid his bill, and walked out into the town, carrying his small overnight bag. He had already booked a room in the Eversley, a quiet hotel which stood back from the front.

"It's up that lane. Gate at the top," said the taxi-driver. "And I can't hang about all day."

Sturrock said, "I'll be about a quarter-of-an-hour."

"If you're much more," said the driver, "I'm going back to Barhaven."

"You could do that," said Sturrock, "but since I haven't paid you anything yet, it wouldn't be very sensible."

He turned and strode off up the lane. The taxi-driver watched him go. The more he saw of his passenger, the less he liked him.

Sturrock found six of the Sunshine Boys drinking tea out of tin mugs. Dennis saw him first, and said, "It looks like ol' Sturrock. I wonder what *he's* doing out here. Hullo, Cherokee. How's tricks?"

"Where's Eric?"

139

"He's down in the town," said Dennis. "He's got some pad down there. We haven't seen a lot of him the last two days."

Sturrock sat down on an upturned beer crate and lit a cigarette.

"I've got a job for you," he said.

"What's in it?"

"What's usually in jobs. Money. But I've got to see Eric. Where do I find him? And what's he up to?"

Dennis showed his sharp, tobacco-stained teeth in a grin. "He's got a friend."

"That so," said Sturrock. "Well one of you can come back with me and show me where to find him. If this job is going to be done, we've got to get it lined up tonight."

The boys considered the matter. It was clear that they knew Sturrock, and were used to taking orders from him. In the end Dennis said, "O.K., Trev can go back with you. He knows where Eric is."

When they got back to the station Sturrock got out, opened his wallet, and held out a ten shilling note.

The driver stared at him.

"I said a quid."

"You said a quid," agreed Sturrock. He was balancing easily on the balls of his feet. "I been thinking about it. And I came to the conclusion ten bob was enough. Of course, if you don't want it—"

"Gimme that money," said the driver, grabbing. Sturrock swayed back, holding the note just out of the driver's reach.

"If you take this, it's all you get."

The driver swore.

Sturrock said, "Five seconds to make your mind up."

The driver said, "All right. Give it to me."

Sturrock flipped the note into the cab, and walked away with Trevor.

"Where we come from," he said, "he wouldn't have started unless I'd paid him first."

"There's a lot of soft touches down here," agreed Trevor.

Chapter Twenty-One

Anthony Discovers a Gimmick

When Anthony got back to his house he went upstairs to change. The blood had caked into a small, black patch on the front of his trouser leg. There were two livid bruises on his leg, each with a jagged cut in the centre. He cleaned the places carefully with disinfectant, and put a square of plaster over each. Then he put on an old pair of flannel trousers and went down to tea.

The real trouble was, there was no one to talk to about it. He saw himself going to the police.

"I wish to report that I was attacked by a man in the train this afternoon."

"Yes, sir. What did he do?"

"He kicked me."

"Why did he do that, sir? Was he trying to rob you?"

"No. He didn't try to rob me."

"Did he make any suggestion to you?"

"He suggested I took a fortnight's holiday."

"I see, sir. And why didn't you report it at once?"

"Because I was afraid."

That was it. Whichever way round you went, whatever side roads you took, that was the spot you came back to in the end. He had been afraid.

It wasn't so much the pain. In a week he would have nothing to show but a couple of blue bruises, less than he might have got in a game of football. It was his manhood which had been threatened. He had been afraid.

Suddenly he found it impossible to sit still. The tea tasted bitter on his tongue. He pushed it aside, grabbed a walking stick of his father's from the stand in the hall, and went out.

He had a favourite walk, which took him through the back streets of Barhaven, across the by-pass, up a farm track, and straight up on to the downs. He connected it in his mind with James Sudderby, who had first taken him that way on birds-nesting expeditions.

He walked fast. By the time he reached the top he was out of breath, but happier. Looking down he could see a little cluster of tents on Caesar's Camp and the smoke of a camp-fire going straight up into the evening air. There was a group of boys clustered round the fire. They would be Sudderby's camping friends. He found himself envying them the carefree joys of youth and managed to laugh at himself. Twenty-three was a bit soon to start posing as an old man. He turned right and set off along the ridge-way path which ran along the top of the downs, and which would take him, eventually, on to Storm Head. From there it was a half-hour scramble down to Splash Point. When he finally reached the Country Club it was eight o'clock and the bar was nearly empty. The early evening crowd had gone home and the after-dinner bridge-and-snooker contingent had not yet arrived.

Anthony ordered himself a pint of shandy and was paying for it when he saw Ann coming in.

She hesitated, for a moment, in the doorway and he turned and waved to her.

She said, "This has always seemed to be a 'men only' sort of place. I was nervous about coming in. All I wanted was something cool and long, like lime-juice and soda."

"Are you on your own?"

"I was playing squash with Molly, but she had a date and had to get back."

"Well now *you've* got a date," said Anthony. "To have a drink with me. Did you say a lime-juice and soda?"

"I did," said Ann. "But I'm not at all sure that this is the best place to drink it, after all."

"Why not?"

"It gets full of old tabbies, of both sexes. Have you got a car?"

"I'm afraid not. I walked here—by rather a roundabout route."

"Well I have. And if you're firm on that offer of a drink, I know a nice little pub out on the Romney Road."

"Good idea," said Anthony. It was only when they were in the car that it occurred to him that it was all wrong. He ought to be taking her out. It ought to be him driving the car, and knowing the place to go to, and taking the initiative.

"I used to come here with daddy," said Ann. It was a tiny pub, just off the coast road, down a short lane.

"When you think of the millions of motorists," said Anthony, "who drive from Hastings to Folkestone on a hot summer day, with their tongues hanging out for a drink, and none of them guessing this place exists. Why don't they put up a sign-board at the end of the lane?"

"Because they don't want a million motorists, I expect," said Ann. She turned her little car competently into the yard behind the pub, said, "Hallo, Tina" to a small girl who was sitting on an overturned wheelbarrow picking her nose, and led the way into the public bar.

Anthony said, "Are you dead set on that lime-juice. It doesn't look to me like the sort of place for drinking lime-juice."

"I'll drink beer," said Ann, "if I can have half-pints when you have pints. I've learned to like it – though why should you have to *learn* to like a drink, for God's sake?"

The place filled up gradually. It was mostly men, and a lot of them seemed to know Ann, but to be chary of saying anything to her when they spotted Anthony. A game of darts dispelled this constraint. First Anthony partnered Ann, against two young men called Ron and Ken, and lost. Then they split up, and Ron and Ann beat Anthony and Ken. Then a very old man appeared, partnered by the landlord, and beat everyone very easily. After each of these games Anthony bought beer for everyone, and at one period in the evening they ate a lot of bread and cheese with green tomatoes.

It seemed far too soon when the landlord said, "Time gentlemen, please. Drink up please. Act of Parliament"; and in no time at all they were in the car, and driving out of the warmth and friendship, into the cold world.

At the top of the last rise before Splash Point, Anthony said, "Do you mind if we stop for a moment?"

Ann looked quickly at him. He could see her face dimly in the light from the dashboard. She said, "All right", and swung the car into one of the little lay-bys provided by the Council for sightseers. By day it was usually crowded with cars. At that moment, it was empty.

He had no idea what to do next, but a sound instinct told him that it would be fatal to speak. As Ann switched off the engine and pulled on the brake he put his arm firmly round her shoulders, and pulled her towards him.

The steering-wheel got badly in the way. Ann said, quite calmly, "Hold it whilst I get out from under this damned wheel. There's more room in the back seat."

A few minutes later, she said, "You'd find it much easier if you took your glasses off," and some time after that, "It's nicer if you open your mouth."

Chapter Twenty-Two

Anthony is Frustrated

When Anthony arrived at the office next morning Ann was slitting his letters open. She gave him a cool, amused look as he came in. It was a look which said "Business only" in black type. She said, "Ambrose has already been on the telephone twice."

"What does he want?"

"He wants to see you. I told him you couldn't possibly manage it. I don't think that'll hold him though. And you've got Colonel Barrow at ten-thirty."

"I'll have to look up that drainage point before he gets here. Ask Bowler to borrow Lumley for me. Mr. Pincott's got a set in his room. And if Ambrose really is going to descend on us, we'd better have a copy of today's *Gazette,* too."

"I tried to get one on the way here, but the two paper shops in our road were sold out."

"That big newsagent in Victoria Avenue is bound to have one."

Anthony glanced through the post. There was a lot to do, but none of it was particularly urgent. He put a call through to the Town Hall and asked to speak to James Sudderby. After the usual frustrating delays he learned that the Town Clerk was not in his office; and that nobody quite knew where he was; but *if* the matter was urgent, he could be asked to ring back. Anthony said that the matter was extremely urgent and left his number, but without much hope.

Ann reappeared. "It's an extraordinary thing," she said, "but Pollocks haven't got a copy either."

"I refuse to believe that the *Gazette* could be sold out at ten o'clock on the morning of publication."

"I tried two other newsagents on the Parade. No dice."

Anthony looked at his watch.

"If I'm going to work out an answer for Colonel Barrow before he gets here, it's obvious I shan't have time to do any letters. Why don't you nip up to the station? They're bound to have a copy. Get two whilst you're at it."

Ann departed and Anthony settled down to study the stout red volumes of Lumley's Public Health Acts (12th Edition). By the time Colonel Barrow arrived he was ready for him.

"It's a swindle," he said, "but a legal swindle, if you follow me. All the proper steps have been taken. But there was no real reason to take them—except to get at you."

"Explain, please."

"When a local authority constructs a sewer, you, as a resident, have a right to connect to it. But it's only a right. It's not an obligation. That's perfectly clear from Section 39 of the Public Health Act 1936."

"Then why is the Borough Council telling me I've got to hitch up to their wretched sewer? I've told them repeatedly that I don't want to have anything to do with it."

"Because they didn't proceed under the Public Health Act at all. That piece of road running along the boundary of your playing-field isn't a 'highway maintainable at the public expense', so they were able to invoke a section of the Private Street Works Act, 1892. Under this section any work they carry out in the street is chargeable to the frontagers. Which means you – all along one side – and that row of terrace houses on the other. You pay half, they pay half."

"Why do you call it a swindle?"

"Because they could have put in exactly the same sewer under the Public Health Acts, and if they had chosen to do so, you *wouldn't* have had to join up to it if you didn't want to, and you wouldn't have had to pay any part of the cost."

"I see," said Colonel Barrow. "Then there's no way out of it, and I've got to pay."

"There's no way out of it as it stands at the moment. But if the Council could be persuaded to 'adopt' Castle Road – which, in my view, they ought to have done years ago, anyway – they couldn't rely on the Private Street Works Act, and they'd have to pay for the sewer themselves."

"Not much chance of that."

"Not with the present lot," agreed Anthony, "but you're going to get a chance to change them next week. Which Ward are you in?"

"Ward?" said Colonel Barrow. "I don't follow you."

"Voting Ward."

"Oh that. I believe I got a paper about it." He searched in his briefcase, and produced a crumpled blue paper. "Would this be it?"

"Marine East," said Anthony. "That's right."

"This says, 'Vote for Jack Crawford, your Independent Candidate'."

"That's just what you *mustn't* do. Vote for Arthur Ambrose. He's the Progressive Candidate. *He's* very keen on the Council adopting more roadway. He told me so."

Colonel Barrow jotted down "Ambrose" in his diary. "You really think it's important," he said. "I've never bothered to vote at one of these things before."

"It's vital," said Anthony. "Tell any of your staff who are on the voters' list to do the same. *And* the parents of all the day boys."

"I'll do it," said Colonel Barrow. "And what's more, I'll let some of the older boys act as canvassers. We're supposed to teach them Civics. I should think canvassing for a Borough Council election would be Civics, wouldn't you?"

"No doubt about it," said Anthony.

He was in the middle of a second attempt to contact James Sudderby when Ann came back. She had a paper in her hand.

"Have a look at this."

"What is it?"

"It's your client, Christopher Sellinge's election manifesto, and if I'm any judge of British character, it puts paid to his chances of re-election."

Anthony read the pamphlet through once, and then again with growing horror. In tones of hectoring arrogance it ordered – there was no attempt at persuasion – it ordered the voters of Marine Ward West to cast their votes for Sellinge *"if they know on which side their bread is buttered"*. This incredible expression was actually used. It went on to say that if Barhaven would elect a Council with a Progressive majority, the present development schemes would be switched from the eastern to the western end of the town ("in which I have a personal interest"), and concluded by pointing out that although such a change of plan would cost money, and might lead to a considerable increase in local rates, ultimately it would produce a brighter and better Barhaven.

"He must have gone mad," said Anthony. "There's no other explanation. How did you get hold of this?"

"They were distributed from door to door last night."

Anthony gave up the Town Hall, who were still, apparently, looking for their Town Clerk and dialled Sellinge's office. His secretary said that he had just gone out. Anthony left a message that he was to be rung, and had started to dictate the first of his morning's letters when Bowler announced the arrival of Mr. Ambrose.

"Tell him I'm engaged."

"He said, if you were engaged, he'd wait."

"Tell him I'll be engaged all morning."

"He's in a terrible state."

"Oh dear," said Anthony. "All right. But when he's been here for ten minutes I want you to come in and say 'Major Ponsonby has arrived'."

"I'll try," said Ann. "I'm not a very good liar."

Anthony could hear Ambrose declaiming as he came down the passage. The words "scandal", "corruption" and "freedom of the press" floated ahead of him, like flags in a following breeze.

"What's happened now?" said Anthony. "Do sit down."

"Were you able to get a copy of the *Gazette* this morning?"

Anthony stared at him. "As a matter of fact, no."

"Nor was anyone else in Barhaven – unless they had it on order. And even some of them didn't get it."

"What on earth—"

"A gang of boys went round every newsagent's shop in town, as soon as it opened, and bought up every single copy."

Anthony restrained an idiotic inclination to laugh, and said, "How many copies did they get?"

"Between seven and eight thousand. The whole thing was very carefully organised. They had an old car and a trailer. They went from shop to shop, bought the whole stock, dumped it in the trailer, and carted it off."

"Someone spent some money on that little lark," said Anthony. He was making a quick calculation. "You sell at threepence. If they got eight thousand, that cost them a hundred pounds."

"It cost them more than that," said Ambrose. "In most cases they simply waylaid the boy who was going out with his papers for delivery and paid him a fiver for the lot."

"It sounds like a pretty skilful bit of sabotage," said Anthony, "but surely your next move is perfectly simple. You reprint another ten thousand. Once this story gets round, they should go like hot cakes."

"That was the first thing I thought of, naturally," said Ambrose, impatiently. "But I'm afraid I can't do it. I'm out of paper."

"Out of paper?"

"There's been some hitch at the mills. I can't understand it. I'm going over to see them today. Normally they're quite happy to let me have a month's supply on credit. We always pay them at the end of the month, when the distributors pay us. It's the normal arrangement. Now, quite suddenly, we've been told the system's changed. It's cash on delivery."

"And you haven't got the cash?"

"The bank will let us have it, but it's going to take a day or two to fix."

"Curious," said Anthony, "that it should have happened just at this particular moment. Who are your suppliers?"

Ambrose gave him the name, and Anthony jotted it down.

"I should get moving fast on this," he said. "You want next Friday's issue to come out, don't you? That's the polling-day issue. When they hear what happened this morning, I should think your readers will be waiting for it with their tongues hanging out. You'll never write a more influential editorial in your whole life. Do you realise that?"

"By God, you're right," said Ambrose, his eyes shining. "The *Barhaven Gazette* cannot be gagged."

"I'll see if I can check up on your suppliers. If someone has been getting at them, it may call for drastic action—"

Ann opened the door at this moment, but instead of announcing Colonel Ponsonby she said, "It's Mr. Sellinge – in a hurry," and stepped aside to prevent herself being knocked down by the infuriated estate agent.

He had a crumpled paper in his hand.

"Have you seen this?"

"If it's your election manifesto, yes. I read it just now."

"*My* election manifesto," said Sellinge, his voice rising to an alarming pitch. "I never saw the bloody thing before in my life."

"You didn't write it."

"Do you think I'd write a lot of—a load of—"

"I think you'd better go," said Anthony to Ann. "I have a feeling that Mr. Sellinge wants to express himself more freely. Take Mr. Ambrose with you. I'll ring you up later if I have any news for you, Arthur. Now—what's all this about?"

Sellinge took a deep breath, and said "Some — has — well gone beyond the — limit."

"Then I gather you weren't responsible for this curious effusion."

"You gather — well right."

"All right," said Anthony. "You've made your point." He was re-examining the manifesto. He turned it over and looked at the back.

"Whoever produced this has let themselves in for a stiff fine. It's against the law to publish a document without publishing the name of the printer."

"They've let themselves in for a stiff backside if I get hold of them."

"Who distributed these?"

"A lot of boys, so I'm told."

"I imagine it was the same lot who bought up all the available copies of Ambrose's paper this morning."

He told Sellinge about that.

"In that case, I know who they are," said Sellinge. "They're a crowd who are living in old army tents up at Caesar's Camp."

"We'll get the police to move them on before they get up to any more mischief. Meanwhile, you'd better get busy. When's your real manifesto coming out?"

"On Monday."

"Who are doing it?"

"The Barhaven Press. They've set up the type, but I don't think it's printed yet. I've got a proof here."

Anthony said, "If people simply get another, different manifesto on Monday, they won't know what to make of it. What you'll have to do is to get the printers to add a paragraph – in black type – at the end here. Let me see—"

He picked up a pencil and a sheet of paper. "'Stop Press. You may have had, delivered by hand, last Thursday, a pamphlet purporting to set out my views. This was a vicious forgery and a criminal contravention of the Municipal Elections Act' (I think we can safely say that). 'You will know what to think of a party which descends'—"

"Sinks," said Sellinge. "Sinks."

"Yes, that's better – 'a party which sinks to practices of this sort.'"

"You don't think that's libellous."

"It's impossible to libel a political party."

"All right," said Sellinge. "I'll get that set up."

As soon as he had gone Anthony telephoned Dudley Powell.

"How are things going in the sleepy township of Barhaven?"

"Warming up," said Anthony. "Do you think you can find something out for me? You remember you looked up the file on Carlmont Properties. And found out the other companies which the two nominee directors were interested in?"

"I do. I've got a list of them here somewhere."

"Would it be possible to find out if any of them had any connection with the East Kent Paper Mills?"

"Easily. We act for the Ballard Group – they're about the biggest people in the paper business. They'll know who owns what bits of it. What's it all about?"

"The East Kent Paper Mills are holding up supplies to the local paper here –the *Barhaven Gazette*. It looks as though they've been got at. If the Ballard Group would like a new customer, now's the golden moment. The *Gazette* isn't enormous – about twenty thousand copies a week – but they must be worth having."

"I'll get on to it right away," said Powell.

After that, Anthony rang up James Sudderby's house. He heard the telephone trilling at the other end. It went on for some time, then, just as Anthony was about to ring off, there was a click. Somebody had taken the receiver off its hook.

Anthony sat listening. No one spoke. After a minute there was a further click as the receiver was replaced, and there was the burring sound of line disengaged.

He said to Ann, "I'm going out."

"If anyone wants you, where are you?"

"Ungetatable," said Anthony.

Inspector Knox was a big, slow-speaking Sussex man. Anthony knew him slightly having cross-examined him in a running down case and got the worst of the exchanges.

"I must have a word with your boss," said Anthony.

"The Inspector's very busy at the moment."

"I'm busy too," said Anthony. "So the sooner we get this over the better for both of us."

Inspector Knox looked at him, a glint of amusement in his eyes.

"Well," he said. "We won't quarrel about it." He rolled off and Anthony sat for five minutes studying a poster illustrating the feeding and mating habits of the Potato Worm. It was very quiet in the charge room. Behind the desk Station Sergeant Porter was filling in a form in long-hand, using a pen with a squeaky nib. A bluebottle buzzed against the dusty windowpane.

Inspector Knox came clumping down the stairs. He said, "You can go up, but if you'll take a word of advice, I should keep it short. And keep to the point. The Inspector's got a lot on his mind this morning."

Anthony nearly said, "So have I", but realised that Knox was trying to be friendly and kept his mouth shut.

Ashford was behind his desk, his bulk filling the chair and overflowing from it. There was a pile of dockets on the desk and the telephone, which he had evidently just finished using, was perched on top of the pile. He jerked his thumb towards a chair. "What's up now?"

"I wanted to find out what the police were planning to do about the gang of London boys who are hanging round up at Caesar's Camp."

"We've had no complaints about them."

"Then you're getting one right now," said Anthony and told him about the events of the night before and that morning.

"You're sure it was these boys."

"They were recognised. And more than one person took the number of the car they were using. I've got it here. If that is the car up at the camp site – Charlie Andrews says they've got an old car there – then I should think that's good enough, isn't it?"

"Good enough for *what*, Mr. Brydon?"

"To get them run out of town."

"I can't run anyone out of town. You're a lawyer. You know that. I can arrest them, if they do anything to justify it. And I can charge them – if there's anything to charge them with. Otherwise they've as much right to be in Barhaven as you or me."

"And you don't call interfering with the process of a municipal election illegal."

"It's certainly illegal. Is that what they've been doing?"

"Is it—?"

"According to what you've told me, they bought a lot of copies of the *Gazette*. That's not a crime, that I know of. And they acted as distributors of a pamphlet which you say is forged. You may be right.

153

It's not proved. But even if you are right, the person to be charged would be the forger, not the boys he'd paid a few shillings to distribute it for him."

"So you won't do anything about it."

"I don't see that there's anything I can do."

"In that case," said Anthony, "I won't waste any more of your valuable time. The only person who can help me is the Chief Constable. I'll have a word with him."

"You could try that," agreed Ashford. "If that's all—I've got a lot to do."

When Anthony had left Ashford made no immediate move. He sat, quite still, in his chair, but there was nothing peaceful or reassuring about his immobility. It was the immobility of a pile of uranium.

He put out a big hand, lifted the receiver and asked for a number.

The woman who answered the telephone said, "I'm sorry, Inspector. Colonel Davy can't speak to you at the moment. He's got someone with him. I'll get him to ring you back as soon as he's free."

Ashford replaced the receiver. The look which Anthony had noticed on a previous occasion was back in his eyes. The present had ceased to exist. He was looking at something which stood at a great distance from him, either in time or in space.

Chapter Twenty-Three

The Chief Constable Postpones his Luncheon

Colonel "Peter" Davy, late of the Royal Engineers and now in his last year of office as Chief Constable of Barhaven, was painting a picture. He was standing in the box-room on the north side of his house, which he had converted into a studio. He was savouring the smell of oil-paint and turpentine, the snowy white canvas on its stretcher, awaiting the assault of his inventive brush, the pleasant disorder of the atelier.

It was the last hour of the morning, the moment when official matters had been disposed of and only a pink gin stood between him and lunch; the moment when inspiration visited him most liberally.

He was visualising the Mojave desert. He had never been in Arizona but he had seen coloured picture postcards of it; huge buttes, tawny yellow with purple shadows; cacti—

Downstairs a bell rang. Colonel Davy smiled. His wife could be counted on to keep callers at bay. He unscrewed a tube of chrome yellow, and squeezed a fat dollop on to the palette. Then he paused. Incredibly, footsteps were coming up the stairs. His wife appeared.

"I know you don't like being interrupted," she said—

"Who is it?"

"If he hadn't been so insistent."

"My dear," said the Colonel, with ferocious good-humour, "all you had to do was to say that I was out. He could hardly have knocked you down, and made his way up here over your prostrate body."

When he talked like this Mrs. Davy knew that her husband was really angry. She said, "Oh, he isn't that sort of person at all." Indeed, she was wondering exactly what it was about the caller which had made her brave her husband's wrath. "He gave me his card."

Colonel Davy looked at the pasteboard for a long moment. Then he said, "I'll come down. Put him in the dining-room."

The caller rose politely from his chair on the Colonel's entry.

"Detective Chief Superintendent Brennan," he said formally, "from Central."

"So I saw from your card," said Colonel Davy. "Sit down, please. What can I do for you?"

"The best thing, I think," said Brennan, "would be for you to read this. It's a summary of a much longer report."

The Colonel grunted, took out his reading glasses, and sat down in the chair with his back to the light. As he read the three sheets of paper his face set in a frown of formidable displeasure. Superintendent Brennan did not, apparently, notice it. He was admiring the reproduction of Murillo's "Beggarboys" on the wall above the sideboard.

"Where did this come from?"

"Various sources," said Brennan. "But chiefly from the editor of your local paper. A Mr. Arthur Ambrose."

"The crackpot."

"I'm interested to hear you say that," said Brennan. "You think he's an unreliable witness."

An instinct of caution, bred of long dealing with officials, checked the Colonel's automatic answer. He said, "I didn't say he was an unreliable witness. But he's a man who likes to stir up trouble. Before we go any further, Superintendent, perhaps you'd tell me exactly what you're doing down here. How do you come into this?"

"I'm here to ask for your co-operation, sir, in investigating these charges against Inspector Ashford, and, to a lesser extent, against two of his Sergeants."

"And if I tell you that, in my view, Ashford is the best policeman I've ever had working under me, with a first-class record of crime prevention and detection, and that I wouldn't investigate Crippen or Jack the Ripper on the say-so of a sensation-mongering journalist like Ambrose—well?"

"I'm sorry, sir. But even if you told me that, I should still be bound to carry out an investigation. It would be a great deal more unpleasant, and a great deal more difficult. But it would have to be done."

"Barhaven is a Borough. It controls its own force. And I happen to be in charge of it."

"I quite agree," said Brennan. "You are entitled to refuse the investigation. Before you do so, you might like to see this letter."

The Colonel slit open the envelope and read the letter on the buff writing paper. It had been signed by the Home Secretary personally and its contents seemed to cause the Colonel no pleasure.

"It's blackmail," he said.

Brennan said, with sudden sympathy, "Look here, sir. If you wouldn't think it impertinent of me—but I've been concerned in this sort of thing before. If we do it together, we can get through it quickly and quietly. Last time it only took three days from the time I arrived to the time I made my report. Which, incidentally, exonerated the officer concerned. I've nothing against Ashford. I don't even know him. If this is a trumped-up case, we'll soon find out."

"Well—" said Colonel Davy. He was being offered a chance to climb down easily, and he knew it. "There's something in what you say. The only thing is – damn it – this couldn't have come at a more awkward moment."

"Why is that, sir?"

"It's the Borough Council elections, next Friday. Two of the Watch Committee are fighting for their seats. They're going to have quite a fight, too, I believe."

"Yes," said Brennan. "We shall have to work through the Watch Committee. Who are they?"

"Chap called Southern is committee Chairman – he's Vice-Chairman of the Council, and next in line for Mayor. Quite a useful man. His number two's Jack Crawford. He's—well—he's not everybody's cup of tea. Let's leave it at that. Those two really run it.

The other two are General Crispen. He's very old, and he doesn't turn up much. And a tiresome old tabby called Miss Planche. Oh, and the Lady Mayoress is a member too, ex officio."

"I see," said Brennan. As he did. He saw a Chief Constable close to retirement, who must have been one of the last of the ex-Service appointments, before the policy was changed in 1948, and senior policemen began to be promoted to their own top jobs. He saw, behind him, a weak Watch Committee, a Council hamstrung by elections; a lot of local pride; and the strongest possible argument for amalgamation of this anomalous little private army into the county police force.

He said, "If we go about this the right way, I don't see that we need stir up a lot of local interest. Not at once, anyway. I'll need a quiet room, preferably not too near the police station, where I can talk to these witnesses, and take their statements. And I'm afraid you'll have to take Ashford off duty for the time being. Could he be given some leave?"

"He came back from leave a month ago."

"Sick leave?"

"Yes. We could do that."

"Who's second-in-command at the moment?"

"That'd be Inspector Knox."

"There've been no allegations against him. Is he a good man?"

"A bit slow. But quite solid."

"I've a feeling you're going to need someone fairly solid in the next few days. I travelled down in the train yesterday with a man called Sturrock. His nickname is 'Cherokee'. He's got a face like a Red Indian. And the habits of one, too."

"What's his line?"

"He's a professional trouble-shooter. Or trouble-maker. He'll throw oil on to the water, or petrol into the fire – all you've got to do is pay him the right money. I got the impression he'd been roughing up the other man in the carriage—but he didn't complain, so I didn't do anything."

"Couldn't we get rid of him?"

"There's no charge on his sheet that I know of. And if you did get rid of him, presumably you'd still have his friends to deal with. They're a rough crowd, from the Camberwell area. I'd say the better plan would be to leave Sturrock alone until you can see what he's up to."

"All right," said the Colonel. Now that some sort of action was imminent, he seemed to have recovered his spirits. He went to the door and shouted for his wife. She came out of the kitchen, looking worried.

"Inspector Ashford's been on the telephone to you, twice," she said. "And there's a man in the front drawing-room who insisted on seeing you. He's been kicking his heels there for the last half-hour. He's a solicitor, called Brydon."

"If Mr. Brydon insists on kicking his heels in my front room," said the Colonel, genially, "who am I to stand in his way? Let him kick. I shall go out by the back door. And if Ashford rings again you can tell him that I'm on my way round to see him—now."

"What about lunch?"

"There are moments when even lunch has to wait."

Mrs. Davy looked surprised, as well she might. The Colonel had not gone without an adequate luncheon, at the proper hour, since the last day of the retreat to Dunkirk.

Chapter Twenty-Four

Anthony Pays a Late Call

Anthony kicked his heels for two hours. He studied a series of Colonel Davy's early, and less successful water- colours, and a remarkable collection of sporting trophies which started with crossed silver spears on a mahogany shield (Champion Pig-Umballa, 1922) and ended with the previous season's mixed four-ball at the Splash Point Golf Club.

Towards four o'clock, conscious that he had missed his lunch and would shortly be missing his tea as well, he raised the siege. Mrs. Davy let him out with her kindest smile. She would *certainly* inform her husband of his visit, and she had *no* doubt that her husband would telephone him as soon as he returned. Anthony accepted defeat with a good grace, had something to eat at one of the cafés in Grand Avenue, and got back to the office just before five, to find Ann waiting for him with a pile of letters and a worried face.

"Wherever have you been?"

"I've been starved into submission," said Anthony, and told her what had happened.

"I thought the opposition had kidnapped you. I was just thinking of ringing up the police."

"You wouldn't have got much change out of them," said Anthony. He spotted a fresh entry in his diary. "I don't remember this one. When did we fix it?"

"It's Mr. Southern. He rang up after lunch. Something about a company matter—"

"Oh Lord, yes," said Anthony. He had done nothing about Southern's company scheme.

"I tried to put him off. I said I didn't know when you'd be back. He said, the later the better as far as he was concerned, so we made it half-past five."

"I'd better start reading the papers, then. Damn."

This was the telephone. It was Ambrose, incoherent with gratitude.

"That was a *very* good turn your London colleague did me," he said. "There's been some *exceedingly* dirty work going on about our paper supplies, no doubt about it. When we offered them payment for last week's – the bank were prepared to back us – they started making fresh difficulties. So I got *straight* on to your Ballard people – gave them the name of the director your friend knew – and arranged for *all* our future supplies to come from them. At slightly better terms than our existing ones with the East Kent Mills, too!"

"Will you be able to reprint this week's issue?"

"Not in time for that, alas. But next week's issue is *guaranteed*. I'm starting on the editorial now. It's going to be a killer, I can tell you."

"Splendid," said Anthony. "Splendid." He tried to sound enthusiastic, but it was an effort. He had been gripped by an unexpected feeling of frustration.

"Do you know, you actually gnashed your teeth then?" said Ann.

"If I did," said Anthony, "it expressed my feelings very accurately. Whenever I think I'm making progress, I butt into some invisible obstacle."

"Like a lobster in a lobster pot."

"I can think of more elegant similes, but that is roughly the position. There's no need for you to hang about. Southern will probably keep me talking for hours. I'll get Bowler to lock up when we go."

Ann was smiling to herself as she went downstairs. No talk now, she noticed, of giving up the fight. She was certain that something had happened to Anthony on his second visit to London. It had been at the back of his mind all the time that he had been out with her that evening. (Well, no. That wasn't strictly accurate. There had been a period at the end when his mind had been exclusively on other things.) But something had certainly been worrying him. He would tell her about it sooner or later.

It was nearly six o'clock when Raymond Southern arrived.

He said, "I'm glad you don't mind working late. I enjoy it. Now, what have you been able to find out for me?"

Conscious that the extent of his researches was a quick canter through the papers in the past forty-five minutes, Anthony embarked on his exposition. Fortunately the points which interested Southern most were tax points, and tax was one of Anthony's specialities.

Raymond Southern's views on tax were simple. Tax was tribute; it was Danegeld. You paid it under duress, and solely because the extractors had the power to extract it. It was no different, in kind, from the protection money which a club proprietor paid to an organised gang of bullies who had it in their power to make it hot for him if he didn't.

"We've got a new Inspector here," he said. "He's a nasty little crook, with a Hitler moustache and glasses. He had the nerve to put up for the Splash Point Club."

"I don't suppose he got in?"

"You're right, he didn't. When I'd finished canvassing, the ballot box was hardly big enough to hold the black balls. Now—let's have another look at that case you quoted. It looks as if they may have lowered their guard there a bit, doesn't it?"

"It's a loophole," said Anthony. "The trouble is that the next Finance Act will probably block it up and then you'll be worse off than before."

"Exactly. When they get beaten, they squeal to the umpire to alter the rules. I think we might give it a run, though—it's going to turn on some rather nice timing. Suppose we altered the company's accounting date—"

They discussed the timing, in detail, and Anthony discovered, when he next looked at his watch, that it was half-past eight. He suddenly realised that he was very hungry.

"Come and have a bite with me," said Southern. "I owe it to you for keeping you here so late. There's a little restaurant behind my office – it hasn't been open long enough to get spoilt – they grill quite a decent steak."

Over dinner Raymond Southern refused to talk business. He talked about cricket, chess, roses and, with the coffee, about local politics.

"I've thought a lot about resigning," he said. "I wouldn't have stood this time, if it hadn't looked like being a close fight with the Radicals. I couldn't back down and present them with a walk-over, although I believe Masters is quite a good chap as Reds go. I shan't stand again, though. Once we've got this development scheme through—of course, I forgot, you're on the other side, aren't you?"

"Well—"

"No need to be embarrassed about it. Someone's got to put both sides of every case. I'd sooner you were on the other side than some smart lawyer from London who didn't know any of the people concerned."

"Speaking as a lawyer," said Anthony, "it'd be a damn sight easier if one *didn't* know most of the people concerned."

"Something in that," agreed Southern and signalled for the wine waiter.

Over the brandy he reverted to local politics. "Your father would have made an excellent Town Clerk," he said. "He could have had the job, for the asking, in 1945—and again when Preston left in the late fifties, and Sudderby took it on.'

Anthony said, "He never told me that."

"I don't suppose he did," said Southern, with a grin. "Since you were the reason he turned it down."

"I was—"

"If he'd left the firm old mother Pincott wouldn't have been able to keep it going for three months. Incidentally, it looks as though another vacancy's coming up."

For a moment Anthony thought he was talking about the firm. Then he looked up sharply, "You mean Sudderby's retiring."

"He's retired."

"When?"

"Macintyre told me this afternoon."

"Why on earth did he do it? It isn't as if he was well off. He—" Anthony realised that he had been on the point of committing a breach of professional confidence, and bit the sentence off.

Southern was still smiling.

"If you were going to tell me," he said, "that James Sudderby was hard up for a bit of ready cash, I knew it. He borrowed £200 from me this afternoon."

"Did he say what he wanted it for?"

"He told me a long story. I won't bore you with it, because I didn't believe a word of it. James is a rotten liar. The truth is, he's got himself into some sort of tangle."

"Corporation funds?"

"Could be. I don't believe he's a crook, though. I think it's something quite silly. And I'm quite sure he'll pay me back. Otherwise I shouldn't have lent it to him. I'm a businessman, you know."

"Oh, quite," said Anthony.

When they parted Anthony set off on foot. The breeze, as it sometimes did, had turned at dusk, and brought in a drizzle of fine sea rain. It wouldn't last long. By midnight the sky would be clear again. Anthony turned up his coat collar and walked steadily. He was heading for Boscombe Avenue, where Sudderby's little bachelor house stood in its pocket-handkerchief of neat garden.

He was far from clear what he was going to say to the Town Clerk. Two thoughts were jostling in his mind. The first was the simple thought that Sudderby was in trouble, and that he might be able to help him. The second was more complicated. Sudderby, in the days before his town-clerk-ship, when he was in private practice with Mentmore, had helped to form the Carlmont Property Company. This didn't necessarily mean that he had any interest in it. Solicitors often formed companies for clients and handed them over lock stock and barrel once they had been formed.

But it did mean that Sudderby *must* know who was behind the company. And that knowledge had suddenly become very valuable.

At the corner of Boscombe Avenue he stopped to clean the misty rain off his glasses. Sudderby's house was the third one along and there was a street lamp in front of it. He was on the point of moving when he checked himself. Someone was coming down Sudderby's front path, and coming fast. The gate swung open and Anthony saw that it was a boy. He saw him quite clearly, under the light of the lamp. He had fair, crinkly hair, eyes with a slight upward slant to them which gave the face an oriental look, a short, almost snub nose and a wide mouth. Normally it would have been an attractive face, but at that moment it was distorted with an ugly look, half-panic and half-calculation.

The gate slammed, the boy turned on his heel and scudded away along the pavement. Anthony hesitated for a moment, then opened the gate, walked up the short path and pressed the bell-push.

The Westminster chimes died into thick silence.

He stepped back and looked up at the house. The ground floor was in darkness. Upstairs, it was not so easy to see. The windows had leaded panes and the curtains were drawn. He thought there was a glimmer of light from what he guessed would be the main bedroom.

The water was trickling from his hair down the back of his collar, and his glasses were getting misted up again.

He knew the lay-out. The flagged path led round to the kitchen door at the back. He followed it. The pantry window beside the back door was open, but was blocked with a sheet of thick gauze mesh. The kitchen window itself was shut. Anthony turned the handle of the back door and found that it was unlocked.

He went in, located the light switch, and clicked it on.

Someone had been eating a meal at the kitchen table and had abandoned it in a hurry. There was a thick slab of fried bread, on which the grease was whitening as it grew cold, an uneaten rasher of bacon, most of a fried egg and a cup half-full of coffee. None of this looked like Sudderby who was a good cook and a fastidious eater. This was a meal the boy had prepared for himself and had abandoned half-eaten.

Anthony opened the door and tip-toed out into the hall. The faint light from the fan over the hall door showed all the familiar objects. The pipe full of walking sticks and umbrellas, the hat-stand, the round glass of the barometer.

He said, his voice sounding curiously husky, "Mr. Sudderby. Is anyone home?" When he said it again, louder, he thought he heard a faint moan. He pressed down the switch, and the light jumped out. There was nothing to be seen. The noise had come from somewhere above him. He ran upstairs, tapped on the door of the room immediately ahead of him, heard another moan and went in.

The only light came from a red-shaded bedside lamp. James Sudderby was lying, fully-dressed on his bed. For a moment Anthony hardly recognised him. His face was paper-white, drained of all blood. There were livid patches under his eyes, his jaw had dropped open. There was spittle on his beard and he was breathing in heavy, laboured gasps.

An empty bottle stood on the table beside a nearly empty glass. There was a thick white sediment at the bottom of the glass.

Anthony ran out of the room, and down the stairs. The telephone was in the hall.

He found Dr. Rogers in.

"I'll be there as quick as I can," he said.

"Anything I ought to do?"

"Yes—ring this number and get hold of an ambulance."

Anthony did so. The name of Dr. Rogers seemed enough for the dispatcher, who said the ambulance would be with him right away.

Anthony went back upstairs.

Sudderby was lying as he had left him, but there was a difference. His eyes, which had been shut, were now open. There seemed to be some message behind them.

Anthony leaned forward. It was difficult to say if it was speech or simply a change in the tortured breathing.

He thought he heard the word "paper". He could easily have imagined it.

He heard a car draw up and ran down to let in Dr. Rogers. The doctor switched on the overhead light, took one look at Sudderby, and said, "See if you can find me a basin. And two large towels." Whilst Anthony was looking for these the ambulance arrived. One man, who carried a black leather satchel, went upstairs. The driver stopped in the hall.

Anthony said, "I suppose I ought to have telephoned the police, too."

"Dispatcher will have done that," said the driver. "If this is going to take a bit of time, what do you say we make ourselves a pot of tea, eh?"

"The kitchen's back there," said Anthony. Then a thought struck him. "Only I don't think we ought to touch anything in it until the police get here."

A look of interest came into the driver's eyes. "One of those cases, is it? Well, here they are, anyway."

It was Inspector Knox. He said "Hullo" to Anthony, and went straight upstairs to have a word with the doctor. It was a quarter-of-an-hour before he came down again.

"How's it going?" said Anthony.

"They're doing what they can," said the Inspector. "I'd like to know just how you come into this. Suppose we go in here." He opened the door of the room which Sudderby called his den, followed Anthony in and shut the door, leaving the disappointed driver standing in the hall examining the barometer.

Anthony told the Inspector what he knew.

"This boy – where'd he come from?"

"From round the back of the house, almost certainly."

"Did you see him?"

"No, but the front door was shut, and if he'd come out that way I'd have heard him slam it. Besides, he'd been in the kitchen, eating a meal – one he'd cooked for himself, I'd judge. Come and have a look."

They walked along together.

"You don't think this was something Mr. Sudderby was cooking?"

"I'm quite sure it wasn't," said Anthony. "Sudderby wouldn't eat a hunk of fatty fried bread. This was a meal the boy was cooking for himself and he was disturbed in the middle of it."

"By what, would you suggest?"

"It's not difficult to guess. He heard some noise, went up, and saw—what I saw."

"And ran away? Without telling anyone? That wasn't very nice, was it?"

"He was in a blind panic—I say."

"Yes, Mr. Brydon."

"I wonder—you know those boys up at Caesar's Camp. They were protégés of Sudderby's. Do you think—he might have been one of them?"

"It's a possibility," said the Inspector. "It'll need checking."

"For God's sake," said Anthony. "It's not checking it needs. It needs a police car up there at once."

"What makes you think that?"

"You didn't see that boy's face. I did. As soon as he gets there, the whole lot'll up-stick as fast as they can."

The Inspector sat, swinging one leg over the other. At last he heaved himself to his feet with a sigh. "We'll take a chance on it," he said. He went out, and Anthony heard him telephoning and giving orders. When he had finished he didn't come back into the room, but Anthony heard his feet clumping upstairs and along the passage. There was a murmur of voices and a door shut.

Anthony sat on. There was a great load of weariness and reaction and sorrow on him, a weight which pressed on his shoulders and bowed his head.

Hours later, so it seemed, he woke with a start. People were coming downstairs, slowly. They were carrying something. The shuffling feet passed along the hallway, the front door opened, there was a pause and the ambulance started up. A single pair of footsteps returned and Dr. Rogers came into the kitchen.

Anthony said, "He's dead, isn't he?"

"Ten minutes ago," said Dr. Rogers. His voice was professionally unmoved. "There was very little chance of saving him. He'd taken about sixty aspirin tablets, I should say."

He took a quick look at Anthony, and added, "You did the best you could by calling us at once. Incidentally, you look as if you could do with a night's rest. I'll run you home."

"I'd rather walk," said Anthony.

When he got outside he found that he had been right about the weather. The wind had driven the last cloud away, and the sky was a black dome, freckled with a million stars.

Chapter Twenty-Five

The Sunshine Boys Depart

Anthony was in Dr. Rogers' surgery, and the doctor had strapped an instrument to his arm to test his blood pressure. The pain in his arm was excruciating. "It's the highest blood pressure this instrument has ever registered," said Dr. Rogers, his face grave. "Can you feel a throbbing in your head?" Anthony nodded weakly. He could feel a distinct throbbing in his head. It was the telephone on the table beside him. When he tried to reach for it he found that he had been lying with his right arm doubled under him and had lost all power in it. He fumbled for the receiver with his left hand and succeeded in knocking it off the hook. Whilst he was picking it up an impatient voice started addressing him.

"I'm sorry," he said. "I was asleep." "Sorry about that, sir," said Inspector Knox, with the total lack of sympathy of a man who has himself been up all night. "How quickly do you think you could get round here?"

"I'd like to shave, and have some breakfast—unless it's too urgent for that."

"It's nine o'clock now. Could you be here by ten?"

"I could try," said Anthony. "What's up?"

"Identification parade. And we've got a lot of people waiting."

"Oh, all right," said Anthony. "I'll skip my breakfast, but I insist on shaving."

At the police station he was conducted into a waiting-room by Sergeant Appleby, a rosy-cheeked little man with twinkling blue eyes.

"We've got 'em lined up in the canteen," he said. "Inspector's with them. You know the drill, I expect."

"I'm afraid not."

"You go right down the line, and take a careful look at 'em all, without saying anything. Then, supposing you've spotted anyone you recognise, you come back, and point him out, and say, 'That's the one.' Only look at 'em *all* first. If you don't, the lawyer who's defending usually makes something out of it. Ready?"

They marched in. There were a dozen boys lined up against the wall, some of them had clearly been roped in from the streets and were enjoying it. Some of them looked serious, and Anthony guessed that they were the Sunshine Boys. He recognised his boy as soon as he came into the room, but dutifully paraded down the whole line before coming back and pointing.

"You're sure this is the one you saw coming out of Mr. Sudderby's house?"

"Quite sure. He was directly under the street lamp."

"Right," said Knox. "You lot can go, and thank you very much. You six, I'll want your names and addresses, and someone to identify you, then you can go home, but you're to stay home when you get there. You may be wanted as witnesses, or there may be other charges. Do you understand that?"

The six signified with a murmur that they understood, and Sergeant Appleby herded them away. They seemed subdued.

"What are you going to do with me?" said the fair-haired boy.

"You'll be charged, and brought up in front of the Magistrate this morning."

"What's the charge?"

"Larceny from a dwelling-house."

The boy thought it out.

"You mean you think I stole that money."

"That's the idea."

"I suppose it's no use telling you it was given to me."

171

"You can tell the court that. If they believe you, that'll be all right, won't it?"

"It happens to be true."

"What would Mr. Sudderby give you two hundred pounds for?"

The boy said, with a perfectly straight face, "He was fond of me."

"It's as crazy a case as I've ever come across," said Inspector Knox to Anthony, when the boy had been taken off. "We went straight up, and found the whole gang of them, packing up to go. Ten minutes later, and they'd have gone. And once they'd gone, I don't believe we'd have seen hide or hair of them again."

"The police in London would have been able to trace them, surely."

"The others, perhaps. I'm not so sure about that boy. He's a card, is Eric."

"Eric?"

"That's the only name we know. The other boys don't know any more about him than we do. He's the boss. He organises the outings. When the outing's over, they don't see him again, till next time."

"If he organises things," said Anthony, slowly, "he must do it *from* somewhere. He must write letters. In fact, I seem to remember Mr. Sudderby told me he'd had quite a correspondence with him."

"So he did," said the Inspector. "We found some of the letters when we were looking over the house last night. They were all written from the rectory at St. John's Church, Southwark. I had a word with the rector on the telephone this morning. He knows almost as little about Eric as we do.

"He used to let him use the church room to organise his Sunshine Boys, and the rectory as an accommodation address."

"Then all you know about him is his Christian name?"

"I don't know even how old he is."

"If he's under age, surely it's for him to object," said Anthony. "If you give it a bit of a splash in the papers, his parents will come forward quick enough."

"I expect they will," said the Inspector. "But it's not the way we like doing things. Suppose his father turns out to be a Member of Parliament, or someone like that."

Anthony considered the matter. Eric had spoken in the curious, flat, classless accent which was the product of universal education and universal television. He might have come from any sort of home.

"Have you traced that £200 yet?"

"Not yet."

"Then I may be able to save you some trouble. Have a word with Councillor Southern. I think you'll find he lent £200 to Mr. Sudderby yesterday. Were they new notes?"

"Brand new, and in series."

"Then you shouldn't have much difficulty identifying them. Mr. Southern drew them from his own bank yesterday, and if they're a new issue, the bank should have a note of the numbers."

"It'll be nice to be able to check *something*," said Inspector Knox.

As Anthony was going, a thought struck him. "Where's Inspector Ashford?" he said.

"At home," said Knox. "A touch of gastric trouble. The court is sitting at eleven. A special session, just to deal with this case. You'll have to give evidence of identification, and I'll ask for eight days remand."

After the court proceedings Anthony went to his office, letting himself in with his own key. Since it was Saturday morning the whole building was quiet and empty. He got out the files of the planning appeal and settled down to do some work on them. The hearing was on top of them, and he was sadly behind in his preparations. Two of the witnesses were London experts, suggested by Powell. They had submitted preliminary proofs, but their evidence needed a lot of sifting out and co-ordinating. Really, he ought to see each of them separately, with Counsel, and run through what he was going to say. And the witnesses were in London, and he was in Barhaven. And they had precisely two clear days to do it in.

Anthony got out his diary and found Dudley Powell's home number.

A woman answered the telephone and said that Mr. Powell was out, but would be back for his lunch at any moment. Anthony guessed that this must be Mrs. Powell and introduced himself. Mrs. Powell said, "Oh, yes. I've heard about you. We really are keen on the idea of coming to Barhaven, you know. The boys haven't stopped talking about it since we told them. *Do* try to find us a house."

Anthony said he would do his best. He thought Mrs. Powell sounded rather nice.

Half an hour later Powell came through and Anthony explained the problem to him.

"Why don't you come up here on Monday morning," said Powell, "and stay the night with us? We could give the witnesses a preliminary canter on Monday and you could be back in your office by Tuesday lunch-time to settle up any last-minute paper work."

"Could you really put up with me?"

"I'm sure we could. Hold on a moment." Anthony heard him shouting at his wife. Then he came back, and said, "That's fixed. I expect you at the office about midday on Monday."

When Anthony put down the receiver he sat quite still for a few moments. He thought that it would be nice to have a partner who could do some of his thinking for him; and, even more, that it would be fun to have a wife you could shout at and who would arrange, at a moment's notice, for a stranger to stay the night.

He went back to his papers. The case had been a muddle before, but one or two pieces seemed to be falling into place at last.

As the shape of the coming battle looked clearer through the mist of depositions and plans and notes and letters the memory of James Sudderby's tormented face faded a little.

Chapter Twenty-Six

Anthony Shifts his Base

BOROUGH OF BARHAVEN-ON-SEA

"The Councillors representing the undermentioned Wards being due to retire by rotation, the vacancies so created will be filled, by ballot, on Friday next, July 29th. Nominations of candidates, qualified for election, and duly proposed and seconded, have been handed to the Deputy Returning Officer as follows:

WARD	CANDIDATES	
The Liberties	*William Law*	*Robert Stitchley*
Victoria Park	*Ralph Masters*	*Raymond Leofric Southern*
	Gerald Lincoln-Bright	*Harold Joseph Hopper*
Marine East	*John Evelyn Crawford*	*Arthur James Ambrose*
Marine West	*Leonard Ames Mossman*	*Christopher Sellinge*

Polling stations will be open from 6.30 a.m. until 8 p.m.

Anthony read this announcement on his way to the station on Monday morning. He stopped for a moment to study the Christian names. Who would have suspected Southern of being a Leofric? Or

Crawford of being an Evelyn? There was something else about the notice which interested him. It was only when the train was drawing into Victoria that he pinpointed it. It was the expression "Deputy Returning Officer".

The person who actually dealt with the nomination papers was, as he knew, little Mr. Pitt, at the Town Hall. So Mr. Pitt was probably the "Deputy Returning Officer" referred to. In that case, *who was the Returning Officer?* Anthony suspected that he knew the answer, and if he was right, it led to a further and even more perplexing question.

He got off his bus at the end of Chancery Lane and made for the Law Society's Hall. It took him a few minutes to locate the point he wanted. He looked up a couple of cases in the Law Reports, jotted down the citation references in his diary and went on his way.

Dudley Powell said, "You look uncommonly thoughtful this morning."

"I was thinking," said Anthony, "how very little law a solicitor in general practice actually knows. He does a bit of conveyancing and probate work, and dabbles in tax and estate duty problems. But think of all the stuff he probably never touches from the moment he takes his Final – Municipal Law – Ecclesiastical Law, Patent, Agency, Sale of Goods, Bills of Exchange—"

"What do you think Counsel are for?"

"Counsel are very useful if you know what the problem is. But supposing you don't even realise that there *is* a problem?"

Dudley inspected Anthony closely, and then said, "You look to me as if you need a good iron tonic."

"As a matter of fact, I have been having rather a time of it lately."

He told him about it as they walked towards the Temple. Powell listened in silence, and said at the end, "How perfectly bloody. I suppose your Town Clerk was homo, and the boy was blackmailing him."

"It looks like that. The funny thing is, that I've known him for years. I never had any idea."

"People never do. Here we are. We've got Breamore, the planning man, this morning, and Colonel Passmore, the drainage expert, is coming along this afternoon. You'll enjoy Passmore. What he doesn't know about sewage isn't knowledge."

Mr. Breamore was small and round, had plenty of auburn hair, worn rather long, and looked like a junior don. He arrived carrying a big, black cylinder of maps. These soon escaped, and, as the morning wore on, covered Mr. Hiscoe's tables, bookcases, chairs and, finally, whole areas of his carpet. Mr. Breamore bounced from map to map. As he went Sandling seemed to expand in front of Anthony's eyes into a Metropolis, larger than Blackpool, shinier than Brighton, noisier than Southend.

Mr. Hiscoe prodded, from time to time, with a question and finally dismissed him.

"A very sound man," he said, "but inclined to get carried away. We must hope he will stand up to cross-examination."

After lunch, with Colonel Passmore, a thin, bald man with a corvine face and an attractive, bass speaking voice, they plunged into another world, a private world of pumpage and pipage, with its junctions and termini and catchment areas; a world in which sewage ceased to be sewage and was transformed into effluent, a thing of strange beauty, with a subterranean life of its own.

It was four o'clock when they surfaced.

"I think we might have some tea now," said Powell.

"There's one question I'd like to find out the answer to, now I'm here—only I don't suppose it'll be possible to fix it in time."

"Name it," said Powell, "and I guarantee we'll find someone to answer it. In this square mile of London you can find an expert on any topic, from Welsh Church Law to Chinese divorce."

"This is Municipal Law."

"Money for jam."

He disappeared into a call-box and came out five minutes later.

"Miss Spurling, who has her Chambers at No. 15 King's Bench Walk, will be delighted to see us. She is in court at the moment, but her clerk says she will be free by five o'clock, so we've time for a cup of tea after all."

Miss Spurling wore rectangular spectacles and had thick black eyebrows which met over the bridge of her nose. She listened attentively to Anthony's exposition, studied the papers he had brought with him and consulted a volume from the bookshelf. Then she said, "It's a curious point. But I should say, quite definitely, that you were right. The position could be rectified, of course, if the Mayor resigned before the election."

"It would mean resigning the mayoralty."

"Certainly. The other office derives, ex officio, from the mayoralty."

"But it would put it right if the Mayor had resigned before polling day?"

"That was the point I was in some doubt about. But there's a case – it's on Parliamentary election law, but it seems to me quite valid in the context of Municipal Law. It is authority for the proposition that these honorary functions only hold good for the day of the election itself."

"I wonder," said Anthony, "if you could give me a short written opinion on that. It might be difficult, otherwise, for me—"

Miss Spurling smiled grimly and said, "I appreciate your position, Mr. Brydon. You shall have your written opinion. Who am I instructed by? Messrs. Moule Mainwaring, or yourselves?"

"You'd better send it to Moules. There's no great hurry about getting it, as long as I know that it's coming."

"Curious, don't you think," said Powell, as they walked away, "that anyone should actually be keen to jump into bed with that woman."

"Does someone?"

"Good heavens, yes. She's been living with — for years. We thought he might give her up when he was made a High Court Judge, but not a bit of it."

Anthony finished that evening playing four-pack racing demon with Powell and his two sons, losing tenpence in the process. He slept well and was back in his office by half-past two on the following afternoon. Ann said, "Mrs. Lord telephoned. Something about an appointment."

"That's right. I rang her up from Victoria."

"She's coming in at four o'clock."

"And how has Barhaven been behaving in my absence?"

"Barhaven's getting worked up," said Ann. "The Progressives had a meeting at the Drill Hall last night. And it ended in a free fight."

"Who fought who?"

"Some men from London. There were half-a-dozen of them – real East End tough boys. You know Walter – the man who takes visitors out lobster fishing—"

Anthony dimly remembered Walter, a huge man with a face the colour of a bar counter.

"One of the toughs butted him in the face, and Walter crowned him with a notice board."

"It sounds like a keen meeting," said Anthony. "What happened next?"

"The police turned up. They didn't arrest anyone, though."

"Didn't—or wouldn't?"

"Oh, I think they would have done, but the people who started the trouble had cleared off. The police scattered a few warnings round. I heard something else. Ashford's been rusticated."

"Inspector Knox said he had gastric trouble."

"That's only a cover story. He's sulking, like Achilles. In his bungalow out at Cliffside."

"How do you know?"

"One of Ambrose's reporters went out to see him. Ashford kicked him down the front steps and threw his camera into the sea."

"Start this story at the beginning. If someone has suspended Ashford from duty – and about time, too – it must be either the Chief Constable or the Watch Committee—which would mean Raymond Southern—"

"There's an odd story going round," said Ann. "People say there's a Home Office Inspector in town, and that he's taking evidence. No one quite knows who he is, or where he's hanging out, but that's the story, anyway."

"One of the reasons Dudley Powell wanted to come to Barhaven," said Anthony, "was because it was such a quiet place. Let's see if we can't deal with some of those letters."

Mrs. Lord arrived punctually at four o'clock. She said, "I gathered from your telephone message, Mr. Brydon, that you had some advice for me. An urgent communication, or so I was informed."

"It's urgent in this sense," said Anthony, "that if you decide to act on my advice, you will have to do so before Friday."

"Expound."

"You remember telling me that you waived your emoluments as Mayoress."

"That is correct."

"It was only when I saw the election notices that I remembered something. As Mayoress you are ex officio Returning Officer in any election in which you are not, yourself, a candidate. It didn't arise on the last two occasions, because you *were* a candidate—both times."

Mrs. Lord considered this. Her face, which sometimes looked foolish in repose, was now as sharp as a needle.

"That's quite correct," she said. "This is the first year in which I have been Mayoress, but not a Council candidate."

"As Returning Officer, you are paid a salary. It varies with the number of voters on the Register. It's not a princely sum – in your case it would be something like nine pounds. But it has this peculiarity. It cannot be waived."

"You mean I can't say 'no' to it?"

"Not effectively."

"Then how was I able to refuse my mayoral salary?"

"Because it wasn't salary. It was honorary emoluments. They would only be paid to you *if you claimed them.* The Returning Officer is a post which carries a fixed salary. You could refuse the money, of course, but you'd still be entitled to it. You'd have been 'in occupation of a paid office'."

"You're sure of all this?"

"When I was up in London yesterday, I took the opportunity of consulting learned Counsel on the matter. What I'm giving you is the gist of what I was told. I'll be getting a written opinion soon, but I'm afraid it'll only confirm it."

There was a long silence. Mrs. Lord sat still. Even her hands had ceased to flutter. Her bright black eyes were focused on a point over Anthony's shoulder. He thought, most of her vagueness is a front. She's a very sharp old lady. She isn't missing a trick.

"Then if I occupy the position of Returning Officer, even though I do none of the work, and even if I refuse to touch a penny of the money, I jeopardise my tolls."

"You wouldn't lose your tolls. But it could mean that the whole of your receipts that year would be subject to tax."

"And afterwards?"

"Possibly."

"You put the matter very clearly, Mr. Brydon. Do I understand that there is no way out of it?"

"There *is* a way," said Anthony. "But I'm not sure that it's going to appeal to you. Your position as Returning Officer doesn't arise until polling day. Until then the work is done by the Deputy Returning Officer. So if it could be arranged – before next Friday – that you were not Returning Officer—"

"I'll resign at once."

"I'm afraid it's not as simple as that."

"Oh, dear."

"The reason that you are Returning Officer is *because* you are Mayoress. It's an *ex officio* appointment. The one depends on the other."

"That's quite clear, then. The only way I can get out of it is by resigning as Mayoress."

"I honestly can't think of any other way."

"Before Friday?"

"Before Friday."

There was a further silence. Then Mrs. Lord, who had surprised Anthony more than once that afternoon, surprised him once again. She rose to her feet and said, with a sweet smile, "I think you're a very good lawyer, Mr. Brydon. You're wasted on Barhaven." Anthony got to the door just in time to hold it open for her, and watched her sweeping down the stairs. Ann was waiting at the bottom with her coat. Bowler held the door open. It was a regal exit.

181

"I can never make my mind up," said Ann, "if she's a wonderful old lady or a perfect old fraud."

"Certain Central African tribes," said Anthony, "are ruled by elderly widows. Such people are felt to have acquired a strength and independence of judgement which enables them to deal effectively with any circumstance, however difficult."

"It's a pity you're not an elderly widow, then."

"Oh?"

"Because I guess you're going to need all your strength and independence of judgement to deal with the gentleman who's been prowling round your waiting-room for the last half-hour."

"Ambrose?"

"No."

"Sellinge?"

"Guess again. It's Hamish Macintyre."

"Macintyre! Did he say what he wanted?"

"He said it was to do with the public enquiry tomorrow."

"That sounds fairly irregular to me. He's on the other side."

"He said that what he had to say was off the record, and wouldn't take very long."

"What we need in this office is a professional chucker-out."

Macintyre came straight to the point.

"I'm told that crackpot Ambrose will be giving evidence for you at the enquiry."

"We don't have to declare the names of our witnesses in advance."

"I know that. But *are* you going to call him?"

"Why don't you turn up tomorrow and find out."

"All right," said Macintyre. "Keep your cards as close to your chest as you like. What I came to say was this. Ambrose has been going round this town spreading lies about me. It's been word-of-mouth stuff. So I haven't been able to pin them down. But I'm warning you, if he gets up at the hearing and repeats them, I'm taking action."

"Repeats what?"

"You know what I'm talking about."

Macintyre's face was so ugly that it had a sort of metaphysical attraction, a power of twisted compulsion, which a more primitive people would have acknowledged, only crossing themselves as they did so.

Anthony drew back in his chair and said, as coolly as he could, "I haven't the faintest idea what you're talking about. Suppose you tell me."

"You've got a brass nerve," said Macintyre, "coming butting into this thing. I suppose you're in it for legal fees. Well let me tell you, some money's too hard-earned. You'll find out."

"Suppose we leave me out of it for the moment," said Anthony, "and stick to the point." He had suddenly realised that Macintyre was not only angry. He was frightened, as well. "You burst in here, uninvited, and start telling me what I'm to do and what I'm not to do. You say that people have been spreading stories about you. But when I ask you what they are, you seem curiously unwilling to tell me."

Macintyre made a small, angry gesture, but kept silent.

"Very well. Let's put a few cards on the table. There *are* stories going round about you. I didn't start them, and I haven't repeated them, but I've heard them."

"Such as—?"

"Such as that you've got shares in the underground garage on the front—"

"Which is a lie. You can look at the Share Register."

"Of course your name wouldn't be on the Register. The shares would be held by nominees. But the courts have got the power to go behind nominee holdings—"

"What courts? What are you talking about?"

"If it was established, as I think it might be, that you had a hidden holding of shares in the only existing garage *and* had been consistently using your position as Borough Engineer to block any other garage being built on the front, I can't help thinking that a criminal charge would lie."

Macintyre said, in a thick voice, "You repeat *that* in front of witnesses, and see what happens."

"There may be no need."

"What do you mean by that?"

"I mean that if the Progressives get a balance of seats on the Council at the forthcoming elections, the first item on the agenda is going to be looking for a new Borough Engineer. And the second item will be an investigation of the affairs of his predecessor."

Macintyre said, "Anyone can make any bloody investigation he bloody well chooses. I bloody well couldn't care less."

"Then don't let me keep you," said Anthony.

Ann, coming in a few minutes later, found Anthony leaning back in his chair at an extreme angle, whistling.

"Well, you look happy," she said.

"I feel happy."

"It's more than Macintyre does. When he went out just now he had a face on him to curdle the milk."

"Do you remember Lewis Carroll's lobster?" said Anthony. "When the sands were all dry, he was gay as a lark, and would speak in contemptuous tones of the shark. But when the tide deepened, and sharks were around, his voice had a timid and tremulous sound. Macintyre is a lobster. He can see the waters creeping up on him, and the ugly snouts circling round and he's scared. Have you brought me my letters to sign?"

It was seven o'clock by the time Anthony dealt with the last of the letters. One of his managing clerks, he noticed, was getting into a snarl over the repairing covenants in a lease. Those letters would have to be rewritten. The rest he signed. Since the staff had all gone he walked down with them himself to the post.

A man on the opposite pavement kept pace with him.

When Anthony came out of the post office he paused. There was little point in going home. When he left for London on Monday he had given Mrs. Stebbins a week's leave to visit her sister in Seaford. There would be tinned food in the house, and he could cook himself some sort of meal, but he felt no inclination to do so. Equally, there wasn't much attraction about the idea of a solitary meal in a restaurant. If he'd thought about it sooner he could have asked Ann to come and have a meal with him. She'd be home, by now, though, and her mother would think it odd—

He looked up, aware that someone was standing in front of him, blocking the way. It was a face that he recognised, but could not place.

"You are Mr. Brydon, aren't you?"

"That's right," said Anthony. "Do I—?"

"We haven't been introduced," said the man. "But we travelled down from London in the train together the other day."

"Good God," said Anthony. "Of course, yes."

"I was wondering if there was somewhere we could have a word together. By the way—" he slid a card out of his case, and Anthony read "Detective Chief Superintendent A. J. Brennan."

"They've got some very nice Red Barrel on draught at the Prince Consort," said Anthony. "Perhaps we could talk there."

Over their first pint Brennan said, "By the way, did I gather you were having a bit of trouble with that character in your carriage?"

"Yes," said Anthony. He still felt ashamed to talk about it.

"I was in the next carriage, and I thought I heard a bit of a rumpus. What did he do to you?"

Anthony said, "He kicked me, twice, on the shin. It doesn't sound very—I mean—"

"I know exactly what you mean," said Brennan. "You didn't feel you were getting your money's worth."

"That's right," said Anthony. There was something comforting about this stout, disillusioned man. "Caving in because he hacked me on the shin. When I thought about it afterwards it seemed so silly. If he'd pulled a gun on me—or a knife—"

"Real professionals don't carry weapons. They're afraid of getting picked up. They use their hands, and their feet, and their heads. Cherokee started life in a circus. I shouldn't be surprised if he hadn't got a bit of Indian blood in him. He's got a lot of funny little tricks."

"What does he do?"

"Anything you're prepared to pay for. Except murder. I don't *think* he's killed anyone yet. He's gone fairly close to it. There was a jobbing builder at Walthamstow getting awkward. Two of Sturrock's boys held him down and Cherokee jumped on his stomach. He was in hospital for three months, and he's still on a diet of slops."

"Why wasn't he arrested?"

"The only person who could prove anything was the builder. And he won't talk."

"Why not?"

"Because Cherokee told him, if he opened his mouth, they'd do the same thing to his wife. You're right, you know. This stuff's good. Drink up and I'll get you another pint."

When he came back he said, "I think you'll have to watch out for yourself for the next two or three days. After that it won't be important. The planning enquiry will be finished, and the elections will be over. They're on Friday, aren't they?"

Anthony nodded. "What exactly did you mean, take care of myself?"

"I don't think you ought to sleep in that house of yours. You're all alone there. And it's an isolated part of the town. I'd be happier to have you down for the next three days in my hotel – the Eversley – it's quiet but it's very comfortable. In fact, I've booked a room for you there."

"But—" said Anthony.

"You've got your pyjamas and washing things with you, I take it, seeing you've been staying in town."

"Yes—"

"Then there won't be any real need for you to go back to your house tonight at all."

"Look here," said Anthony. "Are you sure you've got this right? I'm not all that important now. The enquiry would go on, whether I was there or not. I've done my part. Hiscoe's the important man, now."

"I've arranged for Mr. Hiscoe to stay at the Eversley, too." The Superintendent took a further pull at his beer, and said, "I'm not saying the police couldn't protect you in your own house. If they put a couple of men on to the job. But it'd be a bit of a business, and they haven't got a lot of men to spare. Now the Eversley's convenient. It's only a street away from the police station—and it's got a night-porter, and it's in a well-lit street."

"You still haven't told me why you think anyone should want to get at me."

Brennan stared into the amber depths of his glass tankard, gave it a little swirl, and watched the bubbles steam up. Then he said, "I'm down here on a job. It's nothing to do with local crime or local politics, but I'm working on it with your Inspector Knox—"

"Not with Ashford."

"Not on this job," said Brennan, blandly. "One of the things I heard from Knox I didn't much like. You were in Sudderby's house the night he died, weren't you?"

"Yes. I found him."

"When did you leave?"

"Just after midnight."

"When the police and the doctor left."

"That's right. I think Doctor Rogers was actually the last man out. Why?"

"When the police came back the next morning, they found the house had been broken into and ransacked. Two or three men on the job. They'd been through every drawer and cupboard and bookcase in the house and taken away every scrap of private paper they could find."

Chapter Twenty-Seven

Wednesday

At four o'clock on the following afternoon Mr. Parnell, the Inspector sent down to Barhaven by the Ministry of Housing and Local Government, coughed, looked at his watch, checked it with the clock on the front of the gallery in the Council Chamber and said, "I will resume tomorrow at ten o'clock, gentlemen."

Mr. Hiscoe murmured to Anthony, "Can you get hold of Mr. Sellinge for a few minutes? And is there somewhere we can talk?"

"There's a small committee room upstairs. We could use that. I'll catch Sellinge."

When they reached the committee room they found Mr. Hiscoe perched on the end of the table swinging his long legs.

"I got the impression," said Sellinge, "correct me if I'm wrong, Mr. Hiscoe, that our side didn't bat too well today."

"I think the opposition have had the best of it so far," agreed Mr. Hiscoe. "And that's what I wanted to talk to you about. In theory, I'm appearing for the appellant, Mr. Shanklin, but I gather, in fact, that you're instructing us."

"I, and a group of people I represent, have undertaken for the costs, if that's what you mean."

"That's exactly what I mean," said Mr. Hiscoe. "There's an old saying that he who pays the piper calls the tune. You all saw what happened today. First, the Council trumped one of our aces very neatly, by agreeing to support an amendment of the plan which would put a row of shops in the next road to Haven Road. That took most of the sting out of our local witnesses. Then, I'm afraid Mr. Breamore went rather too far, and got roughly handled by Paradine."

"On the other hand," said Anthony, "I thought that Colonel Passmore gave better than he got."

"I think he did. But, if I might adopt Mr. Sellinge's metaphor, this isn't a match in which it's any use playing for a draw, is it? We shan't achieve anything by showing that a western development is *just as good* as an eastern development. If that's all we do, the Inspector is almost bound to come down in favour of the existing plan."

"He'll do that, anyway," said Sellinge. "He was against us from the moment he first opened his mouth."

"I've appeared before Mr. Parnell on a number of occasions," said Mr. Hiscoe. "He's a senior man—indeed, it reflects the importance which Whitehall must attach to this enquiry that he should have been sent down here at all. And there's no denying he has a considerable sense of his own dignity. I'm afraid Mr. Ambrose upset him with his ill-timed interjection."

"I tried to collar him," said Anthony, "but I just couldn't get hold of him in time."

"Ambrose is a silly ass," said Sellinge: "Clever, mind you. But dead stupid, too, if you follow me. The thing is, though, what are we going to do next?"

"As I see it," said Mr. Hiscoe, "we have two choices. Either we go quietly, or we go the whole hog. So far, all that we've managed to say is that the eastern development is bad planning. We've now got to make up our minds whether to go further and assent that it is dishonest planning."

"Which would mean calling Ambrose as a witness."

"What about subpoena-ing Macintyre?"

"I'm afraid that a planning tribunal has no power to subpoena witnesses."

"Then it's Ambrose or nothing."

Anthony tried to visualise the editor of the *Barhaven Gazette* in the witness-box. He visualised him being cross-examined by the Belial-like Mr. Paradine, under the austere correction of Mr. Parnell. Ambrose would certainly lose his temper. He would go wildly beyond his script. He would create an enormous sensation and would very likely put paid to their chances of success. On the other hand, if they didn't call him— He said to Mr. Hiscoe, "By the way, what about libel? Does a witness in a planning enquiry enjoy the same absolute protection as a witness in a court of law? Macintyre as good as told me that if we tried to drag his name into it, he'd sue us."

"Curiously enough," said Mr. Hiscoe, "the point has never been specifically decided. My own view, for what it is worth, is that he does not. A planning enquiry is an administrative, not a judicial tribunal. He would have qualified privilege, of course."

"Which means what?" said Sellinge.

"As long as he says no more than he honestly believes to be the truth, without malice, he will have a defence to any proceedings for defamation."

"Without malice?" said Sellinge, thoughtfully.

"There's another point," said Mr. Hiscoe. "I doubt whether the Inspector would allow Ambrose to get very far. If he started some irrelevant attack on Macintyre, he'd shut him up at once. He could even order him out of the room. I've known him do *that.*"

"It's no good ordering Ambrose out," said Anthony. "You have to carry him out."

"I can't think that such an undignified proceeding would do our case a lot of good," said Mr. Hiscoe.

"Now there I disagree," said Sellinge. "Don't let's take our eyes off the ball. Strictly within these four walls, I don't care a damn if we win or lose this particular appeal. The object is to ventilate our feelings about the Council – and about people like Crawford and Lincoln-Bright, who've got property at the eastern end of the town—"

"But *not* in the development area."

"True. But they want the development to go east, not west."

Mr. Hiscoe thought about it. The ultimate responsibility, as he well knew, was his. He was, as Anthony had discovered that day, a very different man on his feet to his cautious self in chambers. He enjoyed a fight and was the last person to avoid one merely because it spelled unpleasantness. But there was a limit beyond which aggression became stupidity.

He said, "I think we shall have to rely on my cross-examination of their witnesses, and on what I can do for you in my final speech."

"And *not* call Ambrose."

"No."

"Someone will have to stun him then," said Sellinge.

"And a large gin for my friend," said Crawford.

"How do you think it went, Jack?"

"I thought it went very well, didn't you, Raymond?"

Southern said, "Very well. And if that prize cuckoo Ambrose goes on talking out of turn, it'll go better and better."

"The Inspector didn't give him much rope, did he?" said Lincoln-Bright.

"Enough to hang himself with," said Crawford.

The bar of the Country Club was filling up steadily as the offices emptied. Apart from Saturday night this was the busiest time at the Club, the oasis of the gin hour.

"Is it true what I heard about the Mayoress?" asked Lincoln-Bright.

"Perfectly true," said Southern, lowering his voice. "Her resignation was handed in, in writing, this afternoon, to be effective as from this evening."

"What happens now?"

"I'm not sure. Normally, her term of office wouldn't end until October. Either we shall be without a Mayor until then or the next senior alderman will take office at once and hold it for fifteen months."

"The next senior alderman being you, Raymond."

"That's right," said Southern. He sounded preoccupied.

"What happens in Council?"

"The Mayoress was Chairman ex officio. In her letter of resignation she made it clear that she wanted to give up the chairmanship too."

"Did she say *why* she was doing this?"

"No. I happen to know that she went to see her solicitor on Tuesday afternoon, and the letter of resignation was written on Tuesday evening. It doesn't mean that there's any connection between the two things, of course."

"Who *is* her solicitor?"

"Anthony Brydon."

"That young man," said Crawford, "is showing signs, I'm afraid, of growing too big for his boots."

"I wouldn't say that," said Southern. "I think he's a very clever young man."

"As long as he doesn't get too clever. The same again, please Jack, and not so much water in mine this time."

"If *you're* Chairman now," said Lincoln-Bright, *"you'll* get the casting vote."

"Certainly," said Southern, "Why? Are you getting cold feet about the election, Gerald?"

"I'm not worrying," said Lincoln-Bright. "I think it'll be a walk-over – particularly if this planning enquiry is the big flop it looks like being. From that point of view it couldn't have been better timed. But one's got to face possibilities. *If* we lost three seats, and the opposition picked them up, we should be eight-all. Then the Chairman's casting vote *would* be vital."

"Talking about the election," said Crawford, "do you know that there's been some highly unofficial canvassing going on in your Ward?"

"Who by?"

"Castle House School boys. The headmaster gave them the day off yesterday, and told them to take a practical lesson in Civics by doing a little door-to-door canvassing."

"I call that very enterprising," said Lincoln-Bright. "One up to the old usher, I'd say."

"Except that the whole lot of them were rooting for your opponents."

Lincoln-Bright spluttered into his drink – and Southern burst out laughing.

Anthony went back to the office after the hearing to clear up a little of the work which was piling up. He toyed with the idea of asking Ann to have dinner with him at the Eversley and funked it. When he had finished at the office he walked home. There was a young policeman at the corner of his street, and he felt a momentary gratification at the thought that he should be important enough for police protection.

The policeman ignored him, and he walked up the path and let himself in by the front door.

Although the house had only been empty for three days it felt dusty, chill and forlorn. Mrs. Stebbins, as was her custom when she was preparing for a thorough clean, had rolled up the carpet on the stairs and in the hall. Anthony picked up half-a-dozen bills and circulars which had tumbled through the letter-box, and then stumped upstairs, his feet clattering on the bare boards. As he reached the top, he thought he heard another footstep, ahead of him, but knew that it was imagination.

He dumped his shirt and collar in the laundry basket, put on clean stuff and packed a spare shirt, two collars and some handkerchiefs and socks in his grip and came downstairs again.

As he was on the point of slamming the front door a thought struck him. He had left the house before the post arrived on Monday. Mrs. Stebbins would have taken in Monday's letters and put them on the table in his father's study.

He went back and looked into the study, a dark little room on the left of the hall. He had hardly been into it since his father died. There were three letters lying on the table and he saw, with a tightening of the muscles in his throat, that the nearest was addressed to him in the thin, scholarly writing of James Sudderby.

"I thought that chap Southern spoke rather well," said Mr. Burgess to Mrs. Burgess as they came down to dinner at the Eversley Hotel.

"Very well," said Mrs. Burgess. "Good evening, Mrs. Foster. We've just been to an election meeting."

"Sooner you than me," said Mrs. Foster. "I can't take much interest in politics. As my husband says, they're all as bad as each other."

"Oh, I don't know," said Mr. Burgess. "Someone's got to do it, haven't they."

"I don't see why."

"There are certain municipal functions. Someone has to carry them out. I think it's very public-spirited of the people who take it on."

"My husband says they're all in it for what they can get out of it."

"I think he's just being horrid and cynical," said Mrs. Burgess. "*My husband is thinking of standing as a candidate for our Council.*"

"Oh well, if he does it, I expect it'll be all right," said Mrs. Foster.

"Good heavens," said Mr. Burgess. "Look who's here. That tall man, with the bald patch, who's just come in. It's old Hiscoe."

"Isn't he a Q.C.?"

"I don't think he's actually a Q.C., but he's a very well-known barrister. He appeared for one of our clients in a most important tax case last year."

Mrs. Burgess said, "Let's go over and say hullo to him. Perhaps he'd like to share our table." Since their only son had reached an age at which he preferred to take his holidays with his own friends, Mrs. Burgess had been conscious of something lacking. She was fond of her husband, of course, but there was a limit to the entertainment to be got from someone as predictable as Mr. Burgess.

"I don't think we ought to intrude," said Mr. Burgess. "I see that his table is laid for two and – yes – this looks like the person he is waiting for."

Anthony had appeared, and was making for Mr. Hiscoe's table. It was clear, even across the width of the room, that something had upset him badly.

Chapter Twenty-Eight

Thursday

The Council Chambers had been uncomfortably full the day before. Now a second row of chairs had been squeezed in at the back and it looked as if it was going to be oversubscribed.

Walking to the hearing that morning, Arthur Ambrose had noted the signs. Groups of people on their way to work who had stopped to talk, a rash of rosettes, mostly the red of the Progressive party, two vans with loudspeakers operating along the crowded pavements. There was thunder somewhere behind the bright sunshine.

The hall was filling up as Ambrose reached it and squeezed his way in to the press benches, which had been inconveniently located at the far end of the room. The young reporter with him touched his arm and said, "I'm sure I've seen that chap before somewhere." Ambrose looked where he was pointing. The man was sitting in the corner at the back, reading a folded newspaper and glancing from time to time over the top of his horn-rimmed glasses. He had a face like a tired whale. It was familiar to Ambrose, too, but he couldn't place it.

"He was here all yesterday," said the reporter.

"Slip across and see if you can find out who he is. The attendant may know. Good morning, Mr. Brydon."

"Good morning," said Anthony, shortly. Ambrose thought he looked worried. Before he could say anything more, Mr Hiscoe appeared with Chris Sellinge, and the three of them sat down together in the roped-off section at the top of the line of tables. Ambrose, straining his ears, thought he heard his own name mentioned, and then the three of them were looking in his direction and beckoning to him.

He moved across quickly to join them.

Mr. Hiscoe said, "Oh, Mr. Ambrose. Sit down a moment, would you. We talked things over yesterday evening, and we came to the conclusion that it wouldn't be necessary to call your evidence after all." He added, with a smile, "Sorry to disappoint you."

Ambrose ignored the smile. A slow flush spread over his face, starting at his cheekbones and working its way up to his forehead.

"Not necessary? Why?"

"It's always difficult, before an enquiry begins, to know exactly how it will shape. In the light of events yesterday, we've had to change our plans somewhat—"

"You mean," said Ambrose, "that you can't trust me not to make a fool of myself."

Anthony who was staring down at the table and looking sick said, without lifting his head, "It isn't that at all, Ambrose."

"Don't mind me. Say it if you think it. My feelings aren't important. It's the case that matters."

"That was our view too," said Mr. Hiscoe, smoothly.

"Tell me this, though. If I don't give evidence for you, how the hell do you imagine you're going to upset their case?"

Before Mr. Hiscoe could answer, the door behind the dais had opened and Mr. Parnell had walked in. As he took his place he glanced around him. The extra chairs were already full, and latecomers were pushing their way through the entrance and distributing themselves round the room. The four window-sills had been commandeered as seats, and people were standing behind the back row of chairs and jamming the open space in front of the door.

"It's rather hot, isn't it," said Mr. Parnell. "Perhaps we might have another window open. That's better. Now, Mr. Paradine—"

"My next witness," said Mr. Paradine, "is Frederick Hinton. Mr. Hinton is the Deputy Town Clerk of this Borough, and I should explain that he is deputising, at very short notice, for the late Town

Clerk, Mr. Sudderby, who took his own life, in tragic circumstances, four days ago."

The Inspector said, "I had heard something of that. We will make every allowance for Mr. Hinton's difficulties."

Mr. Paradine bowed gracefully to the Inspector, and then turned to Mr. Hinton, who was looking worried and fingering a large-scale plan. In fact, he acquitted himself very well. When Mr. Paradine had finished with him, Mr. Hiscoe, without getting up, said, "I congratulate Mr. Hinton on his very able performance as an understudy at such short notice. Since, however, he has told us nothing about this plan which we did not know already, I will not waste the Inspector's time by attempting to cross-examine him."

Mr. Paradine looked surprised, Mr. Hinton looked relieved, and the Inspector said, "I should like to be clear on one point, Mr. Hinton. This plan, for the development of the town to the east, has the full support of your Borough Council, I take it."

"That is correct, sir."

"It is the official plan, worked out by your Council?"

"Yes, sir. We had the services of a firm of architects and planning consultants, Messrs. Grey Dorfer & Co., to help us—"

"One of whom I now propose to call," interjected Mr. Paradine.

"Very well," said the Inspector.

"Mr. Dorfer, please—"

Mr. Dorfer who, like all Town Planners, seemed to have no objection to the sound of his own voice, held the floor for most of the morning session. Mr. Hiscoe's cross-examination was brief. He said, "We have listened with close attention, Mr. Dorfer, whilst you expounded to us the merits of the Council's pet plan for the development of Barhaven to the east. It has been described by the learned Inspector, as the 'official plan', although I take it that, as an expert in these matters, you would agree with me that this is an incorrect description."

"Well—yes—"

"There can only be one official plan, and that is the five-year plan, produced by the County Council."

"Certainly. But the Borough has a delegated authority to work out the details."

"I'm not disputing it. But if you look at the county plan you will see that considerable areas both east *and* west of Barhaven are zoned for residential development."

"That is so."

"So that, had the Borough Council decided, instead, to develop in a westerly direction, there was nothing in the *official* plan to prevent them from doing so."

"No—no. I must agree with that."

"I felt sure you would," said Mr. Hiscoe, with a smile, and reseated himself.

Mr. Paradine said, "In view of the observations which my learned friend has seen fit to make, it is perhaps opportune that my final witness should be Mr. Lincoln-Bright. He was Chairman of the Lands Development Committee, set up more than two years ago by the Council, and will be able to tell us something of the careful thought and deliberation which went into the preparation of what I understand I am not allowed to call the official plan—"

Mr. Paradine directed a knife-edged smile towards Mr. Hiscoe, who grinned.

"—and which I will therefore call, if I may, the Council Plan. Mr. Lincoln-Bright—"

The member for Victoria Park arose to his feet with a flashing smile. He may have been reflecting that this public tribute to his hard work during the past two years could hardly have come at a more opportune moment. By the time Mr. Paradine sat down he felt that he had done himself more than justice. He straightened his tie, cleared his throat and faced with confidence whatever barbs Counsel for the opposition was preparing to place in him.

Mr. Hiscoe seemed, for a moment, doubtful whether he wished to question him at all. He rose, almost hesitantly, to his feet, and said, "Was your committee aware, Mr. Bright, when it decided to employ them, that the firm of Grey Dorfer & Co. was a part of the Greyslates Organisation?"

"Certainly."

"It didn't occur to you that it might have been better to have planning consultants who were independent of the builders who were going to do the work?"

"I'm afraid you've got the order wrong," said Lincoln-Bright with a smile. "We only chose Grey Dorfer & Co. *after* the Greyslates Organisation had won the tender for the work."

Mr. Hiscoe considered this answer for a long moment whilst a puzzled frown puckered his child-like face. It was a nice piece of acting, which impressed everyone except Mr. Paradine, who was busy working out what was coming and wasn't liking it much.

"You'll have to clarify that for us, Mr. Bright," said Mr. Hiscoe. "If you already had the job out to tender, you must already have decided which way you were going to develop."

"Well—yes. We had."

"And if you had decided to go east *before* you employed Messrs. Grey Dorfer & Co., how were they able to advise you which way it was best for you to go?"

Lincoln-Bright hesitated. He didn't like being addressed as Mr. Bright, and he didn't like Counsel's tone. He made the mistake of snapping. "I should have thought it was quite obvious to anyone who knew anything about this sort of thing. Grey Dorfer & Co. had nothing to do with the decision about which way we went. That was purely a Council decision. They advised us on the detailed lay-out."

"In that case," said Mr. Hiscoe, "we appear to have wasted a great deal of time this morning. We have been listening for nearly two hours, whilst Mr. Dorfer expounded the technical merits of developing east but apparently *none* of these arguments was in front of the Council when it made its mind up."

"Well—no."

"What arguments *were* in front of it?"

Lincoln-Bright looked round for support. It seemed to him that he had been jockeyed into a false position. He said, "We thought the matter out as best we could, on general grounds."

"On general grounds. Not on personal grounds?"

"I'm afraid I don't follow you."

"I mean," said Mr. Hiscoe, "that no member of the Council, in coming to this decision, had any personal motive whatever for preferring the eastern to the western development."

A dead silence had settled on the room. Even the coughing and shuffling had stopped. Lincoln-Bright arranged his features into what he hoped was a dignified, and even intimidating look, and said, "Any suggestion of that sort is defamatory and untrue."

"Allow me to correct you on a point of law," said Mr. Hiscoe. "It could only be defamatory *if* it were untrue."

The Inspector said, "I take it, Mr. Hiscoe, that these suggestions are not being made to the witness without your having grounds for them."

"I can assure you," said Mr. Hiscoe, "that I should not have made them unless I had the most cogent grounds for doing so," and sat down.

No one seemed to know what to do next.

Mr. Paradine looked uncertainly at Lincoln-Bright, and said, "I have no more questions," and the Inspector said, "Then in that case—"

"Before addressing my closing remarks to you," said Mr. Hiscoe, rising again, "I should like your permission to call one additional witness. My instructing solicitor, Mr. Anthony Brydon—"

Anthony got up. His face was white and strained.

"I assume that there is some reason for him being called out of turn."

"Certainly, sir. The document I am going to ask him to produce only came into his possession late last night. It is a personal letter, to him, from the late Town Clerk, James Sudderby, whose name has already been mentioned to you."

The silence in the room was painful.

"How—?"

"I should explain, sir," said Mr. Hiscoe, who had dropped his bantering note, and was speaking with great simplicity, "that owing to his engagements Mr. Brydon had not been home between early on Monday morning and yesterday evening. He did not, therefore, see a letter which had been posted late on Friday night and, as sometimes happens with local deliveries, did not reach him until Monday morning. With your permission I will ask him to read it. I will put in the whole document of course. But since parts of it are personal, I will ask Mr. Brydon to read only from the top of the second page."

In a voice drained of all feeling Anthony read out the paragraphs which he now almost knew by heart.

"—I think it is time that everyone knew the truth. There were three of them in it. Southern, Macintyre and Ashford. There were other, smaller people too, but I see no point in dragging their names into it now. And I'm not trying to excuse myself, either. I did what I was told. If I hadn't—"

Anthony stopped, looked at the Inspector, and said, "The next bit deals with an incident in Mr. Sudderby's past. I don't want to read that now—"

The Inspector nodded.

Anthony read on. "These three men were all in it for what they could make out of it. Macintyre had a controlling share in the underground garage, which he extracted from the developers as his price for getting the development through the Council. He also undertook to use his official position to stop rival garage development as far as possible. Inspector Ashford was taking a cut from the profits of the Pleasuredrome, which was put up by the same developers. If it hadn't been paid, he could have found half-a-dozen ways of making life difficult for the proprietors, possibly of closing it down altogether. Southern knew about both of these schemes, although, to the best of my knowledge, he took no money out of either of them. As Vice-Chairman of the Council he was useful to Macintyre and Ashford, but he was after much bigger game for himself. Some years ago he formed a company called Carlmont Properties. His own interest in it was buried under a network of nominee shareholdings and I doubt if more than three people knew of it. This company already held a substantial slice of land north of Haven Road, and Southern was planning, with Macintyre's help, to drive the owner of Castle House School out of business and pick up his property cheap. If the eastern development plan went through, both these pieces of land would be worth between four and five thousand pounds an acre—"Anthony had been aware, as he read, that his voice was starting to compete with other sounds. He was now drowned by the scraping of chairs and the stamping of feet. The representatives of the press were fighting their way through the over-crowded exit. Ambrose was second out of the room. He was beaten by a short head by the stranger in the corner.

Southern sat in his office on the north side of Connaught Square behind a desk that was as neat as he was. He was listening, a half-frown of concentration on his face, to what an angry and agitated Mr. Grey of Greyslates was saying to him on the telephone.

"It wasn't a question of timing," he said, at last. "Brydon left his house before the post arrived on Monday and didn't go back until Wednesday evening. There was nothing more to it than that."

Mr. Grey said something impatient, and Southern's frown deepened. He said, "It's very unfortunate, I agree. But it may have come too late to do any harm. These things take time to sink in, you know. I might lose my seat tomorrow, *if* the ordinary voter hears about it – which he may not – and *if* he cares about it – which he probably won't. But it won't necessarily affect anyone else. Provided my colleagues keep their heads, we'll get this scheme through all right."

"Is that guaranteed?"

"As far as I'm concerned, it's guaranteed. I can't answer for all my associates. They suffer from a wobbly form of morality. They don't mind making money on the side as long as it looks all right, and particularly as long as no one finds out about it. If there's any sort of publicity, they'll wash their hands of it quicker than Pontius Pilate."

"Ambrose's editorial should make interesting reading tomorrow," said Mr. Grey. It was a tribute to Southern's calming influence that his voice sounded almost normal again.

"I told you that I always missed any excitement that was going," said Ann. "I'd slipped out for a quarter-of-an-hour whilst Lincoln-Bright was saying his piece, and when I came back it was all over. What happened?"

"The Inspector adjourned the meeting. He hadn't much option, really. It had practically adjourned itself."

"What *did* you say?"

"I didn't say anything. I read this out to them. It's a copy. Hiscoe has got the original."

Ann read it in silence. Then said, "Poor little Mr. Sudderby. You were fond of him, weren't you?"

"He was very kind to me."

"He's certainly put the cat among the pigeons. Not that pigeons is a very good word for them. Rooks. Crooks." She paused for a moment, and said, "Macintyre and Ashford. No surprise there. But fancy it turning out to be Southern. I always thought he dressed too well."

Anthony said nothing.

"You'll have lost yourself a client over this, I suppose."

Anthony still said nothing.

"However, if he's a crook, he's no great loss to us."

She thought Anthony was going to pass that one up too, but in the end he said, with a note of anger in his voice, "My father once described Southern to me as an honest crook."

"There's no such animal."

"What he meant was that Southern never wrapped up what he was doing. He's out for his own ends, but he keeps inside the letter of the law. Not for any ethical reasons, but because it's easier, in the long run, to work with the law than against it."

"You can talk as much as you like," said Ann, "but you can't get round the fact that he was using his seat on the Council to push through this development, which was going to put hundreds of thousands of pounds into his pocket."

"How do you know?"

Ann looked surprised.

"How do you know which way he voted in the Council?"

"Well, of course I don't. But whichever way he voted, he ought to have *told* people he owned the land."

"Oh. Why?"

"Why—? Well, if you can't see it—"

"All you're saying is that he was out for himself. Who isn't? Sellinge is on the Council. He's fighting just as hard for his own pocket. So's Ambrose. He isn't doing this as a crusade. He's doing it to boost the *Gazette,* and boost himself into Fleet Street."

Ann, who was as angry as Anthony now, said, "You're just saying this because Southern was a friend of your father's, and you happened to admire him."

Anthony came round the desk to where she was standing. She thought he was going to slap her face, and put her right hand up quickly. Anthony caught her wrist with his own left hand, pulled her towards him, got his right arm behind her shoulders, and kissed her savagely.

As soon as she got her mouth away she said, "That's no argument."

Anthony kissed her again, more gently this time, and felt the unmistakable, intoxicating, answer.

They were so deeply absorbed in each other that neither of them heard the door open, and shut again.

Arnold, who was a downy youth of sixteen, hurried back to report to Bowler.

"Snogging," he said. "So busy kissing her, he didn't see me come in nor go out."

"You're making it up," said Bowler.

"That I'm not," said Arnold. "Go and see for yourself, if you like. I don't suppose they'll leave off for hours. Mind you, I don't blame him. She's quite a dish. I wouldn't mind having a bite myself."

"The trouble with you, Arnold," said Bowler, "you're over-sexed."

As opponents had discovered to their cost, Southern was at his best when he was up against it. And for all his confident talk to Mr. Grey, he realised, none better, the trickiness of his position.

First he summoned Lincoln-Bright and Crawford. If he had tried to go and see them, they would probably have avoided him. Since he sent for them, they came; Lincoln-Bright embarrassed and inarticulate, Crawford truculent.

"If you were going in for that sort of fiddle," said Crawford, "you might have had the decency to stand down from the Council first."

"And let in one of our opponents?"

"There's that, of course," said Crawford, thoughtfully.

"Perhaps I've got old-fashioned ideas," said Lincoln-Bright, "but it seems to me that what you did was absolutely unethical."

"Stop talking like a Boy Scout," said Southern. "If I'd offered you a share in Carlmont you'd have snapped it up. And so would Jack Crawford here—"

"You never gave me a chance," said Crawford. "Anyway, it's too late now. The fat's in the fire."

"It's only too late if you sit down and howl," said Southern.

"You're not withdrawing as a candidate, then."

"Good God, no. I'm going to fight this election—and I'm going to win it. There's a built-in Conservative majority in the Victoria Park Ward. You can't change people's convictions overnight. Half the voters won't hear about this at all, and half the people who hear it won't believe it. I'm going to talk to Anderson and Furlong now—they're organising my campaign for me. The line I'm telling them to take is— 'Don't believe malicious gossip'—"

After an hour of this Southern's fellow-candidates went away, if not entirely reassured at least happier than they had come.

Before they had left the room Southern was on the telephone. It was eight o'clock by the time he had finished with his campaign managers. No time to spare for dinner. There were friends to telephone, waverers to chide, supporters to rally. Then there was Mr. Pitt, the Deputy Returning Officer, who telephoned to remind Southern that, as acting Mayor, he was now Returning Officer and would have to conduct certain formalities. Did he intend—

"Of course," said Southern, shortly. "Why not?"

Mr. Pitt said, "I only thought—" and then, sensing from the silence at the other end that he had said the wrong thing, "I'll be seeing you tomorrow morning, then."

"Ten o'clock," said Southern and rang off.

He started to dial Anthony's office number, realised that the office would be shut, and tried his home number. When he got no answer there he jotted down a note on his pad, thought for a moment and looked up Arthur Mentmore's home number. He found him finishing his dinner, apologised briefly, and put a question to him, which seemed to cause that elderly solicitor some difficulty.

He had hardly rung off, when the telephone went again. This time it was Hamish Macintyre, who said, "Do you suppose they've got this telephone bugged?"

"I've been expecting to hear from you," said Southern. "No, I shouldn't think so."

"What line are you taking about all this?"

"I'm taking the line that my private affairs are my own business and no one else's."

"It's all very well for you. You're a bloody councillor. I'm just a wage slave. I'll be losing my job over this."

"I should have thought you'd got enough money not to care."

"No one can ever have enough money."

"No? Then I'll tell you an easy way to make yourself some more. I've just been having a word with Mentmore. He tells me that planning enquiries aren't privileged occasions."

"What the hell does that mean?"

"It means that as long as Ambrose just quotes Sudderby's letter, he'll be safe. If he starts to comment on it, he'll let himself in for damages for libel."

"What makes you think he'll comment?"

"You know our Ambrose."

Southern heard a belly laugh the other end of the line. He guessed that Macintyre would not be unduly worried by the turn of events. He would have foreseen what had happened and would have made his plans well in advance.

When he had rung off he sat for a long moment before making his next call. Then, with a grimace, he dialled a number. Unexpectedly it was a woman's voice that answered.

Southern said, "Oh, Miss Ashford. I wonder if I could have a word with your brother."

"It's Mr. Southern, isn't it. I'm afraid my brother's out."

"Have you any idea when he'll be back?"

"He didn't say. He took his car out about an hour ago. He—he hasn't quite been himself lately."

"I'm sorry to hear that," said Southern smoothly.

"It was Pilot. That was the last straw—"

Southern knew Pilot, a leggy Alsatian that Inspector Ashford was training.

"What happened to Pilot?" he said.

"He ran out into the road, this afternoon. A car hit him. It broke both legs."

"I *am* sorry."

"My brother had to put him down. The vet was out. Poor Pilot was in agony."

"A thing like that would upset anyone."

"He had to shoot him, himself."

"It must have been horrible," said Southern. "When he does get back, would you ask him to give me a ring—at home. It doesn't matter how late—"

As he rang off, he realised how tired he was.

It was partly atmospheric. There had been a metallic glint about the sun all day, and it had gone down into a film of cloud. A clear warning of thunder to come.

He walked across to the window and looked out. Connaught Square stood empty under its orange neon street lamps. A few lights still burned in the municipal buildings on the east side of the Square but the other three sides were offices, and their windows were black and quiet.

As Southern turned to the door he thought he heard a sound.

There was a back door and a flight of steps leading directly up to his first-floor office. He sometimes used it himself to escape importunate clients. The door, at the foot of the stairs, was closed on a catch, and was usually kept locked. As he thought about this he heard

207

a stair creak. Somebody was coming up and was taking care to make as little noise about it as possible.

Unwillingly, and for a moment, Anthony stopped kissing Ann. Their car was parked, once again, in the lay-by on the cliff road to the east of the town.

"It's gone eleven," she said. "If I don't get home soon, mother will be ringing up the police."

"Have you broken it to her—about us?"

"I haven't had a chance," said Ann. "Do you realise, that with one very brief pause for food, we've been kissing each other for about six hours."

"I've got a lot of time to make up."

"When shall we get married?"

"Soon, soon."

"I'd better tell mother early September. She'll need a month to get her wits about her."

"Have we got to wait till then?" said Anthony, putting his arm back round Ann's shoulders. He had found that if he slid his arm under hers, fairly high up, his hand lay over her right breast without any fuss; and that this was a splendid position for the start of further gentle exploration.

Ann stiffened under him.

"What's wrong?" he said.

"Look," she said. "Look. Down there. What is it? What on earth's happening?"

Below them spread the twinkling lights of Barhaven. Into this firmament a new, and fiercer sun was rising.

Anthony stared for a moment, and then he said, "Christ! It's the *Gazette* Printing Works. They're on fire. Come on."

Chapter Twenty-Nine

Friday

Anthony remembered the next bit as a sort of nightmare; flames, billowing smoke, the sharp smell of burning woodwork and hot metal, sparks climbing into the air as the high-pressure hoses hit the building; Ambrose, in tears, at his side. Captain Weekes, the Chief Officer of the Fire Brigade, saying with professional detachment, "She's well away, isn't she?" just as the floor of the print shop fell in, and a heavy press lurched through, to drop into the inferno of the dispatch department. And then, around one o'clock in the morning, a flash which overawed the flames, a roar which drowned the roaring of the lire and the heavens were opened as the long threatened storm burst across Barhaven. In ten short minutes the elements achieved what the united fire brigades of Barhaven, Hastings, Folkestone and Seaford had failed to do in two hours. Under the weight of water poured down upon them, the premises of the *Barhaven Gazette* were reduced to a sullen, smoking shell.

Ambrose, shivering with cold and hysterical with rage and shock, had to be restrained by force from bursting his way in.

"You'll not be able to handle a thing in there for two or three hours," said Captain Weekes. "Even then it won't be at all safe. Better leave it till it's light."

"Has anyone any idea how it happened?" asked the Chief Constable, who had arrived in his official car five minutes after Anthony, and seemed very wide awake.

"We know *when* it started, sir," said Inspector Knox. "A youngster and his girlfriend were walking home, past the building, just before midnight. They saw flames coming out of a first-storey window, and rang up the brigade from a call-box."

Ambrose said, "I was last out. We'd finished by half-past eleven. We'd got the whole of tomorrow's edition printed, and stacked. I locked the place up myself."

"Half an hour," said the Chief Constable. "That's not very long. Suppose someone had dropped a cigarette – something like that – it'd take time, surely—"

"It wasn't that sort of fire," said Weekes.

"What do you mean by that, Weekes?"

"Unless a lot of different people dropped cigarettes in different places. This fire had five or six starting points. And another thing, Mr. Ambrose. Have you any petrol-driven engines in the place?"

"No."

"Just stand here – clear of the smoke – and take a deep breath – through your nose – now."

They all did as Weekes had suggested, and they could all smell it, pungent, volatile and unmistakable.

"The place has been soaked in petrol," said Weekes. "No amount of burning will get rid of the smell. The stuff's been poured in by the bucketful. This place didn't catch fire. It was set on fire. And by people who knew their job, too, I'd say."

At four o'clock, in the first faint light of dawn, a party led by Ambrose forced a door at the back of the dispatch room and started to carry out what remained of that Friday's edition of the *Barhaven Gazette*. The copies were in loose bales of twenty, forty and a hundred, set out on tables, ready for collection. Ambrose picked up the nearest bundle and dropped it with a cry. The wire round it was still hot. The smaller bundles had been burned through. In the larger ones there were a few papers, right in the middle, which had survived the holocaust, blackened at the edges, but still readable. They rescued and sorted out three or four hundred of them.

"I'll deliver them myself," said Ambrose, "and I'll tell every person I hand one to just exactly—just exactly—" his voice trembled and broke.

"Have a bath, and breakfast, before you do anything," said the Chief Constable, not unkindly. "It'll be on the nine o'clock news, anyway. We've had reporters skirmishing round the scrum all night."

Ann reappeared with her car and said to Anthony, "Mother's running a bath for you. And you can have breakfast with us. Why don't we go down to your house now, and collect some clean clothes."

"Clean clothes?"

"You've no idea what you look like. A cross between Old Bill and that horrible chimney-sweep in *The Water Babies.*"

After a bath, a change and breakfast, cooked and served by Mrs. Weaver who turned out to be a small, easy, untroubled sort of person, they walked down to the office together. Anthony was feeling extraordinarily fit and wide awake. He knew from experience that this was the normal result of a lost night. The reaction would come in the late afternoon.

The storm had passed, and it was a fresh and sparkling morning. Barhaven was *en fête*. Loudspeaker vans were blaring, volunteers were distributing handbills, everyone seemed to be wearing a rosette. The electors of Barhaven were exercising their franchise with that curious mixture of gaiety and purpose with which English people carry out a public function. The announcement on the wireless – two bald sentences, with the ominous tag, "The police are working on the theory that the fire was started deliberately" – had left a wide swathe of speculation behind it.

"Poor Ambrose," said Anthony. "He'd have sold every copy of the *Gazette* twice over."

Arnold met them at the door of the office. He was grinning. "We're all in the *Mirror*," he said. "Did you see?"

Ann grabbed the paper from him. It was on the front page. A single word, in the *Daily Mirror's* largest black type – "corruption".

"Good God," said Anthony. "Do you realise we've been entertaining a celebrity. I've just remembered who that man in the corner was. The fat, baldish one, with glasses. I was sure I knew his face—"

The telephone was ringing as he got into the office. It was Sellinge.

"Have you looked in the *middle* page," said Sellinge. "There's a picture of you and me and Hiscoe leaving the hearing. And one of Macintyre. It's so like him it's practically libellous."

"I haven't got to the middle page yet," said Anthony.

It was half-past ten when the telephone rang for the tenth, or twelfth time; Anthony had lost count. He had long since given up hope of doing any work.

It was Mr. Pitt, and he sounded worried.

"You don't happen to know where Mr. Southern is, do you?"

Anthony said, "No, why?"

"He had arranged to meet me here at ten o'clock. As acting Mayor, there are some formalities—"

"He'll turn up," said Anthony. "I expect he's making a final tour of the polling stations." As he put down the receiver a roar of cheering came up from outside. He walked across and saw two open cars with the Progressive candidates, Masters and Hopper, standing in the back wearing enormous rosettes, being manhandled by a crowd of supporters down the far side of Connaught Square past the Town Hall. A group of officials had come out on to the steps and were staring in astonishment at the sight.

"Barhaven *is* letting its hair down," said Anthony.

"This is nothing," said Ann. "Along in the Marine East Ward they've just finished burning Crawford in effigy."

The telephone rang again. It was Inspector Knox. He said, "Mr. Brydon? Would you mind coming across to Mr. Southern's office. Yes, now. As quickly as you can."

Anthony found a lot of people he knew in Southern's office. The Chief Constable was there, talking to Dr. Rogers, and Inspector Knox. Superintendent Brennan was sitting on the edge of the desk swinging one thick leg; and Mr. Temple, Southern's head clerk, was sitting at the other side of the desk with his head down on his hands. He had either been sick, or was trying very hard not to be.

Knox said to Anthony, "Did Mr. Southern get hold of you last night?"

"No—why?"

All of the men except Mr. Temple were staring at him. Mr. Temple still had his face down on the desk, his body heaving.

"We found a note on his desk-pad. He evidently tried, more than once, to contact you. And he was going to do so again this morning."

"He was my client," said Anthony. "It was probably business. Look here, do you mind telling me what all this is about."

"Last night someone killed Southern. Between ten o'clock and midnight. They throttled him into insensibility and broke his neck. Then they stuffed the body into that cupboard. Mr. Temple here found him about half an hour ago."

Anthony looked at the cupboard, a tall, green metal one. The nearer door was ajar, hiding the interior.

Anthony said, "Is he still there?"

"He's still there," said Knox.

Anthony walked slowly round the table until he could see past the open door. Raymond Southern looked even smaller in death than he had in life. He was sitting, hunched up, on a stack of files, his knees to his chin. His head lolled sideways at a grotesque angle like the head of a china doll when the interior cord has snapped. His eyes were brown with exploded blood.

Anthony came back into the room. He waited for a few seconds until he was sure that he had control of his voice, then he said, "Do you know who did it?"

"We were hoping you might help us there," said Knox. "If he had any business enemies you'd be likely to know about them."

"He had plenty of enemies, but none of them could do a thing like that."

"Do you mean they didn't dislike him enough, or they weren't strong enough?"

"Both."

"It was pretty brutal," agreed Knox.

"How did the murderer get in?"

"Up the back stairs. The door at the bottom's a self-closing one. It wasn't on the latch. Whoever came in must have had a key."

Mr. Temple looked up, and said, through grey lips, "Two other people had keys. Mr. Macintyre and Inspector Ashford."

Anthony said, "I don't need to tell you what happened at the enquiry yesterday, do I?"

"No," said Knox, and looked at the Chief Constable, who said, "When rogues fall out, eh?"

At that moment a police sergeant came in, and handed an envelope to Knox, who took out four photographs, said, "Quick work," and handed them to the Chief Constable, who said, "A nice clear set of prints. Those'll be the ones off the cabinet, I take it."

"Could I make a suggestion?" said Brennan. He had been sitting so quietly that they had forgotten about him. "Inspector Ashford started his career in the Metropolitan Police. His prints are on record at Central. If you put that set on to the teleprinter, you'll get an answer in ten minutes."

"It's an idea," said Knox and looked at the Chief Constable, who nodded.

"His prints would have been taken when he first joined as a constable," said Brennan. "If you could give them his Divisional letter and number, it'd be even quicker."

Knox said, "I don't think we've got that."

"Couldn't you ask Ashford?" said Anthony.

"We could if we knew where he was," said Knox shortly. "He hasn't been home since last night. Thank you very much for coming across. Now, I think—"

"All right," said Anthony. "I can take a hint."

There was a lot to do in the office, but he felt in no mood for work. One of the managing clerks who came in with a problem went out again in quick time. He warned the other, "Better leave Mr. Anthony alone for a bit."

He didn't feel hungry enough for a proper lunch and sent Arnold out to get him sandwiches. Whilst he ate them, and afterwards, whilst he desperately tried to turn his attention to work, his mind was running on other things.

It would be Sturrock and his friends who had set fire to the *Gazette* offices. Of that he felt no doubt. Equally he doubted if it would ever be proved. They would have been back in London within two hours of the fire, organising careful alibis for themselves. He wondered if Sturrock's employers would be pleased with the results of his efforts. He thought not. The *Mirror* had trumped, and more than trumped, *that* trick. Anyway, Sturrock wasn't important any more.

If the fingerprints on the cabinet were Ashford's, then it proved two things. It proved that Ashford had killed Southern; and it proved that he was now quite mad. Where was he now? Had he, too, gone back to the London he came from? Or was he hiding at home, and was his sister lying to keep the police away? Who was going to win the election? Whoever won, it was going to be a bumper poll. A bumper poll. Bumper. Bump.

Anthony hit his head on the back of the chair, swore, and sat up. If he stayed in the office, he would go to sleep, and it would be the comfortless, hag-ridden sleep of exhaustion. Movement was the only possible solution. He got up, grabbed his hat and went out.

He thought he would walk home, collect a few more things which he needed, and walk to Ann's house and deposit them there. Ann's mother had offered him the spare room and had sounded as if she meant it. He would gradually move all his things there and make it his permanent base. Their old house could be shut up. He would have to sell it anyway, and it would be easier to sell if it was empty. The only person who would mind would be Mrs. Stebbins.

Anthony half-filled a big suitcase with clothes. He left room in it for some books and papers which he planned to collect at the same time. This reminded him that there was one job which he would have to do sooner or later, the sorting out of his father's private papers. It would not be a difficult job. His father had been as methodical in his private affairs as he was in his business.

Inside the unlocked desk stood a double row of neatly labelled folders. "School", "House", "Insurances", "Charities", "Car", "Holidays", "Tradesmen", "Law Society"— In the "School" folder

Anthony discovered every bill and every report from his first term at his Seaford preparatory school down to his last term at Tonbridge.

"Anthony leaves us with a good character, a proven ability to think straight and work hard, and an enviable athletic record," the headmaster of Tonbridge had written in his neat hand, with its Greek 'e's.

The last folder in the line was labelled "Business—Miscellaneous". It was a thin folder; Mr. Brydon had been a man who conducted most of his business in the office.

The first letter that Anthony extracted was from Raymond Southern. It was dated five years before, and it offered Mr. Brydon a third of the shares in Carlmont Properties Ltd., at cost.

Underneath it his father had written, in pencil, "A very attractive offer. But I said, 'No.'"

At three minutes past eight that evening Mike Viney, prompted by Mr. Pitt, got up on the platform at the end of the Council Chamber, rang a bell and proclaimed, "I formally declare this poll to be closed" and, in a hurried aside, "Is that all I have to do?"

"That's all for the moment," said Mr. Pitt. "The controlling official at each station will have closed it sharp at eight, and the boxes should be coming in any moment now. That sounds like the first of them."

"How long do you think the count will take?"

"We can usually finish it in an hour. It's not like a General Election. There aren't a great many votes to count. Although it looks as if most of the voters turned out today. Some of the stations have reported practically a full list."

"What on earth are you doing up there, Mike?" said General Crispen.

"Some are born great," said Viney. "Some achieve greatness. Some have greatness thrust upon them. I belong to the third category. I was senior alderman after Southern and am now acting Mayor of this Borough."

"Congratulations," said the General. "Have I time to slip out for a drink before they start announcing the results?"

"I should think so—hullo, Miss Barnes. Coming to see the fun?"

"Other people's elections are always fun," said Miss Barnes. "I've never known one quite like this before, though—it must have been that article in the *Mirror.*"

"They've been having a high old time down in Marine East," said Lawrie. "Jack Crawford got shouted down at a rally on the pier and the meeting turned into a free-for-all. Two people got pushed into the sea. Luckily they could both swim."

At a quarter to nine Mike Viney hopped up on to the platform. When it was seen that he was holding two pieces of paper in his hand the noise in the hall spurted and died away, like water cut off at the main.

"Election of Borough Councillors," said Viney. "Marine West Ward. Christopher Sellinge 1553 votes, Leonard Ames Mossman 925. I declare Mr. Sellinge elected. Marine East Ward. Arthur James Ambrose, 1320 votes, John Evelyn Crawford 1262 votes. I declare—"

The rest of the sentence was lost in a roar from the hall, which was now crowded to capacity.

Viney turned round, climbed on a chair, and chalked up the figures on a blackboard which Mr. Pitt had provided.

Anthony, from the edge of the platform, caught sight of Ambrose, his face scarlet, being smacked on the back by his supporters. He himself was trying to do a sum. It was not so much the results as the size of the poll which had staggered him. Barhaven had a population of about 40,000 which meant around 5,000 in each Ward. About half of these would be under age or disqualified for some reason or other. Which meant that almost every person entitled to vote must have walked, staggered, or been carried to the polling station—

"Seven-six and two to play," said General Crispen.

"Seven all, actually," said Anthony. "Southern's opponent would get a walk-over."

"So he would." said the General. "I'd forgotten that. This is getting rather exciting, isn't it? The Progressives need both of the other votes to get a majority."

Other people in the hall seemed to have done the same sum, and the noise grew. It was like a gigantic cocktail party, thought Anthony, a crowded concourse of people, animated not by gin, but by excitement, forced to talk louder and louder, until no voice could make itself heard below a scream. From where he stood, faces known and unknown bobbed up and down in front of him. George Gulland, and Charlie Roper; Colonel Barrow, from the school, keen to view the effect of his first practical lesson in Civics; Arthur Mentmore (how pleased his father would have been, thought Anthony, to see "Old Mental" looking so sour). Bunny Davies, the professional from the Splash Point Club, with his arms round two very pretty girls. Right in front of him was a wispy red-haired little man, whom Anthony took a few seconds to recognise as Mr. Shanklin, the householder of Haven Road, who had provoked the planning enquiry and was thus, in a sense, responsible for everything else that had happened. Mr. Pitt forced his way on to the platform, and Mike Viney rose again. One piece of paper this time.

"Victoria Park Ward," he said. "As you will know, owing to the unhappy death of Mr. Southern, the first seat goes to Masters, by default. I have here the results of the second seat. Harold Joseph Hopper 1295 votes. Gerald Lincoln-Bright 1290 votes—" He held a hand up until the tumult died away. For all his mop of untidy grey hair and his humped back he was a curiously dignified little figure.

"In view of the closeness of the result," he said, "I have ordered a recount, which is taking place now."

"I can't stand much more of this," said Sellinge, who had fought his way to Anthony's side.

"How did it go up in the Liberties?"

"The caravanners turned out in force. But so did the rest of the Ward. The tellers thought at first that it was going to be a walk-over for Stitchley, but by the evening they weren't so sure. A lot of the die-hards got there too."

It must have been about ten minutes later when the door behind the stage which led into the big committee room where the counting was taking place opened again, and Mr. Pitt came out. He had two pieces of paper in his hand, and Anthony could see from the look on his face that something exciting had happened.

He handed them to Viney, who glanced quickly at them, then looked at them again, as if working something out, and then climbed up on the chair. By this time the silence was so absolute that everyone might have been holding their breath.

"First of all," said Viney, in his high clear voice, "the recount of the seat in the Victoria Park Ward confirms the first count. It is, in fact, exactly the same. I therefore declare Mr. Hopper elected. I also have here the result of the Liberties Ward. It, too, was very close, but not so close as to warrant a recount. William Law 1174 votes, Robert Stitchley 1146 votes. I therefore declare——"

The noise burst over the platform like a winter sea over the rocks. Anthony shouted to Sellinge, "That makes it a draw. A great big bloody stalemate."

"It's nothing of the bloody sort," screamed Sellinge. "You've forgotten Mike Viney. As Mayor-elect he's Chairman, and that gives him a casting vote. Which he'll bloody well use."

Some people were forcing their way through the crowd.

It was Inspector Knox, with Brennan and a policeman behind him. They were making for the Chief Constable, who bent his head down to listen.

"It's Ashford," said Knox. "One of the men on Andrews' Farm spotted the Aston Martin in some bushes near Caesar's Camp. He looked into the old spotters' shelter and saw a man asleep on some sacks at the back. He didn't disturb him, but telephoned us at the station. I sent a car up straight away."

"If you've got any transport here, I'd like to go up myself," said the Chief Constable.

"There's another car back at the station——"

"Quicker if you use mine," said Anthony. "It's parked just behind the hall. I can take all three of you."

Knox said, doubtfully, "You'll have to keep your head down. His sister tells me he's got a gun."

As they bumped along in the car towards Andrews' Farm Anthony said, "*Were* the fingerprints Ashford's?"

Knox said, "Yes, both lots."

Nothing more was said until they drew up near the end of the lane.

The police car was parked on the farther side of it. They saw, in the light of its headlamps, one man half-lying, half-leaning against the bank, his coat open, and another man kneeling beside him.

Knox said, "What's happened, Appleby?"

Sergeant Appleby said, "We tried to rush him. He got Jack Tovey through the shoulder. It's not too serious. Lamb is up there, watching him, now."

"All right," said Knox. "You'd better stay here. I'll go up and have a word with Lamb—"

They heard someone shout. Then the noise of a car starting. Then the rising note of its engine as it came down the lane, straight towards them.

"Block the end of the lane," roared Knox. Anthony, who was standing beside his own car with Brennan, heard him and understood what he wanted, but too late. Before he could even get his own car door open the red Aston Martin had come rocketing out of the lane, tyres screaming and scuttering on the rough surface, had swung through a right-angle in a racing turn, hit Anthony's car a raking blow and accelerated away up the road towards Barhaven. "Let's get after him," said the Chief Constable.

"Not in my car," said Anthony. "He's burst the off-side front tyre."

They turned to the police car. The sergeant said, unhappily, "Lamb's the driver. *And* he's got the key with him."

"Quicker to telephone," said Brennan. "There'll be a phone in that farm. I can see the wires—"

Knox went off at a shambling run. The others stood listening. They could hear the noise of the Aston Martin, a sudden spurt of sound as the driver changed down to swing out into the main road; then a steady, diminuendo beat.

"He's heading east, along the coast road," said Anthony.

Since it was the last night of their holiday Mr. and Mrs. Burgess took a longer after-dinner stroll than usual. They passed the end of the promenade extension, reached the spot where the inland by-pass joined the road to Splash Point and walked a quarter of a mile down along it. Here, where the road turned sharply inland again, there was a low wall of cliff, giving on to a strip of rock and shingle. It was a favourite spot for picknickers. The children would bring shrimping nets and dabble hopefully under the seaweed in the rock pools which the tide scoured out and refilled for them twice daily.

"It'd be nice to collect a few shells for the front path," said Mrs. Burgess.

There were half-a-dozen tracks down the face of the bluff, easily negotiable by day.

"No," said Mr. Burgess. "Don't let's risk a sprained ankle. Not on the last day of our holiday. We'll sit here for five minutes, and then walk back."

"It's been a lovely holiday," said Mrs. Burgess. She said this at the end of every holiday.

"I must confess that I'm a little disappointed in Barhaven. As a town, I mean. First, one can't forget the terrible business of James Sudderby. Then that election. It's not what one comes to the seaside for."

"I was wondering. Do you think, next summer, we might try somewhere abroad?"

"Abroad?" Mr. Burgess considered the suggestion. Abroad was not a place he approved of. The language was strange, the water suspect.

"If we did," said Mrs. Burgess, "we might persuade Eric to come with us. I know he does very good work with those Sunshine Boys of his, but it's three years now since we've had him with us."

"Well—" said Mr. Burgess. And then, "Listen to that." A car was coming, very fast. "Speeding, on a road like this. Asking for trouble. Good God, the fool—"

The red Aston Martin braked as it reached the corner. On a clear surface it might have made the turn. On loose gravel and flint it had no chance. The turn became a sideways skid. Wheels locked, the front bumper hit the white painted marker stone on the corner the car turned on its side, hung for a second, and then somersaulted right over and landed on the rocks with a thick crunch, more horrible than anything that had gone before.

Mrs. Burgess recovered first. She shook her husband by the arm. "We must do something. He may be hurt." For some reason, she was whispering.

Mr. Burgess said, sharply, "What's that? What did you say?"

"Oughtn't we to go down?"

"Damned fool. Driving like that. He hadn't even got his headlights on. Suppose we'd been walking on the road. He could easily have hit us."

"Don't you think we ought to go and see—"

Mr. Burgess put one foot on the uprooted marker stone, and peered down. They could see the body of the driver. He had been flung clear of the car, and was lying, face downwards.

"No, I don't," said Mr. Burgess, angrily.

"Suppose he's still alive."

"Don't be a fool, Doris. Does he look as if he's alive?"

Mrs. Burgess shook her head. Her brief instinct of humanitarianism had evaporated. She had no desire to go down and look closely at the thing which was spread over the rocks like a star-fish.

"Besides," said Mr. Burgess, more rationally, "if we get mixed up in this, we shall never get home tomorrow. There'll be an inquest, endless delays. Much better leave it."

Driven by the night breeze the tide was coming in fast. It splashed over the rocks, bursting into little heads of spray, lipped over the shingle, filled up the pools. As it drove in it smoothed out the footmarks, picked up the flotsam and jetsam, washed away the debris and mess of the day.

It washed away a lot of blood, too.

Chapter Thirty

Afterwards

Almost exactly a year later, Anthony said to his wife, "I heard something today which made me wonder whether what we went through last summer was really worth it."

"Of course it was worth it," said Ann. "What did you hear?"

"Sellinge and his group have signed up with Greyslates to do the western development."

"Who told you?"

"Colonel Barrow."

"He ought to be pleased with the way things came out."

"I'm not sure. He'll want to quit sooner or later. If we hadn't stopped the eastern scheme, he could have sold the school grounds at a fat profit and made enough to retire on."

"You did what was right," said Ann, "and that's all that matters."

"I wish," said Anthony, "that someone would prove to me, factually and statistically, that you improve matters by doing what's right. We've made a lot of money for Sellinge and his friends, and Greyslates will reap a handsome profit. We've put the Progressives into power, by the narrow margin of a casting vote, and that means that it's a bad and ineffective Council. I'm told that Arthur Ambrose talks so much that they can never get any business done, and I don't believe that any of the new people are in the same class as Raymond Southern. And who have we got in place of Ashford? Useless Eustace! He can't keep law and order in the town. You can say what you like about Ashford's morals, we didn't have Mod-and-Rocker riots when *he* was in charge."

"You've got rid of Macintyre, anyway."

"A fat lot he cares. He got all the money he wanted. He's suing the *Gazette* for libel and the Council for wrongful dismissal – *and* he had the nerve to ask *me* to act for him."

"The world isn't perfect," said Ann, "but look what you got out of it. A lot of credit, and a lot of new clients, and Dudley as a partner— and me—"

"That's true," said Anthony.

"And Gerard."

Gerard Brydon was lying on his back on the floor staring at the ceiling in an unfocused manner.

"I was working out the other day," said Anthony. "He ought to be through his Law Finals by 1990."

Gerard gave a thoughtful burp.

MICHAEL GILBERT

CLOSE QUARTERS

An Inspector Hazlerigg mystery

It has been more than a year since Canon Whyte fell 103 feet from the cathedral gallery, yet unease still casts a shadow over the peaceful lives of the Close's inhabitants. In an apparently separate incident, head verger Appledown is being persecuted: a spate of anonymous letters imply that he is inefficient and immoral. When Appledown is found dead, investigations suggest that someone directly connected to the cathedral is responsible, and it is up to Hazlerigg to get to the heart of the corruption.

'…brings crime into a cathedral close. Give it to the vicar, but don't fail to read it first.' – *Daily Express*

THE DOORS OPEN

An Inspector Hazlerigg mystery

One night on a commuter train, Paddy Yeatman-Carter sees a man about to commit suicide. Intervening, he prevents the man from going through with it. However, the very next day the same man is found dead, and Paddy believes the circumstances to be extremely suspicious. Roping in his friend and lawyer, Nap Rumbold, he determines to discover the truth. They become increasingly suspicious of the dead man's employer: the Stalagmite Insurance Company, which appears to hire some very dangerous staff.

'A well-written, cleverly constructed story which combines the unexpected with much suspicion and dirty work.'
– *Birmingham Mail*

MICHAEL GILBERT

THE DUST AND THE HEAT

Oliver Nugent is a young Armoured Corps officer in the year 1945. Taking on a near derelict pharmaceutical firm, he determines to rebuild it and make it a success. He encounters ruthless opposition, and counteracts with some fairly unscrupulous methods of his own. It seems no one is above blackmail and all is deemed fair in big business battles. Then a threat: apparently from German sources it alludes to a time when Oliver was in charge of an SS camp, jeopardizing his company and all that he has worked for.

'Mr Gilbert is a first-rate storyteller.' – *The Guardian*

THE ETRUSCAN NET

Robert Broke runs a small gallery on the Via de Benci and is an authority on Etruscan terracotta. A man who keeps himself to himself, he is the last person to become mixed up in anything risky. But when two men arrive in Florence, Broke's world turns upside down as he becomes involved in a ring of spies, the Mafiosi, and fraud involving Etruscan antiques. When he finds himself in prison on a charge of manslaughter, the net appears to be tightening, and Broke must fight for his innocence and his life.

'Neat plotting, impeccable expertize and the usual shapeliness combine to make this one of Mr Gilbert's best.'
– *The Sunday Times*

MICHAEL GILBERT

FLASH POINT

Will Dylan is an electoral favourite – intelligent, sharp and good-looking, he is the government's new golden boy.

Jonas Killey is a small-time solicitor – single-minded, uncompromising and obsessed, he is hounding Dylan in the hope of bringing him into disrepute.

Believing he has information that can connect Dylan with an illegal procedure during a trade union merger, he starts to spread the word, provoking a top-level fluttering. At the crucial time of a general election, Jonas finds himself pursued by those who are determined to keep him quiet.

'Michael Gilbert tells a story almost better than anyone else.'
– *The Times Literary Supplement*

THE NIGHT OF THE TWELFTH

Two children have been murdered. When a third is discovered – the tortured body of ten-year-old Ted Lister – the Home Counties police are compelled to escalate their search for the killer, and Operation Huntsman is intensified.

Meanwhile, a new master arrives at Trenchard House School. Kenneth Manifold, a man with a penchant for discipline, keeps a close eye on the boys, particularly Jared Sacher, son of the Israeli ambassador...

'One of the best detective writers to appear
since the war.' – BBC